IMMORTAL MEI

POSSESSED

EMMA SHELFORD

This is a work of fiction. Names, characters, places, and incidents either are the product of the author's imagination or are used factitiously, and any resemblance to any persons, living or dead, business establishments, events, or locales is entirely coincidental.

POSSESSED

Kinglet Books
Victoria BC, Canada

ISBN: 978-1989677209 (print)
ISBN: 978-1989677216 (ebook)

www.emmashelford.com

First edition: March 2020

DEDICATION

To Merlin: the character, the legend, and the inspiration.

CHAPTER I

Marie de France is today's discussion topic in class, and I've been looking forward to it. History knows little about her save her name, attributed to several fine tales in verse from thirteenth century Brittany. Since she was my seventh wife, I know a little more.

"Many assume Marie was an abbess, as only religious women and those of noble birth had the education necessary for poetry. However, she was in fact a wealthy secular woman, and never took vows with the church," I tell the class. Some look interested, some bored. A young woman at the front scans her phone with a frown, then she raises her hand.

"It says here that nobody knows who she was for certain."

"I have my sources," I say with a wave of my hand. "Don't believe everything you read on the Internet. Marie wrote primarily narrative poems, with their subjects drawn from Celtic or Breton legends. She drew her inspiration from wandering jongleurs that frequented the local taverns. Visiting those establishments would have been frowned upon for a woman of her class, so we should be grateful that she was rebellious enough to grace us with this poetry."

She used to disguise herself by wearing her servant's surcoat and wrapping a headscarf over her hair in the peasant style, but nothing could conceal her uncalloused hands and bright, inquisitive eyes that speared me through as I sang. The innkeeper said she was a fixture in the inn for months before she approached me. Marie told me my chansons about Arthur and his court were some of the finest she'd heard, and she wondered where I'd drawn my inspiration. I told her, eventually.

The students and I discuss the meaning behind Marie's poems—some students discovering far more depth than Marie or I had ever intended—and it's a shock when the clock

1

indicates that class is almost over. I open my mouth to remind them about the readings for next time, then my eye catches Minnie Dilleck, the oft-repeated love of my life, standing against the back wall. She sends me a sweet smile when she catches my eye, and I can't help beaming back at her.

The students rustle at my silence, and a few crane their necks to see what I look at. I clap my hands for attention.

"Check the syllabus for your readings. As always—"

"Don't bother coming if you haven't read it," a full third of the class recites with cheeky grins.

I wave them away and they shuffle en masse out the door. Minnie waits until the aisle is clear before she walks down to join me. My arms wrap around her middle and I press my lips against hers with fervent attention.

"Every time we meet, you act like it's been forever," she says. Her smile is teasing, and she squeezes my bottom. "I like it."

"It feels like forever, every time." And it's true. Although she has been with me for most of my life, reborn again and again in different bodies but with the same spirit, I never knew it. I've endured many centuries of loneliness, and now that I finally know the truth, I never want Minnie out of my sight. She's Minnie, Josephine, Gretchen, Marie, Nimue, and so many others, finally back in my arms. And this time, I know it's her. The pleasure is so strong it's almost painful.

"I liked your subject matter today," she says as we walk toward the door, hand-in-hand. "Do you often teach about Marie, or was that in my honor?"

"Your poetry is eternal, my love." I hold the door open for her and she breezes through. "It is as relevant today as it was in Marie's time, and it happens to be an excellent example of troubadour poetry in the chivalric style. Also, many of your tales have survived the ravages of time, mostly intact. But I won't deny that I've always made sure to include them on my syllabus to remind myself of you."

2

Minnie squeezes my fingers.

"You really are a wonderful teacher," she says. "A natural."

"Nothing is natural when you've had centuries of practice. I'm good at everything now."

"And so modest, too."

"Modesty is an overrated virtue."

Minnie shakes her head with a wry smile.

"A leopard won't change his spots, I see. But, truly, I think teaching is a good fit for you. You bring a passion to it that 'centuries of practice' wouldn't give you. Maybe you've finally found your calling."

That gives me pause. Not that teaching might be my calling—I like it and I'm good at it, but if I stuck with a single profession throughout my entire life, I would go mad—but that I need one.

For so long, I believed my purpose was to wait for Arthur's return. It was a faint hope based on a vague prophesy and the belief in rebirth from my childhood upbringing that influenced me more than I wanted to admit. That hope kept me going for so long, through times when I couldn't see the point in persevering through my senselessly long life by myself.

But now, Arthur and the others are back. Furthermore, they've returned again and again, if only I'd had the wit to see it. There is no need to wait any longer, because my greatest desire has been realized. I'm no longer alone.

It begs the question: what is my purpose now? Simply living with my lover and friends, enjoying their return to me, has been reason enough for the past month of bliss. But, what does the future hold? A strange void grows in me, one that teaching isn't enough to fill. Now that my usual life's purpose is complete, what does that mean for me? And what was the purpose of the prophesy?

"Perhaps." I don't want to dwell in uncertainties, not with Minnie by my side. These unsettling thoughts are better left to solitude, so I change the subject. "What do you think about me getting a new car?"

Minnie looks at me in surprise.

"That's unexpected. I thought you loved the speed of your Lotus. Looking to upgrade to something faster? What brought this on?"

"The Lotus is a two-seater. It was always an issue—don't tell Jen I admitted that—but it's even more of one now that you're here. I can't give anyone else a ride, and I find myself with more friends than I've had in a long while."

Minnie brushes my shoulder as we stroll down the boulevard. Leaves drift gently around us like large flakes of snow. Students rush to classes but give us a wide-enough berth that we can ignore them.

"It's a nice feeling, being loved," she says. "Having a village to depend on."

"That phrase has a much different meaning since I was actually born in a village." I shake my head at the memories of a cluster of huts on a rainy mountainside where I grew up. "My village was not particularly accommodating."

"I think more seats is a great idea." Minnie chuckles. "Do you remember what I desperately wanted when I was Josephine?"

I sift through memories until a grin crosses my face.

"A Volkswagen van, if I recall."

"That's it! I was so envious, but by the time they came out, I was too old and not hippie enough for one."

"We could have done it, anyway. What did we care what the neighbors thought?"

"I don't know. Why didn't we do it? Then, I got sick and it was too late." She is silent for a moment. "I wish we had. That van would have been great. Don't leave until tomorrow what you can do today, right?"

"That expression means a little less now that you know you're continually reborn."

"But it's still true." Minnie squeezes my hand in her

4

earnestness. "Moments pass, opportunities are lost. We may still be here, but experiences come and go like leaves in the wind." She sighs, a little wistfully. "It was going to be royal blue."

"What do you remember as Josephine?"

Minnie recalls far more about her past than does my friend Alejandro—recently revealed as my earliest comrade Arthur in a past life—but her memories are still not always complete.

"Most things, I think. The bungalow we lived in on the lake. You baking the most gorgeous cakes for my birthday, even though your eyes were so sad every time I grew a year older. Swimming to the floating dock in the summer and diving so deep that I almost got lost in the weeds. Watching the kingfishers when we visited my hometown in southern Texas." Minnie's words come faster, and she starts tripping over them as if she can't push them out quickly enough. "Painting the hall that garish goldenrod color. Making love under the willows by the river at midnight. Finding the dog under our porch and nursing it back to health. Drinking with Jerry and Sue at the fireworks on Independence Day."

Minnie stops and leans against my shoulder, gasping and clutching her forehead. I wrap my arms around her and hold her up while she recovers. My brow creases in a frown. These episodes of Minnie's have occurred off and on since she found out who she really is. She describes it as an overload of memories, one piling on top of the other until she can't handle any more. Alejandro doesn't suffer the same effect, and I have had years to process my own memories, so I'm at a loss of how to help her.

Finally, her breath quiets, and she rubs her cheek against my chest.

"I'm okay now." She gives me a wan smile. "Come on, we're almost at the car."

I drape my arm around her shoulders and support her as we walk.

"Where do you want to go? Home to rest? I know we were going for lunch, but our plans can change. What would you like?"

"Can you drop me off at the beach? I don't have any clients until three. I'd feel a lot better after being on the water. Maybe some peaceful paddle boarding." Her face is pale, and she avoids my gaze.

"Do you want some company?"

"Not today, please." She glances at me. "I'm sorry. I just need to get my head on straight."

"Anything you need," I reassure her. I wish there was something I could do to ease her into this new life, but the only thing I can think of is to reintroduce her to memories, which only sends her spiraling into overwhelm.

After dropping a pale Minnie off at the beach, I return to the front of a classroom to give a lecture on the fifteenth century autobiographer Margery Kempe. The students look bleary after a long week of classes, but most try gamely to pay attention. One young man, whose eyes flutter, is the target of my next attack. He's aware of the consequences of sleeping in my class, and it's too much fun to deny myself the amusement. This one is more likely tired from a Thursday evening start to the weekend.

"So glad you volunteered, Carson," I say loudly. Carson startles awake at the sound of his name. "Tell us for what purpose Margery Kempe wrote her book."

Carson's eyes widen at my demand, and the class titters. He sits up straight and his mouth opens and closes like a gasping fish.

"Sorry, couldn't hear that," I say. "Speak up, please. Make Margery proud."

Carson mumbles a few poorly paraphrased sentences from the textbook. I finally wave at him to stop, and he slumps in his chair, his forehead moist.

"Uninspired, but correct in essentials," I say to the class. "What you may not know is, despite having birthed fourteen children, Margery…"

Halfway through my story, the door at the back of the classroom quietly swings open, and a young woman enters. Her straight brown hair swings across her soft, pretty features as she slides into a vacant seat.

My eyes narrow in question. She looks vaguely familiar. She's not one of my regular pupils, although occasionally my classes are audited by interested students. She meets my gaze with an enigmatic smile, and her chestnut brown lauvan swirl calmly. I nod and resume my lecture, although the mystery of the young woman preys on my mind. It doesn't help that her eyes never leave my face, and she doesn't take notes or do anything other than smile bafflingly.

After the rest of the class files out at the end of my lecture, she remains. I place my books in my satchel then turn to her.

"Can I help you?"

"Perhaps." She moves with unhurried grace down the aisle. "I've wanted to meet you for some time, Merry Lytton."

"And how do you know of me?" I wrack my brain to figure out where I've seen her before, but nothing comes to mind. Is she a student? A friend of a friend? The sister of a woman I've slept with?

"Hard not to, in my position." She boosts herself onto the front table and swings her legs as she gazes at me. "Why, we're practically family."

"My family is long dead," I say. Who is she?

"I don't think there's a human word for what we are." She strokes her chin thoughtfully. "Nor an elemental one. Not that we generally use words. This physical body is fascinating. What an experience. Definitely worth the headache of getting

7

one."

My blood chills in my veins as I get an inkling of who this might be. My suspicions are confirmed at her next words.

"What would it make us?" She tilts her head in question. "If I am your father, reborn? His essence, but wiped clean and, dare I say, improved?"

Absolutely nothing, I want to say, but the words stick in my dry throat. The successor has come to Earth. Somehow, despite the odds, the successor found a way to transcend the boundary between worlds and find a body. It hits me, then: the young woman before me was a Potestas member. I saw her during a meeting, back when I was undercover in the organization. The successor must have possessed her body.

My stomach churns. Had she asked to be a body donor? Did she understand the consequences? Was she still in there, somewhere? She is so young. Human lives are too short to throw them away before their time.

"Surprised to see me?" She holds out her hands, inviting me to marvel. "It was a piece of work getting here, no thanks to you. But I managed, and without sacrificing your partner, I might add. That has to make you happy."

"That you didn't murder my love?" I croak. "Happy is an odd word choice."

She waves my words away.

"Semantics." She leans forward to get closer to me. "Words are tricky. You've been living on Earth a long time, haven't you?"

"That's an understatement," I say under my breath. My mind still whirls from the news of the successor sitting before me. How did this happen? Is March Feynman, former leader of the cult Potestas, back in town? What sort of spell or ceremony did they perform?

"It's all rather new to me," she says. "I'd love for you to show me the ropes of living on Earth. I have so many questions. How do you harness the elements from this side?

What's your favorite earth move? And where can I find the best pizza in town?"

My mouth gapes open. After nearly killing Minnie, after taking over this girl's body, the successor wants me to play tour guide. I close my mouth with a snap. I don't know what sort of game she's playing, but I don't want to burn any bridges until I figure it out.

"That's an interesting proposition," I say with an attempt at my former composure. "I'll think on it. In the meantime, what shall I call you?"

Her eyes light up.

"A name! What a uniquely human construct. Of course. What should I be called? Perhaps Xenia, or Christopher, or Madison."

"Not particular on gender, are you?" I ask.

"Another human construct. Elementals are reborn of themselves, so there is no need for genders. Besides, I might change in the future." She winks at me, but I have no idea what she means.

"Xenia, then." I pick the first name mentioned. "That will do."

"Xenia and Merry. They sound good together. A perfect team." She leaps off the table and nudges my arm. "Looks like our introductions will be cut short."

She nods to the door, where a few students are wandering through. I'm not done with this conversation, but Xenia sashays up the aisle.

"Later, Merry," she calls over her shoulder. "I'll be in touch. This is only the beginning of a beautiful alliance—I can feel it."

I'm frozen for a long moment, until the clatter of desks startles me out of my state. Now that the successor is here, what does she want? With her ruthlessness and disregard for human life, it can't be anything good. I have a bad feeling that she shouldn't be allowed to roam freely. But what do I do now?

CHAPTER II

I drift through my other classes in a daze, my mind flitting from one concern to another. Half the time I'm formulating plans to stop the successor when she approaches me again— she said herself that she wasn't well-practiced at using lauvan on this side of the divide—but the other half has me wondering. Now that she's here, perhaps the danger is over. She has a body, she's in the physical world, and now she wants to explore a little. Does she truly need to be stopped? I could learn more about the elemental plane from her. If she can cross over in this direction, what would it take for me to go the other way?

The next morning, wind flutters tree branches that line the road below my apartment. With one look out the window, Minnie's Saturday plans necessarily include something wind and water related.

"Are you sure you don't want to come?" she asks as she slips on her shoes. "Surely, you've picked up a little windsurfing at some point. I could teach you. And my friend Pia wouldn't mind you tagging along. You've been quiet since yesterday."

I wrap her in my arms and plant a kiss on her soft cheek. Her citrus scent fills my senses when I bury my nose in her hair. I haven't yet confided in Minnie about my visit with Xenia. I don't want to worry her, especially since I don't know if there is anything to be worried about yet. Xenia may simply want to taste pizza for the first time.

Furthermore, she might have answers to the litany of questions that have blossomed in my mind since her departure from my classroom. Here, at last, is my chance to learn everything about the elemental world. I know so little.

"It sounds far too cold and wet for my liking. You have fun with Pia. Just don't forget to come back to me."

I say it in jest, but we both know I mean it with far more

11

sincerity. Minnie's eyes crinkle, and she rubs her warm hand along my jaw.

"Always," she whispers. Then she pats my chest and steps back to pick up her wetsuit and purse. "How are you going to fill your time this blustery Saturday morning?"

"Jen's back in town. I thought I'd see if she's free."

Right after the Potestas cave incident and her big Guinevere revelation, my friend Jen was whisked away to Peru on a job, hired as a trusted interpreter for a business associate of her father's. Almost a month later, she is finally back. I've missed her more than I expected to. Minnie—and all her past selves— was an alluring distraction, but now that Jen is back, I find myself looking forward to her company. Does she represent a simpler time before the insane revelations that shook my world? Or is it that she is—was—Guinevere, Jen, and many other friends that I likely enjoyed spending time with? No matter the reason, it's time for a visit.

While I would never give up knowing who Minnie, Alejandro, and Jen truly are, a part of me misses the simple friendship Jen and I shared. Her dropping in with sushi to watch a movie seems like a distant memory now.

"That sounds perfect," Minnie says. She opens the door and flashes me her heart-stopping smile. "Say hello for me."

When Minnie disappears into the elevator—taking a piece of my heart with her, as always—I find my phone on the kitchen counter and dial Jen's number. Three rings purr in my ear before she answers.

"Merry." Her voice is flat. Or is it guarded? Whatever the case, it's a far cry from her usual enthusiasm and joie de vivre.

"Hi, Jen. Glad to hear you're back. Let me take you out for coffee this morning, and you can tell me all about your travels in Peru."

"I'm a bit busy this morning," she says with hesitation, but I've lived long enough to recognize evasion when I hear it.

"I'm sure doing your laundry or washing your hair can wait.

No coffee, then, but how about a walk? I'll be at your place in fifteen minutes. See you then."

She splutters but doesn't say no outright, so I hang up and grab my keys.

Fifteen minutes later, my car purrs to a stop outside Jen's apartment at the south end of Vancouver proper. The bridge to the adjacent city of Richmond peeks between buildings at this vantage. Jen must have been watching for me, because before I close my car door, she's already walking down her path to the sidewalk.

"You don't take no for an answer, do you?" she says in way of greeting. I throw her a roguish smile.

"I wouldn't get my way if I did, would I? Come on, let's walk to the park. What was the best thing about Lima?"

Jen's stiff lauvan gradually loosen as she describes her time in Peru. I listen to her words, enjoying the familiar sound of her voice and a gradual increase of her enthusiasm. When she mentions Machu Picchu, I interject.

"I walked up there years ago, maybe in the nineteen twenties? It's amazing how little it has changed. I suppose once something is in ruins, there's not a lot to go wrong, especially since the terrain there isn't favorable to plant overgrowth."

Jen's lauvan tense up again, and she doesn't respond. I frown.

"What's the matter?"

"Nothing," she says, but her tight golden strands tell a different story. I let the silence billow around us for a moment.

"You don't like me mentioning the past," I say. Her lips tighten, and I know I'm right. "Is it bothering you, knowing? Are the memories too much? Talk to me."

"I'd rather not," she says in a pinched voice. "Let's drop it."

I'm astonished by her attitude. Can the memories truly be upsetting her this much? I regret her absence more keenly now that I know she has suffered in silence for the past month, while Alejandro and Minnie and I have been reminiscing joyfully. Surely, it would have helped for her to be among friends instead of stewing on her own for so long.

She clearly doesn't want to talk about it, so I resolve to leave the topic for now. Another day, perhaps, she will be more amenable to discussing it. I cast around for a neutral subject.

"I'm thinking of getting a new car," I say. Jen glances at me with confusion.

"Really? Why?"

"The two-seater is becoming a problem, now that Minnie is around. We can't give anyone a ride once she's in the passenger's seat."

"I've been telling you that for ages," she says with a hint of smugness. "A two-seater is a terrible idea. What's your budget? Never mind, if you sell the Lotus, you'll have plenty."

"Money's no object," I say. I've lived long enough to always maintain a substantial nest egg. It pays to have access to ready cash, especially if I must flee my situation. Jen narrows her eyes but doesn't comment directly. Perhaps she fears a return to our earlier uneasy topic.

"You should get an electric," she says. "Get away from gas, good for the environment. If I could afford it, I'd trade in my Prius for one. Maybe one day."

I shrug.

"Perhaps. I was thinking something a little more retro."

"Well, you're not going to get electric and retro together, that's for sure." Jen pulls out her phone and checks the time. "We need to head back. Cecil's picking me up in a few minutes. I have actual plans, you know, not just laundry or whatever you were thinking."

Our conversation is stilted on the way back. It crosses my mind to tell her about Xenia, but something stops me. What's the point? Jen will only be alarmed over nothing. I leave her standing in front of her doorway to wait for her boyfriend Cecil, my borrowed umbrella warding off a drizzle. I'm flummoxed. She clearly suffers from her revelations but won't talk about it to unburden herself. I would push harder, but I fear I'm part of the problem. Perhaps someone else might have better luck, like Minnie, someone who understands what she went through but isn't the root of it. My foot presses the pedal harder. Yes, I'll convince Minnie to speak to Jen. If Minnie can't make Jen speak freely, no one can.

CHAPTER III

Dreaming

Celeste steps down from the carriage with a sharp exhalation. Her steel-gray hair is coiled in elegant whirls and studded with ruby-tipped pins that complement her wine-red gown. She grips my hand tightly.

"I am not pleased with aging in this fashion," she says with a pert tightening of her lips. The French accent she never fully lost sweetens the words on her tongue. "Why should my knees ache so? It is abominable."

"Made worse by seeing me unchanged, I suppose." I tuck her hand into the crook of my arm, and we step with slow dignity to the front door of the public ballroom. It is never fair that my wives age and I remain unchanged. I care not—they are always themselves, beautiful in every form—but I know my agelessness must chafe at their confidence.

"No, Merle, never that." Celeste squeezes my arm. "Your handsome face is what helps me bear this aging body." She shakes herself a little in preparation then sends me a sly smile. "Are you prepared for this party? I have two aims this evening."

"What are they, pray tell?"

Celeste entered upper-crust British society a few years ago, and it has been her mission to become a delightfully obnoxious busybody. It is not entirely her nature—she is a sweet and caring woman—but the change in scenery provided an opportunity to create a new personality. She enjoys understanding the inner thoughts and motivations of others. With the identity of Lady Meryton, elderly aunt of Lord Meryton, she can gossip in a more forthright fashion.

"I must discover what Miss Raeburn thinks of Colonel Gordon," Celeste says with glee. "He pines for her, but she is the coldest fish I've ever had the displeasure of knowing. I will win her over, however."

"You always do. What is your second aim?"

"To ensure that Mr. Royce bequeaths a larger dowry to his sweet daughter instead of saving it as inheritance for that worthless son of his. Young Merritt will only make something of himself if he is forced to, and Miss Royce is the dearest creature of our acquaintance. She deserves her choice of the eligible young men and having a significant dowry will secure her decision."

"You have a full evening ahead of you," I say with a laugh. We approach the doorman, and I say for his benefit, "I wish you the best in your endeavors, dear aunt."

"Enjoy the dancing, dear nephew," she says with a wink. "Perhaps you'll indulge your old aunt in one dance later this evening. I doubt my knees could take more."

"Of course." I bend to kiss her hand and she squeezes mine in return.

An acquaintance sweeps Celeste away as soon as she is noticed—for all her forthrightness, Celeste's true caring nature is evident and has won her many friends—and I am left to my own devices. Dancers bow and twirl in long lines down the center of the hall, and a hum of chatter from surrounding tables fills the room. A servant offers me a glass of punch and I accept. The milky sweetness of syllabub coats my throat, and I wish for something stronger.

"Lord Meryton." A light voice, familiar and welcome, interrupts my refreshment, and I turn.

Miss Jeanine Vernon smiles at me, her chestnut ringlets framing a face bright with youth and round-cheeked beauty. She holds out a gloved hand in greeting.

"Miss Vernon." I take her offered hand and press my lips to it. "It is a pleasure to see you."

"And it is a relief to see you." She sweeps her hand to encompass the ballroom. "This hall is filled with insipid young ladies and fawning gentlemen. I almost despaired of encountering two sensible words strung together until I saw you."

"I'm happy to be of service."

Jeanine heaves an impressive sigh, given the inevitable corset under her empire-waist gown.

"Father insists on my dancing with Mr. Landon," she says in a grave tone better suited to discussing funeral arrangements. "Twice."

"Twice?" I look at her in surprise. "Is there something I should know?"

Jeanine's rosy bottom lip nearly disappears when she bites on it in her agitation, and her yellow lauvan twitch.

"I am expecting a proposal at any moment." Her voice drops to a loud whisper. "Father told me Mr. Landon has already requested his permission. Father said yes, of course." She twists her gloved hands together.

"And what will you say?" I ask gently.

"I cannot say anything but yes," she snaps, then her eyes glance at me with guilt. "Apologies, Lord Meryton. I did not mean to castigate you. I am simply so disturbed."

"It is forgotten," I assure her.

"Father told me that I must marry Mr. Landon. If I do not, he will never consent to another proposal, and I will be a spinster for the rest of my life."

I frown at this unwelcome news.

"That is a severe announcement. Is Mr. Landon such an excellent prospect?"

My eyes rove across the company until they land on the gentleman in question. He has handsome features, but they are marred by the pallor of ill health. His russet-orange strands are liberally sprinkled with knots.

"He is." Jeanine's head droops. "Money, land, and a title to be inherited shortly, once his aging father passes. It is doubtful that I will receive such an offer again. And he is a perfect gentleman—I do not wish to cast aspersions on his character.

18

If my father were not insistent that I marry him, I would likely accept his proposal with joy and gratitude."

"You wish for the choice to be yours." I peer at the gentleman in question once more. "If you do accept his hand, you might be in luck. Mr. Landon does not appear in good health."

"With my luck, I will be his nursemaid until I am past my prime," she mutters, then she waves her hand to dismiss our talk. "Oh, we should not discuss the demise of my suitor. It is cruel and unseemly."

"And yet, there are many freedoms as a widow of your status," I say quietly. Jeanine's eyes grow distant as she ponders my words.

"I could decide for myself what I wanted," she says. "I could do what I wished. I love to sing. Perhaps I could study music and be the next Angelica Catalani. And I could choose to marry again, someone I desired, if anyone would have me."

Her gaze falls upon a young man nearby. His military uniform marks him as a middle-ranking officer. His open, eager face speaks with animation to two more uniformed men. I glance at Jeanine's wistful eyes and raise my brow.

"If Lieutenant Arron proposed to you, would you say no?"

Jeanine starts, and her cheeks redden. Her chin tilts up in defiance.

"If my father allowed it, I would consider an advance from Lieutenant Arron favorably."

"You would lose your widow's income if you married again, and you are too coddled to be a soldier's wife," I tease her. "Soldiers cannot afford pearls and sumptuous townhouses in London."

"Oh, and you believe that you know what it is like to be without?" Jeanine says with heat.

As it stands, I do know very well, but she sees me only as the pampered Lord Meryton, and I am not ready to disabuse her of the notion.

"At least I would know it to be my own decision," Jeanine continues. "And the censure or approval would fall squarely on my shoulders. I wish to steer the ship of my own destiny."

"An admirable sentiment," I say with a slight bow. I pity Jeanine, despite her station. Although I have endured much hardship over my long life, I have been fortunate to never endure the constraints of being a woman. I open my mouth to say more, but an older gentleman glides in to interrupt our conversation.

"Jeanine, come with me now," he says. "Mr. Landon is looking for you. It is almost time for the next dance."

Jeanine steps back.

"But Father, I wish to—"

Mr. Vernon wraps a meaty hand around her delicate wrist.

"You will dance with Mr. Landon, as we discussed earlier." He attempts a pleasant smile for my sake, but his eyes flash. Jeanine deflates.

"Yes, Father."

She bows her head, but her mouth is set in a firm line. Before her father leads her away, I speak.

"Will you dance the quadrille with me later?"

"Yes, Lord Meryton," she says with relief. "It would be my pleasure."

CHAPTER IV

Sunday morning, Minnie slips her purse over her shoulder and smooths her hair at the front door of our apartment. Technically, it's my apartment, but Minnie plans to give up her lease since she spends every night here. And with our history, it seems foolish to pretend that we're anything other than a fully committed couple. We're not married, in Minnie's current lifetime, but we might as well be.

I wonder if I should fix that.

"What are you up to today?" she asks me. I still clutch a cup of coffee, my hair unkempt, clearly not ready to bolt out the door.

"Undecided. Enjoy your brunch with Inna and the others."

She kisses me back then pats my chest and opens the door.

"Love you," we say in concert and grin at each other.

When Minnie disappears down the elevator, I rub my chest to ease the pain of her departure. It doesn't work very well, and I sigh and wander to the living room to find my phone. Maybe a distraction this morning will help.

"You have the morning off, right?" I ask Alejandro when he answers the phone. "Up for some fresh air?"

"Where do you want to go?"

"There's a lauvan cable near the Fraser River I want to check out."

"Is there a problem?"

Alejandro sounds worried. I hasten to reassure him, although I conceal the real reason. Do the cables feel different now that Xenia is on Earth? Perhaps she will sense me there and contact me once more. There is so much I want to ask her.

"Simply something to do. I could be reading essays, but that sounds far too dull."

When Alejandro climbs into my car outside his house, his dark green lauvan swirl in contented loops. Ever since he touched the grail—the ancient cup found by March and myself in a shipwreck—and discovered his past lives, most notably as Arthur from my earliest memories, he has exuded a happy calm. He has always been cheerful, but there's an inner peace about him that rubs off on me. Knowing his whole truth has been good for him.

The only times that he grows troubled is when he thinks about Jen. She wasn't interested in picking up their relationship after the revelations, and Alejandro has taken it hard. The only saving grace is that Jen was away for the past month, and Alejandro can pretend like nothing has changed if he doesn't see the evidence of her coolness before him.

Jen's reaction to her memories is so different from Alejandro's. Where he is peaceful, she is in turmoil. Is there something Jen can learn from Alejandro? Would she be willing to listen?

"Tell me another memory," Alejandro says once we're on the road. He closes his eyes in preparation. This is a pastime we have enjoyed since his revelation. I describe to him a memory of mine that he's in, and he fills in the blanks if he remembers. Often, the exercise triggers recollections, and it's now one of Alejandro's favorite hobbies.

"You're young," I say slowly, trying to pull details from my mind. "Shorter than me, with that mop of curly hair. We're at the banks of the river near your father's house. It's raining and our cloaks are wet, but it doesn't matter today. We're planning to get far wetter. I reach for your lauvan, twisting you into the shape of a—"

"Fish," Alejandro whispers. "When I dissolve and reappear, the air suffocates until you throw me into the cool water. There's a huge splash which frightens me, then your human body shrinks into a silver minnow. We swim for ages. A pike almost catches us once, but we hide in a rotten log until it passes."

Alejandro opens his eyes and beams at me. I blink a few

times. Often, during these memory sessions, joy and gratitude at the return of my friends threaten to overwhelm me. I love it, more than I can express, but sometimes it's too much.

Alejandro must sense my emotion, for he doesn't ask for another memory. I cast about for something to say.

"I'm thinking of getting a new car," I say. "Jen wants me to go electric, but I don't know. I like some power behind me."

"Merlo," Alejandro says with a shake of his head. "Expensive electric cars can go from zero to sixty in less than three seconds. How fast do you need?"

I look at him in consideration.

"I didn't know that."

We're quiet until I pull off the highway and into a park above the Massey Tunnel that descends below the Fraser River. The cable I want to plug into runs straight through the park. When the car purrs to a silent stop in the parking lot, I hold up my hand and pull out my phone.

"Give me a minute," I say to Alejandro. "I need to check something first."

A website for used cars shows me what I need, and I call an acquaintance in the engineering department at the university. A few minutes later, he has eagerly promised to work with a local body shop to create my custom order for an exorbitant price, and I hang up, satisfied. Alejandro looks at me with raised brows.

"Custom work? What are you having done? Good thing you have deep pockets."

I chuckle.

"Love makes us all foolish. And the vehicle is a secret, for now. Come on, let's examine this cable."

The air is brisk with a hint of rain in the distance. A few runners with dogs panting beside them pass us, but we have most of the park to ourselves. It's flat and open, here beside the river that used to flood this delta every spring when I first beheld it, and the cable glints with flowing grace across our path. A narrow stream, rushing from a recent rainfall, crosses directly underneath it.

"How long do you need?" Alejandro asks.

"I don't know. Ten minutes? It's hard to tell when I'm in there."

"I'll be by the water's edge when you're done."

He ambles toward the river. I step closer to the cable and push up my sleeves. One last glance around—no one is in sight—and I thrust my outstretched fingers into the glowing mass of threads that pulse and shimmer before me, as tall as my shoulder and far wider.

Sensation overtakes me and my eyes close involuntarily with the painful pleasure. Once I have acclimated, as much as I ever do, I send tendrils of my mind into the cable.

What happens when I do this? Now that I know I can separate my strands from my body, I wonder how this works. My eyes open with immense difficulty—every part of me screams to keep the connection, which is almost impossible with my eyes open—and I'm rewarded by the sight of my slender brown elemental threads slinking from the cable back to my body.

It's a disquieting feeling, having a part of me leave my physical body to connect with the cable, but I push the thought aside. I've been doing this for millennia with no ill effects, so why stop now?

My eyes close once more and I send my lauvan into the cable. Now that I know what's really happening, it's a simple process to connect with the cable. My mind travels upstream for a moment.

A presence in the cable asserts itself, and I'm brought up short, with my heart pounding. What is this? Is it the successor?

The presence pushes me backward, gently yet firmly. I sense no hostility, and the presence doesn't attack. I'm curious and allow the presence to have its way. I hope it's Xenia, but even

24

if it's not, I might have a profitable exchange with an elemental. Wouldn't that be a novel notion?

Back at my body, I pull my mind and lauvan out of the cable. Before I can extract my hands, pressure pulls them downward. Then, a head and torso of shimmering blue strands blossom from the stream below the cable, between my splayed hands. They aren't Xenia's chestnut brown strands, that is certain.

"Keep the connection," a fluid voice says from a gash in the head where a mouth might be. "If you wish to speak."

I suppose it wants my hands left in the cable. Hopefully, that is enough.

"Who—what are you?" I say with an intensity that surprises me. I haven't bothered searching for elementals since the revelations of my friends' past lives. Reacquainting myself with Alejandro and my darling Minnie has taken all my time. But, now that an elemental is before me, even if it isn't Xenia, I can still get answers to the many questions I have about the world beyond this one.

"I am the elemental of this river." Its words flow together in a pleasant rush. "The river has run for a long age, and so have I, through many rebirths."

My mouth opens and closes a few times before a question materializes.

"There is so much I don't understand. About your world, about why you can appear now when you never have before."

"Our world is in turmoil," it says with the splashing cadence of water over rapids. "Since the earth fundamental tried to open the way between worlds, there is very little in our way. No one watches the divide during the unrest. We're not supposed to come to the physical realm in this way, but I wanted to sense it for myself."

Unease trickles down my spine. Xenia's presence here on Earth is more disruptive than I imagined. Is she causing even more trouble by staying here? I suspect the damage is already done. I'm not certain what a fundamental is, but I suppose it refers to the successor.

I don't want to waste my precious time with the river elemental on fruitless pondering, so I ask another question that rises to my mind.

"What can you feel in the cable?" When I saved Minnie in the cave and had transferred my human lauvan to Alejandro so that only elemental strands clung to my body, I experienced little of the physical world. Everything appeared as lauvan clusters, felt through senses that no human has.

"Not as much as I hoped." The river elemental sighs with a burbling sound. "The stories say that a human body is necessary to feel all. I only desired to quickly experience the physical world, but I don't want to get caught. Better to be an elemental of a stable river than to be thrown back into dormancy for breaking the rules."

With every word the elemental speaks, a dozen questions fill my mind. Here, at last, I can gain an understanding of that mysterious plane of existence.

"Dormancy? What does that mean?"

"Not all elementals are as stable as I am. The river has lasted for eons. But what of a flash flood? The power in that flow of water awakens an elemental in dormancy, and it comes alive to revel in the energy. When the flood subsides, the elemental slips back into a pool of dormant elementals and must wait its turn to be awoken once more. My predecessors were once part of that pool, but with the right allies and years of service, they rose to control this river."

The strands of the river elemental shiver.

"I must go," it whispers. "Someone is coming. I mustn't be found breaking the rules. Being the elemental for this river is too important to me."

"Can we talk again?" I'm desperate for more answers from this willing fount of knowledge.

"Come to this spot another time. If no one is watching, I will find you."

Without another word, its glinting blue lauvan sink into the silvery browns of the cable and slither back into the stream.

My hands drop. I can't decide whether I'm frustrated or elated. I didn't get nearly enough answers, but I now have a willing elemental to speak to in the future. I did not anticipate this stroke of luck when I woke up this morning.

"Old men talk to themselves a lot, don't they?" Alejandro says in a conversational tone behind me. I whirl around.

"You would know." If Alejandro's memories serve him well, he's been around on Earth almost as long as I have.

Alejandro grins, unperturbed.

"What was all that about?"

"I met the spirit of the Fraser River. Just shooting the breeze, you know."

Alejandro looks impressed as he falls in beside me on our way to the car.

"Anything interesting?"

"A few things. It was nervous about being watched—contacting the physical world is against the rules, apparently—but it said I could come back for a chat whenever I want." I nod in determination. "I'll take it up on that."

After my Monday morning classes, I chat for a few moments with the most eager of my students until they finally tire of questions. Once they are sated, and the last one wanders out of the classroom with her backpack slung over one shoulder, I pick up my phone and call the body shop where my new vehicle is being assembled.

"I don't know what strings you pulled or who you cozied up to," says the mechanic with a rueful laugh. "But the parts you got sent here arrived early this morning. I've had three of my guys on it full-time since then, plus your engineering friend, and it's really coming together. The handling might be rough if we leave it as is, but we have a few mods that would help that, if you want to talk—"

"Do it," I say. I'll miss the Lotus for its low-slung cornering, so anything the body shop can do to improve my new ride is welcome. "The smoother the better. I'll pay." Wayne waves from across the hall, and I lift my hand in reply and walk toward him while I speak. Wayne is my fellow university instructor, an initiate into my secrets of the lauvan, and a steadfast friend. Our friend Liam stands with him, at ease with his hands in his pockets and a casual gaze wandering over the milling students. "Let me know when it's done."

"Shouldn't be long."

Wayne points at the phone as I slide it into my pocket.

"Was that Minnie?" he says. "If you don't have plans, dinner at my house tomorrow."

"I'll let her know." I don't disabuse him of the assumption that I spoke with Minnie. My car project is a secret, for now. "Hi, Liam. Joining us for lunch club?"

Contrary to the innocuous-sounding name, lunch club is a meeting at Wayne's gym, where a group of his gym friends get together for sparring, mixed martial arts-style. I've attended regularly since Wayne introduced me a few months ago. It's an exhilarating way for my body to recall its fighting past. As a warrior, a knight, a mercenary, and an all-round scrapper, I've lived by my combat prowess for much of my life. This season of peace is more of an oddity than the norm for me. So, when I have a chance to let loose—and I've always thrilled at the adrenaline rush of battle—I jump at it. I've impressed the group with my "improvement" over the time we've been fighting, but it is merely my body remembering its history after decades of stagnation.

"Wouldn't miss it," Liam says easily. As soon as Liam heard about Wayne's group, he pestered Wayne for an invite. He has little training, but his natural skill and genial willingness to be thrown to the floor, learn what went wrong, and leap into action once more, allows him to improve quickly. "But I'm not here just for that. Wayne and I were investigating."

"I had no classes this morning," Wayne says. He leads us to the exit, and we walk down the stairs and across the grassy boulevard that runs through campus. "I should have been preparing my lecture for this afternoon, but we're concerned about the Potestas members."

"What?" I frown at Wayne when we turn toward the street. It's an overcast day with a late September crispness in the air, but it's still warm enough that I don't miss my coat. Liam glances at me with curiosity over my confusion. "Why are you wasting your time on Potestas? They're through, the headquarters are empty, March is M.I.A."

My mouth opens to tell them about Xenia's arrival on Earth, but something stays my tongue. She's not causing any harm, now that she has a body. Between her and the river elemental, I might start piecing together a picture of that other plane of existence that is my heritage. I will tell them soon, just not quite yet. They will only pounce on the news and insist we hunt Xenia right away.

"I always intended on following up with the members," Wayne says calmly. "The ones who were at the cave had their memories messed with, remember, and I wanted to see how they had recovered."

I stare ahead, a twinge of guilt lancing through my stomach. I don't want to feel remorse—they all had it coming, after kidnapping Minnie and almost killing her in the seaside cave— but Wayne's unspoken censure hangs in the air. He has always been concerned with my ability to manipulate minds, and I can't blame him. It's a skill that I've used and occasionally abused in my long life, and sometimes it's difficult to know where the line should be drawn.

Slight changes of mood via lauvan manipulation are permissible in my books, and indeed preferable in some situations. But the modification of memory that I performed on the Potestas members at the cave was extensive, and I doubt many of them remain unscathed. I would do it again in a heartbeat to protect Minnie, but still…

"How are they?" I say quietly. Wayne glances at me, his eyes understanding. Liam, unaware of the subtext, answers my question honestly.

"It varies. Some appear like they're functioning in their old lives okay. Others have changed jobs, houses, companions in their upheaval, and a few show signs of severe post-traumatic stress disorder."

I wince, but it's no worse than I expected.

"No signs of regaining memory?" I ask.

"I don't know how we'd know that," Wayne says. "We're only observing these people from a distance, for the most part. But we can't find any evidence that Potestas has been rekindled, so that's something."

"So, it worked, as well as can be expected." I nod decisively, as if their news is welcome, although I don't savor the clear disruption in these people's lives. Although, it serves them right for being accessories to attempted murder. My shoulders straighten at the thought.

"I saw Anna Green," Wayne says after a pause. "I thought you'd be interested in how she's doing."

I glance at him sharply. While his voice is calm and collected, his lauvan are tight and wiggle with an emotion I have trouble identifying. What is Anna to him, besides my former fling and March Feynman's previous second-in-command?

"And?"

"She works in a coffeeshop on Broadway. We talked to her, and she seems fine, no lasting trauma. She had a period of amnesia, according to her, but her friend's aunt has taken her under her wing."

"Bethany," I say in relief. "Sylvana's aunt, the one who

30

owns the mystic shop down in Steveston. That's good news. Bethany will handle Anna just fine."

Wayne nods, but his lauvan twitch at the mention of Anna's name. My pondering is interrupted by Liam.

"There are a few members we can't find," he says, his easy tone belying the import of his words. "March, of course, is gone as far as we know. Out of the country, from all appearances. But there are a few members who have disappeared."

"What kind of disappeared?" I say.

"Missing-person-report kind of disappeared," Wayne says, his voice grim as he presses the button to cross an intersection. "Two have reports filed, and another is just gone—we must be the first people to check on her. It's too coincidental that they're all Potestas members. Vancouver doesn't have so many missing persons in a month that three connected ones would be expected."

Xenia must be responsible for one of those disappearances, but I don't understand where the other ones went. How did she get here, anyway? A chill settles in my gut. March's ominous note that she left for me in the deserted Potestas headquarters reminds me that she is still intent on gaining spirit powers.

"Worth investigating, anyway," Liam says as he opens the door to the gym for us.

"Sure, but don't let it disturb your life, your work. I can't see how March is up to anything." I say the words to convince myself as well as the others.

"We'll see," says Wayne.

CHAPTER V

Sleep is elusive tonight. Minnie has been breathing softly beside me for ages, but I can't stop my mind from whirling.

The successor's appearance on Earth is a mystery that I can't solve. Keeping secrets from Minnie and the others nags at my conscience like a sore tooth, but I can't bring myself to reveal her presence quite yet. With every passing hour, I expect Xenia to appear and continue our conversation. I have so many questions for her, most of which are churning in my head as half-baked notions. And, if I talk to her, perhaps I can decide how dangerous she might be. Then, I will know what to tell the others.

Xenia isn't the only thing keeping me up. Minnie is not handling her new memories well. She seems to have received them all at once, instead of in dribs and drabs like the others. It's overwhelming her at times, and I want to know why.

Why, and how I can help. Talking about the past sometimes brings her joy, and sometimes swamps her with memories. The only thing that seems to help are her watersports. I'm happy to let the waves soothe her, but I only wish I could help more. It pains me to see her suffer.

My brain clearly has no intention of settling down for sleep, so I carefully rise and slide into pants and a shirt. Minnie doesn't stir, not even when the front door clicks open. I slip over the threshold and twist the handle when I close the door so it remains noiseless. I love having someone in my bed whom I care about enough to preserve her sleep.

Beyond the elevator and the outer door, cold of the cement walkway seeps upward into my bare feet. It's chillier than I expected, and I rub my arms as I walk. My apartment complex has a path that meanders through cultivated gardens and around an outdoor swimming pool, closed for the season. The cold air pries my eyes open and wakes me up more fully than a cup of coffee. This walk might not be the smartest cure for insomnia, but it is refreshing.

A breeze touches my skin and I turn my face toward the sky. Glinting among a few stars visible through the city's glow are air lauvan. They bathe the sky with a gentle, silvery shine like fluid moonlight. I pity those who cannot see through my eyes, for the strands that surround us all can be breathtaking in their beauty.

The air threads flow in a steady pattern, away from the ocean. It must be the offshore breeze, created as the land cools below the temperature of the sea. With steady winds of this nature, the normally chaotic air lauvan coalesce into broad streams of threads that flow in the same direction.

I've often wondered if these clusters of lauvan are like earth lauvan cables, but since they disperse and reform frequently, I've dismissed my notions in the past. Tonight, though, I revisit those thoughts. What would happen if I stuck my hands in the strands? Would more elementals be able to speak with me?

The air cables—if that's what they are—loop and twist with the breeze, now high as a bird, now brushing the ground, like immense serpents of the air. I hold up my hands and ready myself to move when one next approaches. The nearest cable rolls, rises, then drops to the ground.

I run for it and plunge my hands in its mass. It's not as large as an earth cable, perhaps as wide around as my torso, and far more dissolute. Before it can yank itself away, I close my eyes and send my strands and mind into the air.

The whirling, tumultuous atmosphere in the cable nearly brings back my dinner before I adjust. Lauvan flit about in chaotic patterns and hit me like shards of glass tumbling over my skin. The cable jolts and buckles, trying to rise into the air once more, but I act as a grounding and it holds firm.

My mind feels around for sentience. Twice, a presence hits my mind then bounces off. I can't put my finger on it, but something about them doesn't feel like the other presences I've encountered. It feels like the difference between an insect and a human.

It's difficult to keep hold of the cable when it continually wants to wrench itself off the ground, but I persist for a few moments more before admitting defeat. Finding a presence in this mass of air lauvan was only a theory. My strands slither back to me, but before they disengage completely with the air, I feel it.

Faster than a whirlwind, air lauvan slither up between my hands. My eyes pop open and blink rapidly at the jittering strands before me, shaped like an amorphous human.

"I wanted to meet you, earth child," a voice rasps, a whistling overtone in the sound. My heart leaps at the contact, but I feign nonchalance.

"I haven't been called a child in centuries," I say. "How novel."

"What should I call you, then?"

"Merry will do." I frown in question. "Do elementals have names?"

"Nothing that would translate to this language we now speak." The head shape tilts, as if in thought. "We communicate very differently. What would you call me?"

"What about Ailu?" I say after a moment's pause. "It means 'air' in my native tongue. It's a masculine-sounding name, so we might as well make you male for argument's sake."

"Ailu," he says quietly. "That will do nicely. I find you intriguing, earth child Merry. I have never encountered one like you."

"I get that a lot," I say, trying to bring some levity to our exchange and buy myself time to come up with questions I want answered. I really need to write down my list and keep it in my pocket for the next time an elemental pops up. It's a frequent occurrence these days.

"The earth fundamental's physical-born son. What a concept. Back in the day, we all did that, so they say."

"What changed?" I take the elemental's lead in the conversation. Anything it can tell me will be more than I know now.

"We finally understood that the more we interfere in the physical plane, the more disturbed it becomes on our side." The air elemental chuckles hoarsely, its voice wheezing. "Disturbed, unsettled, agitated. Language is a wonderful device. I adore it. We communicate differently over here, but I love listening to humans speak." Before I have time to comprehend the elemental's tangent, it switches back with a business-like manner. "They banned cross-plane visits, for good."

"Who did?"

"The fundamentals, of course." The air elemental doesn't have many features, but what it does have arranges itself into a quizzical expression. "You really don't know much, do you? There are four fundamentals, one for each element. Air is best, of course. We flit about wherever we want, we have speed and flexibility, but we're not volatile like fire."

The elemental's expression looks gleeful before it switches rapidly to a serious look. It's hard to keep up with its changing moods.

"Your father was the earth fundamental," it says. "Same as his successor. They keep us lesser elementals in line." This is said with derision, as if this air elemental doesn't have much use for rules. "They're losing their grip now, since the troubles. I can talk to you here, can't I? The troublemaker himself."

"Me?" What is the elemental implying?

"Rumor has it that the new earth fundamental is making waves because of you. I don't know the details—none of my allies is high enough up the hierarchy—but it's all wrapped up with you and him. It doesn't matter, really, except that I can sneak across sometimes for fun, when they're not paying attention."

"I met a river elemental the other day who said the same

thing, that everything was in an uproar and that it could break rules now." I wonder that Ailu doesn't know about Xenia's crossing over to Earth. Should I tell him? I don't know anything about this elemental, though. Is information like this dangerous?

"Water elemental? Don't waste your time. They don't know anything. Air hears rumors on the breeze. Come talk to me, and I'll keep you in the know."

"How do I find you again?" I can't believe my luck. Another elemental is willing and eager to speak with me. Are they everywhere? Can I push my hands in a cable at any point and find another friendly elemental to chat with? A sudden yearning to explore their world, their strange existence that I can only glimpse, overtakes me. For centuries, I longed to find the land my father came from and despaired of success. Now that I have found it, it calls to me.

"I'm the sea breeze for this region. My wind might be minor, but I'm as stable as they come." Ailu sniffs, a sound that must be an affectation, given that he doesn't even have a nose.

"Forgive my ignorance," I say to stay in Ailu's good graces. He nods beneficently.

"Of course. You know so little, I can't expect you to understand my world. No dormancy for me, not like these little sleepers, here."

"Are those the other presences I feel, the ones that don't talk?" I ask.

"Yes, useless, for the most part. They won't think enough for communicating unless they can work their way up. Their level is so low that they jump back into dormancy every few minutes. Terrible. I'm around all the time, though. If you want to find me, stand in the sea breeze."

With that, the air elemental swishes down and dissolves into the rest of the swirling air threads in my hands. I pull my own lauvan into myself once more, and the cable swings back into the sky, undulating with silent splendor.

My heart pounds with excitement at my encounter. It will take me ages to fall asleep now, but it doesn't matter. I have another elemental at my fingertips. He warned of disruption in the elemental plane, just like the river elemental, but I brush its concerns aside. If the disruption doesn't affect us here in the physical world, I don't care what occurs. The elementals will sort out their own affairs, I have no doubt. A twinge of unease spikes through me, and I hope that Xenia contacts me soon. I need to make sure her presence isn't too disruptive here.

The next evening, after a full day of no word from Xenia, I pick Minnie up from work and we roar to Wayne's house for dinner. I have engagements with friends so frequently compared to my previous years of solitude, and when I'm not busy with friends, I'm at home with my love. I don't think I will ever tire of the company.

"Come in, come in," Wayne says after we ring the bell and he answers the door. "I don't have anything started yet, but there's beer in the fridge and we'll think of something."

"I'll cook," I announce. Preparing dinner will give my agitated hands something to do. "As long as your fridge isn't entirely empty, I can make soup from stones. Lead the way."

"I won't say no to that," says Wayne. "I make do, but the takeout shops get more business from me than my coach at the gym would like."

We file into the kitchen, where Wayne pulls out beers from the fridge and I survey my options.

"Carrots, lettuce, potatoes," I mutter then open the freezer. "Patties." A cupboard yields oil, vinegar, and a bag of buns. "Burgers, fries, and salad. Done."

"Works for me," Wayne says. "Here you are, Minnie."

"Thanks, Wayne." Minnie takes the offered glass of beer.

"Have you heard about the disappearances on the news lately?"

"Yes." Wayne glances at me. "Merry didn't tell you our findings about that?"

"No."

I turn to see two pairs of accusing eyes piercing me. I throw up my hands.

"I have a lot on my mind."

"Two of the missing persons are Potestas members."

Minnie puts her hands on her hips.

"You didn't think that was worth mentioning?" she says to me. "Honestly, Merry. That sounds incredibly fishy."

"I agree," Wayne says. "What's the connection? I don't think March is back from her travels, but who knows. Maybe another member is ringleader now and trying to bring the successor to Earth to gain powers. People will do crazy things for some power."

"I remember," Minnie says with a shiver. I slam a carrot on the counter in my frustration at Wayne's insistence and Minnie's bad memories. She doesn't need to be reminded of that terrible event where she almost died. Neither do I.

I should tell them about Xenia now, but she's only responsible for one of the disappearances. Perhaps Wayne is right, and March is up to something, wherever she is. Could she have brought Xenia and others to Earth? But how could she have, without the grail? It aggravates me not to know, and it eats at me to keep secrets from the others. Both make me surly.

"Even if there's a connection, we don't know what it is," I say. "So, not much point in talking about it. Where's your barbeque, Wayne?"

The others must sense my agitation, because the conversation switches to lighter topics. By the time Alejandro arrives with a store-bought pie, laughter rings out from the open door. During dinner, we flit from one topic to the next, and my heart swells with happiness and gratitude.

Once the pie is finished and we're all satiated, Alejandro stands.

"Merlo, I was thinking," he says.

"Hope it didn't hurt too much," Wayne says with a genial grin.

"Ha, ha," Alejandro says. "Merlo, I know you used to be part of that sword fighting club, back in Lyon during your studies."

It's a complete fabrication, but I play along to find out where Alejandro is going with this.

"Yes. And?"

"It sounds like fun," he says in a rush. "Could you teach me?"

"Really, Merry?" Wayne leans his chair back on two legs. "How did you get into that as a hobby? Sounds like a hoot, though. Count me in, too."

"I don't know how much I remember."

I sound reluctant, but my heart ignites at the notion that I could spar once more. I've always been a fighter, and the past century has had so few hand-to-hand combat opportunities. Wayne's lunch club at his mixed martial arts gym is a pleasant taste, but I crave more.

Minnie reaches for my hand and squeezes it. Her clear eyes see so much, and I know she understands what I'm truly feeling.

"Why don't you go to the backyard and give it a whirl," she suggests. "Wayne's yard is fenced. The neighbors shouldn't mind a trio of armed men swinging pretend overgrown knives through the air."

She gives me a mischievous look. I laugh and pull her to her feet.

"You convinced me. Wayne, do you have any old brooms?"

In a few minutes, Minnie is perched on the back steps to watch, and Alejandro and Wayne stand before me. Alejandro grips a kitchen broom, and Wayne holds the handle of an old mop. I swing my broom with one hand, and Alejandro's eyes follow the motion.

"I have to say, I'm feeling a little undignified with a mop in my hands," Wayne says.

"Hush, apprentice. Let the master teach you the way of the sword," I say. Minnie snorts quietly behind me.

I lead them through a series of simple blocks and slices to warm up their limbs and reawaken their brains. With every motion, the others' movements grow sure and their eyes focused. When Alejandro comes back with an extra thrust that I haven't taught him yet, I know the memories are coming back. His eyes sparkle with the same knowledge.

"All right," I say and walk to Minnie. After I sit beside her, I wave at the others. "Attack each other."

They both stare at me in bemusement. I wave again in exasperation.

"Go on. Do a little roleplay. Alejandro, you're a Saxon. Wayne, the man from Gwent. Fight for your land, your women, and your freedom."

Wayne frowns a little at the unfamiliar name, but lunges forward with sudden movement. Alejandro swings his broom up in haste to block. Their blocks and thrusts are halting at first but soon grow into a flurry of movement.

Minnie sneaks her arm through mine.

"You love this, don't you?" she whispers.

"I've missed swordplay." I touch the broom in my lap with an absent finger. "I've missed fighting with my friends. I've missed the comradery of battle." I turn to her and stroke her cheek with my fingers. "And I've missed you."

Her eyes crinkle in a smile.

"Right answer, you charmer, you."

Alejandro's yell brings my attention to the fighting pair. Wayne holds a wheezing Alejandro by the arm, looking guilty.

"Sorry about that."

"Don't be sorry." I stand and look Alejandro over with a

critical eye. "Alejandro should have blocked better. He'll know for next time. He should be glad you don't sharpen your mop."

Wayne grins at me, and Alejandro straightens and catches his breath.

"Let's do it again," he says breathlessly.

"See?" I pat him on the back. "He's fine."

"Merry?" says Minnie. Her voice is strange, and I turn quickly toward her. She grips the railing with one hand. "I'm not feeling great."

Wayne and Alejandro glance at each other, but I only have eyes for Minnie's pale face.

"Of course," I say. "We should go. Thanks for dinner and sparring, Wayne. Let's do this again."

"Anytime," he says, his face beaming with anticipation. By the looks on their faces, I don't doubt that he and Alejandro will continue their sparring after we leave.

Once Minnie is tucked into the passenger's seat and I buckle my seatbelt, I look at her.

"What's going on, Minnie? You've been poorly off-and-on for weeks. Is it the memories?"

"Maybe," she says with her eyes closed. "It does get a little much at times. I don't know what's going on." Her clear blue eyes open to gaze at me, covered only by two stray lauvan each. "I'll be okay, I promise. A good night's sleep will help."

She should know better than to make promises that she has no ability to keep. Fear clutches my heart at the reminder of so many deaths of this woman I love. A quick glance at her strands indicates that nothing is wrong physically, which lends me some relief. But if her body isn't sick, what's going on? And what isn't she telling me?

CHAPTER VI

A text from my engineer acquaintance working with the autobody shop greets me when I wake up Wednesday morning. He's eager to please, given how much I paid for this custom rush job, and it looks like he's as enthusiastic to show off his handiwork as I am to receive it. I text back to arrange a meeting with the lead mechanic right away.

I'm excited in a way I haven't felt in a long time. I can't wait to see the look on Minnie's face when she sees our new wheels. My life has been defined by the secrets I keep, and I relish being open these days. However, surprises for my love are a different matter, and I'll gladly keep those hidden until the time is right. It will be worth it.

I want to surprise Minnie with the new vehicle tonight after work, so I enlist Alejandro to keep me company. When he exits his front door, I'm waiting for him outside. Cars driving past me give me dirty looks at my illegal parking, but I ignore them.

"Busy?" I ask.

"Not until noon," he replies. "Where are we going?"

"Say goodbye to the Lotus." I swerve into the lane and zip toward the autobody shop. "I'm getting a new ride."

"You can't be serious," Alejandro says weakly when I point out the Volkswagen van in the parking lot, painted a shiny royal blue. "You're trading in the Lotus for—that?"

"Minnie always wanted one." I pull in beside the van and admire its reflective chrome and gleaming paint as we exit the Lotus. "What can I say? I'd do anything for her."

"Wow, you really mean that." Alejandro looks longingly at my old car. "But this one drives so well, and it's just—so much better in so many ways."

"Times change," I say bracingly. "We must adapt or perish. Figuratively speaking for us, of course."

The head mechanic rushes out to greet me.

"It worked up great," he says with a pleased air. "All the mods are top-notch. The engine fit like a dream, and the extra weight down low should really help cornering." He looks over my shoulder at the Lotus. "I know a guy. You want me to sell that for you?"

"If you don't mind." I toss him the keys. "I'm done with it."

The mechanic's eyes bug a little, but he pockets the keys quickly, as if afraid I'll snatch them back. He leads me to the driver's seat, where he gives me a brief rundown of how the van drives. It's simple, and soon enough he holds out the keys to the VW.

"She's all yours," he says.

Alejandro climbs in with a dubious expression.

"It sure looks like new." He rubs the seat, covered in navy blue leather. "They did a good job. How much did it cost you?"

"Money in fair words," I say. "It doesn't matter. What matters is whether Minnie will like it. Here's hoping."

"You probably shouldn't take any highways," he says. "I bet these things have a top speed of sixty kilometers an hour. Putt-putt."

In reply, I press the ignition button. The van blinks a little, but otherwise there is no sound to indicate it's on. Alejandro's eyes widen.

"Did you make this electric?"

"What were you saying about sixty kilometers an hour? Something about zero-to-sixty, perhaps?"

I turn onto the main road and stop immediately at a red light. A young man in a cherry red Porsche revs his engine a few times to show off. I glance at Alejandro and nod toward the car. Alejandro starts to laugh.

"No way," he chuckles, but he chokes on his words when the light turns green and I press my foot hard on the pedal.

43

With seamless efficiency, the van flashes by the Porsche and leaves it roaring behind us. I laugh aloud.

"This will do nicely."

Once downtown again, I drive down a main shopping stretch in my silent van.

"Drop me off here?" Alejandro asks. "I need to buy some lunch. Wait, not here."

I look to where his gaze pierces a young couple on the sidewalk. My heart sinks for Alejandro. It's Jen and Cecil, holding hands and looking very happy and affectionate. I pat Alejandro's shoulder.

"Give her a bit. She's having a tough time with this transition."

"Doesn't look like she's having a tough time," he mutters. I drive for another block before pulling over, and Alejandro finally bursts out, "Why can't she see? We're meant to be. Look at you and Minnie. Why can't she see we could be like that?"

"We don't know that yet," I say reasonably. "Jen hasn't told us all the people she was in the past. This might be the first time you've met since the Arthur days. And you know Jen. She doesn't like to be forced into anything. Guinevere might have been compliant in her early years, but Jen has transformed into a strong-willed woman, a force to be reckoned with. She'll need to come to her own conclusions. And it might take a while."

Alejandro crosses his arms.

"There has to be a way to make her see that we're meant to be together."

"Take it carefully, that's all," I warn. "Don't let your actions push her further away."

Jen agrees to let me buy her lunch today, albeit reluctantly, so I speed out of the university at noon in my little van and park in the loading zone near her work. There's no point in turning the sign blank, since I'll only be a minute, so I hop outside to lean against the van while I wait.

There's still no word from Xenia, and I wonder if she has fallen prey to a human mishap that an elemental might not have anticipated. It's strange that she hasn't contacted me again. Didn't she want help? I am in a unique position to give advice. Now, I worry that my diffidence during our first meeting drove her away. Ailu and the water elemental are amazing resources, but a fundamental would surely surpass their knowledge.

Jen is punctual, as always, and she strides out of the glass doors of a tall office building before me. She looks good, professional in a pencil skirt and crisp white blouse under a peacoat. Her long black hair is coiled up in a bun and she looks older than the bouncy undergrad I first met a few years ago. Change happens so quickly to everyone else.

When she spots me, her face softens a little but not into the smile I was hoping for. She directs her steps in my direction, but they slow as she takes in the vehicle behind me. When she covers her hand with her mouth to hide laughter, the bubbly girl I used to know shows herself.

"What is that?" she asks through giggles. "Who did you borrow it from? Where's your Lotus?"

"Out with the old, in with the new." I hold up my keychain and pat the van fondly. "This is my new steed."

"You're kidding." She walks around to admire it. "It's in pristine condition."

"The body shop worked wonders."

"But it's not you at all," she says. "Why would you choose this car, of all cars?"

"Minnie wanted it."

Jen smiles.

"Enough said."

"I took your advice into consideration, too." I don't want her to think that I've forgotten her, even if she would rather forget me. "It's fitted out with an electric engine, at great expense, I might add."

"Really?" Her eyes widen and her smile reaches her eyes, the first she's directed at me in a month. "That's amazing. And it's not a two-seater! This is a great upgrade. Even if it makes you look like an old hippie."

"Perhaps I was," I say with a grin, but Jen's face tightens. I sigh inwardly. She's still working through the memories. I wonder whether Minnie will have any luck getting through to her. I decide on a truce. "Sorry, I'll avoid talk of the past, all right? This is just lunch with a friend."

"Thanks, Merry." She doesn't look me in the eye, but her tense golden lauvan relax at my words.

Jen doesn't have long, so I take us to a food truck in Stanley Park that serves her favorite falafel. When we dig into our food on a nearby picnic table, I ask her about her work, her trip, her time with Cecil, anything that avoids discussing the past. Speaking about my own pursuits of late is difficult, as my time is often spent triggering memories in Alejandro, reminiscing with Minnie, and now sparring with Wayne. Jen appears happy enough to stick to my questions.

When our falafel disappears, much to the disappointment of a lingering crow, I surprise myself by mentioning Xenia. Perhaps the guilt of secrets is gnawing at me more than I thought. It will be easier to practice on Jen before I bring the news to Minnie.

"There's been an unsavory development," I say carefully. Jen narrows her eyes and her strands tense.

"What is it?"

"The successor is in the physical world."

Jen pales.

"What? Is Minnie okay? How did this happen?"

"Minnie's fine," I assure her. "Trust me, we wouldn't be

having this casual lunch if she weren't. I don't know how it happened, but the successor is prancing around in the body of a young woman who used to be a Potestas member."

Jen sighs and slumps.

"I thought we were past this," she whispers. "I thought Potestas was finished."

"Trust me, I thought so too."

"What did Wayne and Alejandro say?"

I look down at my food wrapper, crinkled into a ball in my hands.

"I haven't told them yet. Minnie, neither."

Jen gazes at me for a moment with strands swirling in contemplation.

"What do you want from the successor?"

I sigh.

"I don't know. Answers, I suppose. There's a whole world that I know nothing about, and yet is a huge part of who I am. I've been in contact with other elementals, but to converse with my father, reborn? You can't know how many centuries I've longed for that." I sigh and look into Jen's understanding eyes. "I haven't told the others yet, because I know they'll immediately be on the warpath. But I should have told them. I'm better than that."

Jen's mouth quirks upward.

"You've always said that."

The fleeting moment of connection passes like a cloud on a windy day. Jen looks down in confusion and her lauvan swirl protectively over her body. She might have meant that I've been like that since she's known me as Jen, but I know better.

I don't comment on her words, even though I ache to. I promised I would stay on modern topics, and I keep my promises.

"I don't know that there's much to do, at this point," I say. "I'm still not convinced that the successor means harm. I supposed I wanted to warn you to keep your eyes open. I don't know what she wants, but she and Potestas have no qualms over hurting those I care about, so I don't want you to be caught unawares." From my coat pocket, I slide out a piece of white paper that I unfold for Jen to see. On it is a sketch of the woman possessed by Xenia. "If you see her, call me right away."

Jen nods, her eyes raking over the sketch.

"Wow, you're a good artist," she says absently.

"Lots of practice," I say. Jen's lauvan slow at my comment, but I don't give her time to react more. I fold the paper and push it toward her. "Keep it, in case you need a reminder."

"Okay, thanks." She opens her purse and shoves the drawing inside the cavernous space.

The picnic bench jolts as someone sits on the other side. I look up in puzzlement. There are plenty of tables available. Why would someone disturb our conversation?

A woman sits beside Jen. She has an attractive face and a shapely figure, enhanced greatly by a tight-fitting leather jacket and leather motorcycle pants. Her auburn hair gleams despite the overcast sky, and she winks mischievously at me.

"Hi, Merry," she says.

Jen lets out a long-suffering sigh.

"I'm so glad you're with Minnie now," she says. "You have too many exes."

"I've never seen her before," I say in bewilderment. "Not that I remember."

"That's even worse," Jen says with a shake of her head.

"Have you thought more about my proposition?" the woman says with a twinkle in her eye. Jen covers her ears with her hands.

"I don't want to hear this."

"I only want someone to show me the ropes," the woman says with a suggestive lean forward, giving me an excellent view of her chest. "You know how this world works, after all, for our kind."

I finally notice the fine strands of brown amid the woman's sandy-colored lauvan. It suddenly clicks, and my stomach drops in horror.

"Xenia," I whisper. Jen looks at me with incomprehension.

"Her name is Xenia?" she says. The woman gives a throaty chuckle.

"I've been having a lot of fun with this body, let me tell you. I love the physical realm. So many new experiences to savor."

Jen looks at me with dawning understanding. I can only stare at Xenia, now possessing a new form. How did that happen?

"Why are you in a new body?" I say hoarsely. Xenia pats her glossy hair with satisfaction.

"Isn't it a beauty? My old body wore out. Humans are so weak. Not really their fault, but I'm the earth fundamental, and there's just so much of me to squeeze into this little vessel. The bodies aren't stable enough to handle me for long. That's all right. Variety is the spice of life, so I've heard. I'm ready to experience a little spice."

She winks at me again, but I can only stare at her, dumbfounded. When I don't respond, she sighs in exasperation.

"Wake up, half-wit. I'm starting to wonder if you're an appropriate guide. Or is it just your human nature overcome by my voluptuous new form? I've had that reaction a lot today."

"What happened to the last body?" I croak.

"Dead, of course. I told you, it wore out. Were your ears not working? I don't know how well humans function day to day. The transfer is much easier, now that I'm in this realm. I only need to touch the next body. Piece of cake. Have you had cake? Lemon is my favorite, so far."

Jen's foot finds mine and pushes down with trembling pressure. I curse my luck. I wanted to make Jen safer, not show the successor who I care about. What can I do now? It occurs to me that Xenia is close, so close, and I could grab her if I wanted to.

But what if she retaliates by touching and possessing me, or worse, Jen? My blood runs cold. I can't risk harm to Jen, even if Xenia is within my grasp.

"I haven't decided yet about showing you around," I say with an attempt at nonchalance. "It's a busy time of year and all that. But let's talk soon."

Xenia taps her fingernails against the table.

"Well, hurry up," she says, irritation coloring her tone. "I've discovered lots, but I could use a leg up. You have centuries of using your powers here. I want a piece of that."

She stands and bends to adjust her boots while giving me an eyeful of her bottom. She grins when she comes upright.

"You could show me other things, too," she says with a raised eyebrow. I rub my face.

"Aren't you sort of my father, in a way? I'm so confused right now."

"Keep it simple," Xenia says. "It's only a body. See you around, Merry."

She saunters toward a parked motorbike and straddles it with practiced ease. She kicks it alive and roars away while Jen and I stare.

"Aren't you going after her?" Jen squeaks when she can finally speak.

"I don't want to leave you alone after that," I say, but I'm lying. There's no danger to Jen now that Xenia is gone. Xenia is clearly the monster I hoped she wouldn't be, and I should chase after her and capture her so that no one else will be hurt. Who was the woman Xenia currently inhabits? A sick feeling descends into my stomach and refuses to budge.

What would happen if I went after Xenia, and she took over my body? I shiver. I don't know nearly enough to combat this foe, not yet. And there is still more to learn. I need to find some way of containing her in a place where I can pick her brain for knowledge.

Another thought occurs to me, with a sinking sensation in

50

my stomach.

"She must be the reason there have been a string of disappearances lately," I say. "Have you seen the missing people in the news?"

"But there were three last week alone," Jen says in a high-pitched voice. I nod wearily, and Jen's lauvan balloon from her body like a large hedgehog. "We have to stop her."

"I'm open to any ideas."

"I'll help," Jen says with a determined glint in her eye. I hate that it took the threat of murder to bring out her old zest, but I'm happy to see it again. "Cecil and I will brainstorm. We'll think of some way to find her. We're on it."

CHAPTER VII

I while away the afternoon marking papers in my office, trying to push aside thoughts of the successor roaming the streets of Vancouver, unchecked. I know, now, that I must tell the others about Xenia and formulate plans to stop her. It doesn't mean that I don't dread the exposure of my secrets.

At the end of the day, I pack up and wander toward the parking lot. I pass my new van without thinking before I realize that I'm not searching for the Lotus anymore. The van perches on its little tires and forces a chuckle from me. The moment of truth is almost upon me: I'm due to pick Minnie up from work. I'll see if she's delighted or horrified by my new purchase.

The van rolls silently to a stop in the loading zone in front of her office. After a minute, Minnie waves goodbye to the receptionist and steps out the glass door. She scans the road for my car, and it takes a full minute before she spots me behind the wheel of the van.

Her mouth drops and her eyes widen fully. Then she releases an undignified squeal, and my face splits open in a smile. She runs toward the van, heedless of passersby, and flings the passenger door open.

"You didn't!" she shouts. "You bought a VW van? For me?"

"Of course, it was for you," I say calmly, although my wide grin belies my casual tone. "I certainly didn't buy it for me."

Minnie climbs in and throws herself around my neck then releases me quickly to examine the vehicle.

"It's so pretty," she breathes.

"Another reason it's for you and not me," I say. She pokes my thigh but continues to gaze around. Her hand strokes the blue leather of the seat.

"It's all done up in my favorite color."

"I'm partial to blue, myself." I reach out and twirl a strand of her navy blue lauvan around my finger. She closes her eyes in pleasure then twists to thank me with her lips on mine.

"It's wonderful, Merry," she says when we finally surface for air. "You remembered."

"It's not entirely vintage, I'm afraid. If you were hoping for sixties-era emissions and old-school speeds, then you will be disappointed. I have to stomach driving the thing, after all."

I press the ignition button and the dashboard lights up. Minnie giggles with delight.

"Of course, love. Make your mark."

Minnie can't stop exclaiming at the van and running her hands over the interior. She twists to look behind her when I turn a corner.

"There's lots of room," she says. "No more two-seater. We can fit the whole gang in here now."

"We're starting to have a gang, aren't we?" I say with a smile at Minnie. She beams back.

"Isn't it lovely?"

The memory of my meeting with the successor sneaks into my mind and colors my enjoyment of Minnie's delight.

"I have some news that's less than lovely." I pull onto my apartment's street. "The successor left the elemental plane, is now currently possessing a human body, and calls himself Xenia. Herself, I should say. The bodies are female, so far. She came to visit me in class on Friday, and then again today in a different body."

Minnie's lauvan freeze in her horror. She gazes at me with her mouth agape, but from a less cheerful emotion this time.

"How?" she whispers.

"That's the million-dollar question." I pull into the underground parking of my apartment. The van slides into my usual spot with a whisper of tires on cement, and I turn the engine off with a sigh. "I don't know. It didn't take killing you, though, and I'm grateful for that."

"What are we going to do?" Minnie twists her fingers together. Her face is pale under the lighting of the parking garage. "The successor can't be allowed to just walk around, can he? She? What does she want?"

"I don't know." I close my eyes, feeling tired. I very much enjoyed the last month of bliss with Minnie, with no Potestas intrigues to worry about. I had hoped that they had given up for good.

"If those murderers wanted the successor here, then she must be bad news," Minnie says firmly. "There's no way she's here for world peace, that's for sure. Where do these bodies come from? Is the previous body now dead? Does the successor murder people for skin suits?"

"Apparently," I repeat dully. "I don't know what she wants, and I don't know how to find out answers without endangering myself or others. She can switch bodies at a single touch."

I'm silent, staring out the windshield at the cement wall before me. Minnie's voice softens.

"You want to know more, don't you?" she says quietly. "You think she has answers about this elemental world that you know so little about, but that is a part of you."

Minnie has only grown more perceptive over the centuries, and she was always insightful.

"You know me well. I need to contain her, but I don't want to destroy her quite yet. Would it help if I promise to take her down the instant she causes trouble?"

Minnie sneaks a hand into mine and squeezes.

"Only if you keep yourself safe, too."

That comment makes me turn my head to look at her with a wry smile.

"I'm a survivor. I look out for number one."

Minnie chuckles and leans forward to kiss my cheek. When she draws back, her face is set with resolution.

"You need to tell the others, too. You're not alone anymore. Get them to keep an eye out. Tell Alejandro, Wayne, Jen."

"I told Jen at lunch," I say. "She's on her guard. But on another note, this past-lives thing is eating her up."

"She needs help?" Minnie asks. I nod my head.

"Yes, but not from me. I only make it worse. Perhaps you could speak to her. She trusts you, and you're in a unique position to understand her issues and to help."

"For sure," she says. "I'll call her right away."

I need to warn my friends—and I will—but right now I need some insight into Xenia's mind. For that, I need to talk to an elemental.

The breeze is strong right now, so once we're in the apartment, I walk onto the balcony in the hopes that the wind elemental Ailu can connect with me there. A minute passes, then another, with no sign from Ailu. How can I make contact? I reach out and run my hands through the multitude of short silver strands that rush past me from the wind. My brown lauvan snake out and touch a few, and I send out my intention to seek Ailu.

Within moments, a thick air cable descends and falls heavily into my hands. I plunge my fingers in and Ailu's head and torso appear.

"Greetings, Merry," he says in his raspy voice. "Another chat already? You must be bored."

"Seeking information, actually," I say. "I won't keep you long. I wanted to tell you that the rumors are true."

"The earth fundamental made it through," he breathes. "I knew it. My sources are never wrong."

"So it would seem." I roll my neck, trying to release the tension built up from meeting Xenia. It doesn't work. "The earth fundamental is currently in control of the body of a young woman. What I want to know is what she wants. She seems keen on learning more about the physical world and asked me to take her under my wing. I didn't give her a straight answer yet."

"Of course she wants to know more," Ailu says immediately. "The earth fundamental has been held in a state of half-dormancy ever since rebirth, just like your father was since you were old enough to disrupt the balance. I can't imagine being forced into dormancy, without even yourself to blame for being in that state. Terrible." He shakes his head and resumes his train of thought. "She wants freedom and to get out from the yoke of the other fundamentals. They've locked her up for long enough, and they have limited power in the physical world, far less than in the elemental realm, anyway. The physical world is a playground of huge proportions, just waiting for an elemental to run wild."

"What does an elemental running wild look like?" I say with trepidation.

"Experiencing physical life, for a start," says Ailu. "It's supposed to be amazing, incredible. We only have stories from before the cleanse."

"The cleanse?" I've never heard this term before.

"When the barriers were put up, and the children of elementals purged from the Earth, elementals were forbidden to enter the physical realm forevermore," Ailu answers. "Before then, the gates were open, but chaos reigned. It wasn't so bad on your end, but a lack of balance from the extra energy—the children of the elementals—threw our realm into imbalance. Elementals are not meant to be created, only reborn from what is already there and excess put into dormancy. With so many children around, our plane was out of control." Ailu's swirling, shifting form glows with his emotion. "Any human with a quarter or more elemental heritage was destroyed, and the way between the worlds sealed."

"While that's fascinating and goes a long way toward explaining why there's only ever been one like me," I say, squinting my eyes in thought. "Let's get back to Xenia."

"Who?" If an amorphous figure of strings can look bemused,

Ailu was certainly giving it his best shot.

"The successor has decided upon a human name." I shake my head. "Trust me, it helps my human brain wrap my head around all this. So, Xenia wants to experience the physical world. She has proven herself capable of murder, since she has used at least two bodies already, possibly more. Anything else I should be worried about? Do elementals have a moral code of any sort?"

Ailu tilted his head in question.

"You mean, the system of rules that humans use to live together in such density without reducing their population numbers drastically? Not as such. We have our own code of conduct, but from what I've heard, it doesn't follow yours."

"Stealing, fighting, murder, none of those faze Xenia, is what you're saying?" I ask with a sigh. "Something else to worry about, then. Joy."

"I do like being right about the earth fundamental traveling to the physical realm," Ailu says in a smug tone. "It shows my allies still have worth. It's good to test your connections occasionally. Alliances can shift if you're not vigilant."

Classes are canceled Friday morning for a protest or demonstration—I didn't listen to the details—and I'm planning Xenia's demise in bed when Minnie pops her head into the bedroom, toweling her hair dry.

"Would you be a love and make me one of your omelets? I'm starving, and they're divine."

"For you, *mon ange*, anything."

While Minnie dresses, I crack eggs into a bowl and whisk vigorously with a fork. When the butter in my pan starts to sizzle and its nutty aroma wafts past my nose, my phone rings. I tuck the device between my ear and shoulder to keep my hands free to pour egg into the hot pan.

"Hola, Merlo," Alejandro says. "Are you busy today?"

"That depends," I say, reaching for cut vegetables on a nearby plate. I need to find Xenia sooner rather than later, but without a plan, there's nothing I can act on. I will speak to Alejandro and Wayne tonight, and we can brainstorm. "What are you offering? If it's interesting, I might be available."

"Ha, ha. There's a new exhibit at the museum, it just opened. I picked up a pamphlet at work." The sound of rustling paper ensues. "Here it is: 'Mysteries of the Dark Ages: Artifacts from Fourth to Seventh Century Britain.' Interesting enough for you?"

The tone of repressed excitement in Alejandro's voice makes me smile. Ever since he found out that he was Arthur in a past life, he's been relentless at remembering everything he can. The memories don't come back as quickly as he would like, causing him frequent frustration, but talking about them helps, as does looking at historical images. He must be ecstatic over the potential memories in this exhibit.

"I suppose I could make time," I say in a disinterested tone to tease him. "I might be available at the end of next week. Let me check my calendar and get back to you."

Minnie walks in and looks at me inquisitively. Alejandro growls.

"Merlo."

"Fine, let me check with my woman." I hold the phone against my chest in one hand and sprinkle cheese on my eggs with the other. "Alejandro wants to go to the museum this morning. Are you busy?"

"I'd love to come, but clients await." She scoots closer and pinches my backside. "I love being your woman."

"That's an affirmative," I say to Alejandro. Minnie holds out two plates and I slide half an omelet onto each. "I'll pick you up at ten."

Alejandro and I stroll through the glass double doors of the museum and into the central lobby. The crisp sunlit morning fades when we enter the dim warmth of the grand building. Marble floors in the entryway echo with chatter and tapping heels from the museum's visitors. Some of the gathered people hold their phones at the ready for pictures to send to friends at home, but a large portion of the visitors are locals, easy to distinguish by their relaxed attitudes and casual attire.

Twice, I open my mouth to tell Alejandro about Xenia. Both times, I glimpse his face, bright with anticipation for this museum exhibit, and my mouth shuts. I will tell him tonight, after he enjoys this visit.

We purchase tickets at the front desk from a cheery attendant who looks thrilled to serve us. My own jaw aches in sympathy for her wide smile that she must use on all the visitors. Alejandro fidgets with his ticket and almost rips it in his anticipation.

"Over here, Merlo. The exhibit is this way. Come on, *anciano*."

"Where is all the "old man" talk coming from?" I say in a wounded tone. "We've already established that you're not far behind."

"Old is as old does," Alejandro calls over his shoulder as he outstrips my measured pace. "Hurry up."

The traveling exhibit fills a solid quarter of the museum's first floor, spanning multiple rooms so we can't grasp the full size of the display. The walls are painted a dramatic black, receding into the background until only the glowing displays shine in the dimness.

A pang of recognition thrills through me. A shield sits by itself in a glass case before us. It is round and far more ornate than most I remember, clearly the shield of a king or noble.

Shining gold in ornate patterns surrounds a raised blue interior, like an inverted bowl. The center glows with a medallion of red enamel. It's a replica, a model of one they found in a burial mound, but the maker has done such an excellent job recreating the shield that I half-expect a warrior to pick it up and race into battle. Loneliness and sadness threaten to overwhelm me as they do whenever I am forcibly reminded of my long past and the people I've lost along the way.

Moments later, the feelings are chased out by a warm glow of happiness. Arthur—a version of him—is by my side, Guinevere is nearby, and my love Nimue waits for me. I needn't long for the past, because it never left me. A smile fights through the frozen mask of melancholy that came over me at the sight of the shield.

Alejandro glances at me. He must see some of the emotion that crosses my features, for he takes me by the shoulder and draws me closer to the shield.

"Tell me more about this," he says softly. "Tell me what it is. Tell me a memory."

"The number of times I've seen you sling a shield like this over your back then climb on your horse," I say with a sigh. "I want to say yours was tooled with blue embellishments, but it was so long ago that I can't be sure."

"Blue with a central red sunburst," Alejandro says absently while he gazes at the shield. When he catches my stare and realizes what he said, his eyes light up. "I remembered!"

My smile grows wide at Alejandro's enthusiasm, and I pull him to the next artifact.

"Is this a water bottle?" Alejandro asks. The leather bag with a small spout hangs from a cord fastened through two loops on the top. The dry leather is inscribed with swirling patterns. I shake my head.

"I doubt it carried water."

Alejandro grins at me.

"Of course not."

We spend the next hour going from display to display. The security guard must think we are the most avid history buffs ever to visit this exhibit. He wouldn't be far wrong. I tell Alejandro whatever I can remember about each item, and at a solid third of the artifacts, he recalls a detail or fragment of memory from his ancient past.

Alejandro is almost beside himself with excitement, and his enthusiasm is infectious. I feel giddy, weightless in a way I'd forgotten I could feel. I yank him away from a gilded shoulder clasp and plant myself in front of a long display of swords.

These are no replicas. Some are eaten away, ravaged by time and weather into fragments of metal carefully pieced together on a frame for our viewing pleasure, but a select few are in a state of remarkable condition.

"These ones were gifted to the exhibit by an anonymous collector," Alejandro says after he reads the placard. "They figure they were never left to the elements, that they'd been passed down from father to son, then when they weren't used anymore for battle, as family heirlooms. They're in amazing condition."

I lean forward, my attention arrested on the leftmost sword, a smaller one than the rest. Although the surface of its once-shining blade is spotty with age and its edge dull, the pommel is intact. The sword tugs at my memories. What is inscribed on the rounded pommel?

"The sign says that this one isn't a broadsword like the others," Alejandro says, his eyes on the words below the weapon. "They say it's more likely a *spatha*, from the Roman occupation. A smaller, one-handed sword."

"It's mine," I whisper.

CHAPTER VIII

Alejandro's head jerks up.

"What?"

"See that carving on the pommel?" I point at the engraving. It's almost indiscernible, but Alejandro's eyes widen after a moment of concentration.

"Your stag," Alejandro breathes. "There it is."

"You remember?" I thought I'd recognized the sword, but to hear Alejandro see the carving for what it is bolsters my faith in my finding.

"How could I forget? You made me polish it often enough when I was a boy."

My stomach cramps with the words. I'll never tire of hearing Arthur's voice from Alejandro, never.

"I can't believe it's here. And looking almost as it did when I had it." My fingers drift toward it until they bump into the glass. I glance down, surprised at their motion.

"When did you lose it?" Alejandro bends down to vainly look at another angle of the sword. My eyebrows contract as I strain to remember, then my heart clenches.

"After you and Nimue died, I wasn't in my right mind for a long time. I lost all my possessions, lived in the woods like an animal. It took me years to recover from my madness. The sword was long gone by then, far too valuable an item to remain undisturbed."

Alejandro gazes at me with open-mouthed horror and pity.

"I didn't know that."

"Why would you? It was a long time ago, you would have no memories of it, and it's not a particularly exciting period of my life. No need to reminisce." I stare at the sword again, and a wistful sigh escapes me. It almost feels like fate, that my friends, my lover, and my sword are all back in my life once more. "I wish I could hold it again."

62

Alejandro looks at the case, then at the nearby security guard.

"What if you could?" he whispers. When I glance at him in question, his eyes are bright with mischief.

There's a long pause while I process what Alejandro is suggesting. When I finally clue in, I chuckle loudly.

"You want to steal the sword?"

"It's yours, after all. Why should the museum keep it?"

"It ceased to be mine when I carelessly lost it," I say, but my mind turns the notion over, examining it. Plans for retrieving it float unbidden through my thoughts. We could do it. I know how. Should we?

Resolution must cross my face, for Alejandro grins widely.

"Tell me the plan. What do I need to do?"

I glance at the security guard, then at the camera winking in the corner. The plan fully forms in my mind.

"Follow me."

In an empty bathroom nearby, we squeeze into a stall together and I get to work. By the time Alejandro emerges, he sports a full head of curly red hair, plenty of freckles, and a garish neon green tee shirt that has seen better days. I follow him, my newly compact arms brushing a fawn brown sweater.

A man washing his hands at the sink looks askance at our emergence from the same bathroom stall. I wink at him, and he quickly exits the bathroom. I eye myself critically in the mirror. Short, sandy hair, brown eyes, lightly tanned skin, medium height, with facial features unremarkable in every way. Beside me, Alejandro stands out like a light in the darkness.

"Still not sure what the plan is," he says while he prods his nose in the mirror. "Where would someone even buy a shirt in this color, anyway?"

"You're the distraction," I say, smoothing my sweater and shaking out my shoulders to get a feel for my new body. "I'm blending into the background. I'll tweak the guard's lauvan to make him more receptive to you, then you'll pepper him with questions while I disable the camera and open the case. Once I've retrieved the sword, we'll meet in the gift shop and I'll switch us back."

"What if something doesn't go according to plan?" Alejandro's eyes are wide, but his green lauvan wiggle with excitement.

"That's why I gave you running shoes."

I flash him a wide grin then slide out of the bathroom door with as smooth a motion as possible. Avoiding detection is my goal during the next few minutes. The bathroom door swishes open behind me and I sense Alejandro's measured movements.

There is a couple walking toward the sword room, hands held and shoulders brushing. I want as few eyes as possible in the sword room, so I walk purposefully toward them.

"Don't forget to see the helmets," I say smoothly when I reach them. A few of their errant lauvan twist my way and I grasp them between forefinger and thumb. With a little intention, I bend their will to mine. "They're really quite spectacular."

Dreamy unconcern slides over their faces, and they drift toward a lit display of masked helmets. Alejandro loiters near a collection of pottery urns, and I stand in front of the nearest display to the guard. I feign intense interest in the three daggers before me—although none are as fine as the blade I used to sheath beside my spatha—and wait until one of the guard's lauvan wriggles my way. With a motion like a striking snake, I grip the strand and concentrate.

A moment later, I pass Alejandro. I meet his eye and nod, and he wanders closer to the guard. His green strands are taut with nerves and anticipation, but they also vibrate with the thrill of the forbidden.

There is one visitor left in the sword room, a portly man with a small backpack and an air of patient observation. He was here before we entered the bathroom, and it looks like he insists on

64

reading every placard in the museum. I can't judge too harshly—Alejandro and I were doing the same thing, albeit for different reasons—but the man's dedication to his education is not welcome. I can't wait for him to move on his own, so I sidle closer.

I've already manipulated three people's minds. What's one more? I feel a pang of discomfort at the thought of Wayne's remonstrations in that vein, but I push it aside. One more, then the sword will be mine again. No harm will come to these people from my meddling.

"I hear they just unveiled a special display in the next room," I say quietly once I'm beside the man. My fingers grip one of his lauvan to make him more susceptible to my suggestion. "The finest collection of spearheads ever discovered. Quite remarkable."

"Really?" The man frowns. "I didn't read that in the event calendar for today. Are you sure?"

"I spoke to the curator." I twist his lauvan tighter, and he nods.

"I'll have a look. Enjoy the exhibit."

He moves off, and I look around. The room is empty except for Alejandro and the guard, who now speak together with animation. Alejandro has positioned himself so that the guard's back is to me, and I nod in approval.

The final precaution is the security camera. My hands rise before me and I spit into my palm. My fingers twist the water lauvan in my spittle, forcing them upward and outward until a tiny white cloud emerges above my outstretched hand. I can't help smiling with satisfaction as I send the cloud floating upward on a silent current of air.

When the cloud is positioned in front of the camera lens, I get to work. Behind the case, the lock hinders me little. With an audible click, the latch swings open. The guard's head starts to move, but Alejandro launches into a spirited question and the guard turns back to him.

I breathe deeply then open the glass door of the case. A tang of metal permeates the air. My hand reaches forward of its own accord and slides around the grip of my sword. I close my eyes, briefly overwhelmed by the familiar sensation, so long forgotten. Then I carefully lift the long weight up and out of the case.

When I open my eyes, the glaring emptiness where my sword used to be draws my attention. Damn it, I didn't consider leaving a replica. What can I put in the sword's place?

My questing fingers in my pocket find only my wallet. With a glance at the still-occupied guard, I slide out an old ten-dollar bill made from cotton paper and attempt to twist its insubstantial lauvan into a passable weapon.

When I'm done, the new sword is too shiny with an insubstantial air, but it will have to do. Alejandro can only distract the guard for so long, and I still have the problem of the real weapon in my hand. How can I disguise my sword?

Despite today's clear weather, an umbrella is always an acceptable accessory in Vancouver's wet climate. With a quick glance at the preoccupied guard, I twist a few choice lauvan around the sword until a passable umbrella emerges, black and nondescript. Although the sword has no lauvan of its own, since no part of it was ever alive, the potential energy it contains hovering above the ground in my hands produces enough strands for me to work with. As long as I don't drop the disguised sword, it will remain an umbrella.

I've lingered long enough. With slow but purposeful steps, I pace toward the end of the exhibit. Alejandro's eyes flicker to me but I give no sign that I know him.

I walk through the gift shop of the exhibit and tuck into a dim corner, out of sight of the cashier and the security camera. With a whisper, my lauvan spring back into place and I am myself again. When Alejandro's red-haired persona strides with jerky steps past my hideout, I yank him toward me. He pants quietly while I unknot his twitching lauvan, then I nudge

66

him gently forward.

"Let's get out of here," Alejandro mutters. I start to nod, then my eye is distracted by a jewelry case at the desk.

"Minnie would love these," I say and beeline to the case. Alejandro makes an exasperated noise behind me but follows. I peer into the case at a replica gold brooch inlaid with chips of gemstone, then my brow creases. "At least, she would have liked them, long ago. I wonder if she still does. Do you get as confused as I do about all this?"

"Just get them," Alejandro hisses. "Or don't. I want to get out of here."

"Stop acting so suspicious," I say quietly then wave at the cashier. "I'll take this one, please."

A tremendous shout echoes through the exhibit when I push the door open to outside. Bells ring with ear-piercing discord, and security guards run past us. Alejandro jumps out behind me and follows my unhurried steps toward the parking garage.

"My replica disintegrated," I say. "Unfortunate, that. I had very little to work with. I hope they don't find it too cheeky that I left a ten dollar bill in place of a priceless artifact."

"That was close," he says. "Too close. I can't believe you stopped for the brooch. It's the umbrella, I assume?"

"Indeed." I swing the accessory over my shoulder, narrowly avoiding Alejandro's head. He ducks with a wince.

"Watch it. That's not an umbrella."

"It didn't even get close. And, as far as cutting things, it's an umbrella right now. Even if it weren't, I doubt it has been sharpened in centuries. Could you imagine the curators approaching a grinding wheel with an ancient sword?" I hold the umbrella out in front of me with a mimed expression of dismay. "There's no way."

"Do you feel like we've done something like this before?" Alejandro says when we start up the steps of the parking garage. "I'd hate to think theft was a common thing for us, but I'm getting déjà vu."

"Oh, do you think you were Arnost?" I stare at Alejandro with interest. "Bohemia, thirteen sixties. Arnost and I got into a lot of trouble, but it was for a good cause. I came back after the Black Death—Africa was a far less depressing location during the horrors—and when I met Arnost, he somehow convinced me to join him at his farm of plague orphans. We relieved quite a few nobles of their coin through means both legitimate and unsavory, and we thrived."

"Do you remember that horse chase? We had stolen a coin chest from a noble's carriage—I still remember how purple he became when angry, like a plum—and we had to race away. The footman almost skewered me with an arrow." Alejandro's gaze grows distant with memory. A flush of warmth suffuses me at the thought of another friend connected to Arthur. So many, over the centuries, and so much needless mourning. I push the thought away and turn my attention to the stairs.

Too late, I notice the purse flopped on its side, expelling its contents over the step. Someone must have dropped it on their way up. I sidestep to avoid tripping, but Alejandro chooses at that very moment to turn to speak to me, and he can't keep his balance when I bump him. His arm flails. Before he grasps the railing, his arm flings out and knocks the umbrella from my hands.

It sails down the stairs, avoiding my reaching fingers and bouncing with a tinny clatter against the concrete steps. Without the benefit of height-induced lauvan, the umbrella dissolves into its natural form.

My sword lies on the landing, exposed to anyone that might spy it. It's clearly no replica, even to inexperienced eyes, and if someone should see it and then watch the news, there would be no doubt over our guilt. My stomach drops at a voice that drifts down the staircase.

"Do you think I left it in the restaurant? Ugh, I can't believe I lost my purse."

Alejandro and I stare at each other for a panicked moment,

then we leap into action. I jump down the stairs two at a time to reach the sword. Alejandro hastily gathers the contents of the purse and climbs the steps. A woman's foot appears around the corner, and Alejandro thrusts the purse out while he barrels up the stairs.

"Is this yours?" he says breathlessly.

I pluck the sword from the floor and hold it behind my back. My fumbling fingers search for the right lauvan, but it's difficult without seeing the sword. I hope I'm doing it correctly.

"Oh, yes!" The young woman reaches for her purse with a relieved expression. "I can't believe it was right here. How did I not notice it fall? Thanks for getting it for me."

I almost drop the sword when it changes shape behind my back, and my knees weaken in gratitude when my fingers touch the fabric of an umbrella. I climb the stairs to join Alejandro and swing the umbrella back onto my shoulder.

"Wow," the woman says, eyeing my accessory. "That's a snazzy umbrella. Way to be bold. Anyway, thanks!"

She disappears up the stairwell. I hold the umbrella out in front of me, and Alejandro snickers.

"Purple polka dots?" he says. "Not very inconspicuous, Merlo."

"That was unintended." I admire my handiwork. "It's more of a gentle mauve. Did you know that Queen Victoria of England adored the color? Mauve mania, they called it. One couldn't get away from it in polite society. I escaped by not being very polite."

"That sounds about right."

We continue to my van. Alejandro glances at the mauve umbrella then at my face.

"What are you going to do with the sword, now that you have it?"

"I don't know." I exhale, unsure why the sight of the sword sparked such a longing to possess it. I don't hold onto possessions, as a rule, except for my sketchbook. I open the back door of the van and slide the umbrella under a seat, where it transforms back into my familiar weapon. "Not much call for a sword these days. All this reminiscing had me thinking about the old days, I suppose. It's pleasant to have something tangible as a reminder, instead of elusive memories that we try to grasp."

"I get that," Alejandro says with a nod. "It's proof, in a way, that this really happened."

It's proof for Alejandro, but I don't need proof, since I've lived it all in my single lifetime. But it's comforting to touch a piece of the past, something that is as old as I am. Not many things are.

We're silent for a minute while I drive past rows of parked cars and ponder the vast swaths of time behind me. Alejandro takes a deep breath and releases it in a rush.

"I think we should tell Wayne everything," he says quickly. I glance sharply at Alejandro.

"Been doing some thinking, have you?"

"He's involved with everything else. I think he deserves to know."

"I didn't want to get others entangled when they didn't need to be. It's a lot to lay on someone, knowledge like that. It doesn't come easily to some."

We're silent again. By the look of Alejandro's twisting lauvan, we're both thinking of Jen.

"Look," I say. "It's not entirely my decision anymore. I'm not the only one with a past. If you think Wayne can handle it, and you want to tell him, I'll stand by you."

Alejandro gazes at me in consideration, his eyes distant as he thinks.

"Wayne can handle it,' he says finally. "I have a feeling."

"I think you're right." I accelerate out of the parking garage and onto the street. If anyone can handle the truth, it's calm and open-minded Wayne. Unfortunately, I've wrongly felt that way about others in the past. "I hope you're right."

CHAPTER IX

After my afternoon classes, I pick up a package that I ordered from a local carpenter's shop at lunch on my way to Wayne's house after work. Alejandro answers the door and ushers me in with an expectant look.

"Are you ready to practice?" he says. "Wayne and I have been trying, but it's hard to get a feel of the moves with brooms."

"Luckily, I thought of that." I hold the package out to Alejandro, who takes it and rips off the paper.

"Wooden practice swords?" Alejandro is half-enraptured, half-annoyed. "I thought you would bring your real sword."

"I'm not marring my beautiful weapon with your clumsy antics."

Alejandro holds up the wooden sword and examines it.

"I stopped using one of these when I was a child, back then."

"And when you master your skills again, you can graduate to a big-boy weapon." I grin at his exasperated look. "Prove yourself worthy."

"That tone is triggering lots of memories, not all of them complementary."

"I was a great teacher," I say in a lofty tone. "You learned from the best."

"You had no idea what you were doing when you started. My father only hired you because of your connection to the druids of Eire." Alejandro tries for a scolding tone, but his amusement drips through. My face splits in a grin at the casual way he mentions the past, even as my heart hurts at what I've been missing for most of my life.

"I made you the man you were. Now, come on, let's get your ass thoroughly beaten by Wayne. It's a bit embarrassing, really, that you don't always best him despite your memories."

Alejandro rolls his eyes then leads me through the house to

the back porch. Grunting sounds filter up from the backyard when he opens the door. I look down at the grass, where Wayne steps around and swings his arms with sharp exhalations of breath.

"You look ridiculous," I call out. Wayne looks up at my voice, and I yank one of the wooden swords from Alejandro's grasp and toss it to Wayne. He catches it with an automatic reflex. "Put something in your hands, at least."

The practice sword is based on the heft and weight of a two-handed broadsword. While it's heavy and unwieldy in my hands, Wayne holds it with casual ease. He grins up at me.

"Come down and call me ridiculous again." He adjusts his feet and body into a fighting stance. "I dare you."

I had a shorter, lighter weapon made for myself based on the single-handed blade sitting under a cushion in my van. I grab it from Alejandro's hands and clatter down the steps, Alejandro following.

"Absolutely ridiculous," I say. "Preposterous. Laughable."

Wayne swings at me and I block his sword with ease. His strike was hard and fast, and it's clear that his strength and skill are much improved even from our previous practice session. He retreats then slices the sword down in a vicious blow, but when I move to block, he surprises me by changing direction and cutting at my side.

I dive to my right, roll on the grass, and leap up to block his next swing. He's getting better, but he's no match for me. An opening to his thigh is too tempting to pass, and my sword sweeps in before he can react.

"Ow!" Wayne steps back and rubs his leg. "You don't hold your punches, do you?"

"Would you like me to? I can be nice if you can't take what I dish out."

Wayne growls, his eyes flashing with a mixture of amusement and fighting spirit. He holds his sword at the ready again.

"Never."

We spar for a while longer until I'm sweaty and Wayne is covered in bruises, then I let him and Alejandro fight while I watch and comment on their form. By the time they throw themselves on the grass, both of their faces are dripping with sweat and shining with contentment.

When they have stopped panting, staring at the darkening sky, I bring up the news that I should have mentioned first. I didn't want to stain our sparring with serious talk, but I can't wait any longer.

"The successor is on Earth," I say without preamble. Alejandro sits up with a start.

"Seriously? How? When?"

"A week ago." I wince, but beyond an exasperated glance between them, neither comments on my tardy mention. "She visited me in my classroom, then yesterday in the park. Goes by the name of Xenia. Wants me to be her tour guide on Earth."

"She?" Wayne says with a groan as he moves his body to a sitting position. "I thought the successor was some reborn version of your father."

"Elementals don't have genders. My father possessed a man's body for my conception, but the successor is currently in the body of a young woman, so that pronoun will do for now."

"Did the successor—Xenia." Alejandro shakes his head in confusion. "Did she tell you what she wants, why she's here in the physical world?"

"Not really," I say. "Some vague mention of working with me, her wanting to figure out how to use her powers on Earth, that sort of thing. No concrete plans for world domination, yet. However, she does trade her skin suit occasionally, and leaves the body for dead."

Wayne whistles, and Alejandro looks sick. They are quiet for a moment to digest the news.

"What about Potestas?" Wayne asks. "Are they involved in

this? Do we have a bunch of amped-up megalomaniacs running around with too much power?"

"As far as I know, Xenia is the only one. March might be behind it, since the first body Xenia used was a former Potestas member, but she didn't use the grail to bring her to this world."

"We need to find Xenia and bring her to justice," Wayne says. "It sounds like she's already destroyed one life."

"It might have been voluntary," I say. "These people were willing, before."

"But they didn't know what would happen, not really," Alejandro says with heat. "Who would willingly give their life so some spirit could take a joyride in their body? I don't buy it. If she's really dead, then it was murder."

I lean my elbows on my knees and rub my forehead. It doesn't scrub away the face of the two young women, filled with the spirit of Xenia then discarded like an old shoe.

"I know," I say. "But what do we do? I have no idea how to find her. And if I did, what then? I don't have any answers."

"I do," Wayne says. "Send Xenia back to the elemental realm, then find March and make sure she can't bring any other elementals to our world. She's the source of our troubles. Xenia wouldn't be here without her."

"I don't even know where to look for March." The weight of responsibility hangs on my shoulders, but Alejandro perks up.

"We'll look, won't we, Wayne? Show us what Xenia looks like now, and we'll find her, and March, too. We'll get them."

Wayne nods with confidence.

"March should be traceable, and if we get the name of the body, we can ask around. We can do this, Merry."

"All right, I believe you." Privately, I think I'd like to have one more conversation with Xenia before Wayne and Alejandro banish her to the elemental realm, but I don't mention that. There will be time for both, I hope.

I stand, and the others look at me in surprise.

"Now, who wants another round of sparring?"

They both groan.

After a final bout, in which I send Alejandro sprawling on his back on the damp grass, he asks Wayne to follow us to my apartment to speak with him about something important. Wayne looks puzzled but agrees.

We wait for his arrival on my couch. Minnie is out with a friend, but I expect her soon. I take a sip of my bottled beer and look at Alejandro sideways. He sits on the edge of the couch with his leg jiggling in nervous anticipation. His lauvan jiggle along with it.

"How do you want to play this?" I say finally. "As a mortal, what do you think is the best way to get through to Wayne?"

Alejandro snorts.

"'A mortal.' Is that what you call us regular people?"

"You are bound by your mortality. *Mort* is the Latin root of mortal, meaning death, a state I haven't personally entered and yet is inescapable for everyone else. So, yes, it's a fitting moniker."

"It makes you sound like you're a god or something." Alejandro's leg stops moving at the distraction of our conversation, so I reply to keep him at ease.

"Many women have made similar comments. What can I say? If the shoe fits…"

Alejandro scoffs and I sip my beer to hide my grin.

There's a knock at the door and Wayne enters. Alejandro's lauvan tense. I place my beer on the table with an unhurried motion and stand to greet him.

"Wayne, there you are. Care for a drink?"

"Maybe later," he says. He paces toward us and glances between Alejandro's taut face and my carefully schooled expression. "Alejandro said you had something important to tell me. Not sure why we had to change locations, though. What's up?"

"Have a seat." I wave at the armchair. Wayne sits carefully on the edge but doesn't take his ease. His eyes dart between us in curious expectation. I remain standing, wondering what to say, where to start. This conversation is so difficult, every single time. It never gets easier. My only saving grace is that Wayne accepted the lauvan with merely a shrug, and that Alejandro is here to help me introduce Wayne to the rest of my crazy world.

Really, after lauvan and spirits and murderous cults, immortality and past lives don't seem so far-fetched. I hope that Wayne agrees.

"I've asked you to accept a number of extraordinary things in the past few months." I clear my throat to reduce the hoarseness from my agitation. "You've taken everything I've thrown at you in stride, far exceeding my hopes. Through it all, you've been a loyal friend and a tremendous help."

I glance at Alejandro, who nods with encouragement. Wayne interrupts.

"Yeah, it's been weird, to say the least." He gives me a lop-sided grin. "But it's fun to switch it up. People can get stuck in ruts too easily. I'm pretty sure, with you around, that the days of spinning my wheels are long gone."

"Indeed," I say. "If you enjoy shaking things up, then you'll love what I have to say next."

I take a deep breath, release it with a whoosh, then grab my beer for a swift drink to ease my parched throat. Wayne raises an eyebrow.

"Go on, spit it out."

"How old do you think I am?" It isn't what I planned to say, but it's as good of a starting line as any. I've used it many times before, with varied results.

"Didn't Jen say that your thirtieth birthday is coming up?"

Wayne's brow creased. "Why?"

"I'm not thirty. I'm fifteen hundred years old."

Wayne and I stare at each other for a long moment. Alejandro is quiet on the couch, and he might be holding his breath. Wayne's eyes narrow.

"What the hell are you talking about? That's impossible."

"As impossible as spirits? As impossible as lauvan?" I break our eye contact and walk over to the wall to lean against it for support. "I never knew why I couldn't die, not until the debacle at the cave, when Potestas almost killed Minnie. I found out that my father is an earth elemental, which apparently gave me the power of immortality." I hold up my hand. "And, before you ask, I have no idea how that coupling worked. That's on my list of questions for the successor, the elemental who was reborn from my father. It's a long list."

Wayne is still for a moment, then he leans back in the armchair with an exhalation.

"So, immortal as in no aging, or are you bullet-proof?"

"Unfortunately, not bullet-proof." I wince at the memory and glance at Alejandro, recalling my most recent bullet hole from the rogue Potestas member Drew Mordecai months ago. "I don't age, and my abilities with the lauvan allow me to heal myself of injuries." I look at Wayne with narrowed eyes. "You're not disputing my claim?"

"Oh, I'd like to say it's all hogwash," Wayne says with a tired laugh. "And if you're pulling my leg, you owe me a case of beer. But after what I've seen, what we've been through, I'd be a fool to discount it."

I nod but stay silent to let him mull over my declarations for a moment. Emotions flit across his face as revelations strike him, and he grips the armrests.

"You're saying you've lived through fifteen hundred years of history," he says with repressed excitement. "You've seen the Lighthouse of Alexandria, you've lived through the Black Death, you've met Martin Luther." His knuckles whiten with the strength of his grip. "You are a history instructor's dream."

"I'm happy to feature in your dreams," I say. "I did see the Lighthouse before it was fully destroyed by earthquakes in the fourteenth century, although the repairs after the initial collapse were not quite as grand as the original, so they said. I fled to Africa during the Pestilence but came back once the worst of it had passed. And I never met Martin Luther—it's surprisingly difficult to know who the memorable people are before they die, especially in the days before global communication. However, I did briefly meet his daughter, Margaret."

Wayne stares at me with an open mouth. The details have convinced him more than my previous words, and now his brain churns through the information to make sense of what it all means. Either that, or he's trying to come up with more questions like Jen used to ask, and his mind is overloaded by the possibilities.

"Merlo was friends with my grandfather in Costa Rica," Alejandro says. "That's how I knew about him. Merlo lived in San José for a time."

"San José," Wayne says faintly, the words clearly not entering his brain. I clap my hands once to snap him out of his stupor.

"You need beer. I'll be right back."

My fridge is well stocked with bottles, as always, and I crack open the cap before I enter the living room once more. Wayne takes the offered bottle with a wordless nod of thanks and empties half of it in one long drink.

"There's more, if you're ready for it," I say quietly.

Wayne chokes on his mouthful and looks at me with watering eyes.

"More?"

"I'm tired of secrets." I sit on the couch and lean back with my hands on my thighs, then I glance at Alejandro. He nods at me with a smile, his expression so like Arthur's.

"Circumstances have changed lately, and I want to be as open with my friends as I can be. Trust me, it's not my default mode, but practice makes perfect."

"Okay, hit me." Wayne grips his bottle with both hands and braces his elbows on his knees. I wave to Alejandro.

"This one's yours, Alejandro."

"But you didn't even tell him who you are," Alejandro protests. "You know, your real name."

"It will sound better coming from you."

Alejandro exhales sharply, then he squares his feet on the carpet and looks straight at Wayne.

"Reincarnation is real. I've lived many lives before this one, and my first life was when Merlo was young. Jen, too, has been reincarnated many times. We were—" He gulps and looks at me, but I only wave at him to continue while I sip my beer. My stomach churns, but my face maintains its calm mask. Wayne glances between us.

"You were what?"

"Who," I correct him.

"You were—who?"

"I was Arthur," Alejandro says in a rush. "Jen was Guinevere, and Merry was—is—Merlin."

Wayne stares at us for a long, breathless moment. Then his face crinkles with mirth and he lets out a great bellow of laughter.

"Oh, too good!" he gasps between chuckles. "You really had me. I'm such a sucker. You'll have to pony up that case of beer, though." He wipes his watering eyes. "Too good."

He finally notices our serious faces, and his chuckles fade. His mouth drops.

"You can't be serious," he whispers. Alejandro nods.

"I know it's hard to believe, but it's the truth. Is it any weirder than the rest?"

"No, just—" Wayne rubs his forehead in distress. "I mean, come on. The experts agree that the real King Arthur didn't even exist, that the legend was based off—"

"An obscure warlord in Southern Wales?" I finish for him. "Yes, I agree that's the likely source of the legend."

Wayne passes a shaking hand over his eyes.

"Give me a minute."

"Whatever you need," Alejandro says. "It's a lot to take in."

Three minutes pass while Wayne sits with his eyes closed. I finish my beer and wander to the fridge for another one. Alejandro plays with a button on his shirt until I press a drink into his hand. It never ceases to amaze me how malleable time is. I've lived for centuries, but three minutes can feel like an eternity.

Wayne finally opens his eyes and looks at us. Alejandro straightens his spine.

"I have questions," Wayne says in a gruff voice. We both nod.

"I imagine so," I say. "I will answer what I know."

"Does everyone reincarnate?"

I frown. It's a good question, and one I've wondered myself.

"Unfortunately, your first question is one I don't have an answer to. It was only a month ago that we discovered Alejandro's and Jen's pasts. Until then, I assumed I was alone."

"The math doesn't add up," Wayne says. "How many billion people are on the planet now? More than ever before in human history. Not everyone can have past lives. So, what causes it? Are there a select few who have the privilege, or are new people being created now due to our population boom, and they will be the first of their line, so to speak?"

"It's an excellent question, and one I'll remember to ask when I contact the elementals again." I trace the bottom of my bottle and ponder Wayne's comments. If everyone I know touches the grail, how many will have past lives?

"And if you three knew each other in the past but only recently found out about your history, how did you know to become friends? Alejandro wasn't even born in Canada, and Merry, you only moved here a few years ago. What are the chances that was random?"

"You think we have some draw, that we pull each other together?" I gaze at Wayne in consideration. I haven't thought this through, not the way Wayne does now. It was a smart decision to bring him into the fold. "That's another good question for the elementals. I'll have quite the list to get through by the time we're done."

"How did you find out about your past lives?" Wayne asks Alejandro.

"The grail," he says. "Remember, the cup that March found on the wreck, and Potestas used to try to sacrifice Minnie?"

"Yeah, I remember."

"When I touched it, memories came flooding back. Not all of them at once—my brain would have probably exploded—but they've been coming in over the past month, more and more." Alejandro's face widens in a genuine smile. "It's incredible. I've been Arthur, yes, but also so many more people, from many different times."

Wayne stares at Alejandro and drums his fingers on his knee, clearly working up the nerve for something. I stare at him.

"What are you thinking?"

"I want to touch the grail." Wayne sets his jaw in a stubborn pose. "I want to see if I have a past."

Alejandro glances at me. I'm not sure what to think, although this is the reason we brought Wayne to my apartment. If Wayne has no past, then nothing will change, really, except perhaps his feeling of comradery with us. I'd like to think he is level-headed enough to shrug off a lack of past, but it's hard to feel different from everyone else and out of the loop.

But if he does have a past, who was he? I'm suddenly desperate to find out. Did I ever know him? What are the chances?

"Are you sure?" Alejandro says, although his lauvan dance

with excitement and don't match his concerned voice. "It's a lot to take in, and your life will be forever different. I know Jen is having trouble adjusting." His green strands droop slightly. "You can't take back this decision."

"My life has already changed forever," Wayne says with a half-smile toward me. "I think we're past the point of no return. Let me do this. It's my life, and my choice."

I sigh deeply then stand.

"So be it. Wayne Gibson, prepare to know yourself better."

CHAPTER X

The grail is perched on the top shelf of my closet, behind a pair of dress shoes and an umbrella. I swiftly untangle the lauvan that hold it in place to protect it from commonplace burglars. Its enameled surface gleams from the light of the setting sun, peacock blues and rusty reds patterning its sides in a wild medley.

Wayne's eyes lock on the fist-sized bowl in my hands when I exit the bedroom. He swallows audibly.

"You're sure about this?" I say when I stop before his chair. "It's all right to say no, or to try another day when you've slept on it."

Wayne shakes his head, back and forth like he's convincing himself. Beads of sweat stand on his bald head.

"Don't try to talk me out of it. We're doing this, and we're doing it now."

I raise one hand in defeat and offer the grail with the other. Wayne takes a deep breath, pauses, then reaches his fingers slowly to the small vessel. When his fingers cup the bowl, I let go.

A shudder travels the length of Wayne's body, and his eyes close. He shivers and shakes, and his face contorts in a rictus of pain. I glance at Alejandro with concern, but he only looks excited.

"That's what happened to me," he whispers.

I look to Wayne, whose eyelids have peeled back to show the whites of his rolled eyes. He must have a past, just like Alejandro, Jen, and Minnie. What is he seeing right now? Who was he? My knees fall to the floor beside his chair while I wait with my breath held for his fit to subside.

Slowly, finally, Wayne slumps against the back of the armchair and takes a deep, rasping breath. My hand grips his forearm tightly.

"Wayne," I say quietly. "Talk to me. What did you see?"

Wayne doesn't open his eyes. Instead, the corners of his mouth turn upward, and I frown. Before I can ask how his revelation could possibly cause him to smile, his mouth opens, and he releases a bellowing bark of laughter.

I rock back on my heels and stare at my friend, flummoxed, while he laughs and laughs, barely able to breathe through his mirth. Alejandro jumps to his feet.

"Check his lauvan, Merlo," he hisses. "Is he sick? Fix him."

"He's fine," I say in wonder. "Nothing physical that I can see. Even the strands around his head don't indicate any great disturbance, surprisingly."

"Then what's wrong with him?"

Alejandro's words must finally cut through Wayne's hysteria, for he stops his laughter with great effort and opens his streaming eyes.

"Take a guess," he wheezes. "Go on, take a guess who I was. Back in the Arthur days."

I look at Alejandro sharply. He stares at Wayne with narrowed eyes, which gradually open wide with astonishment. What does he think he knows?

"No," he says faintly. "That's too obvious. Wayne." Alejandro looks at me with a shake of his head. "Not Wayne. Gawaine."

My backside hits the floor with a thump. Wayne is Gawaine, another good friend from my earliest days. I gaze at Wayne, who gives me a broad smile.

"I don't remember much, but I do remember that. What do you think? Tell me that us being gathered here is a coincidence, and I'll eat that grail." He winces and I jump to my feet, but he waves me off after a moment. "Another memory hit me, that's all. What a weird sensation."

"It is," Alejandro agrees. "Like a dream that fades away when you wake up, but in reverse. The memories get stronger as they come back."

"Yes," Wayne says, rubbing his bald head. "Exactly like a dream, in that it happened to me, but not for real. Does that make sense?"

"Perfect sense," Alejandro says. I shrug.

"I'll take your word for it. Gawaine." I shake my head in amazement. My heart pounds at the revelation that another of my old friends is back. It's both a huge shock and a welcome addition. "I really thought I'd seen it all. And, yet, these past few months have only showed me how little I know. It's highly unsettling."

"The old man is set in his ways," Alejandro loudly whispers to Wayne in a falsely concerned tone, and Wayne guffaws. I throw up my hands.

"You've only just been reacquainted, and you're teaming up on me already? Besides, you're both as old as I am, according to your memories, so that's enough of the 'old man' talk."

They both chuckle like boys, then Wayne sobers.

"There must be more of us," he says. "I refuse to believe this is coincidence. Who else might be one of us?"

"Don't forget Minnie," Alejandro says. "Do you remember Merlin's wife, Nimue?"

Wayne closes his eyes and winces, then he smiles at the new memory triggered by Nimue's name.

"The pretty priestess who tamed the wild womanizer. How could I forget?" Wayne looks dumbfounded. "Minnie is Nimue?"

"Minnie is every woman I've ever truly loved," I say. "So, I have to agree with you, Wayne. Whatever is going on here isn't coincidence. And I'll thank you not to eat my grail."

"Wow," Wayne says. He looks thoughtful. "A real soulmate, huh? There's another theory of mine disproved." He winces again.

"Indigestion or another memory?" I ask.

"You'd be surprised how similar they feel," Wayne says. "No, another memory. Merry, do you have paper and a pen? I

86

need to start writing these down. This is incredible. There's a reason I teach history—I love the stuff. Hey, do you think that's why I teach history? Because I somehow knew about this?"

I shrug and shake my head as I search in my satchel for a pen.

"Your guess is as good as mine." I pass him a few pages ripped from the back of a student's notebook. "Here, write away. But, be warned, if you've been around since Gawaine's time and reborn many times since, then I hope you have a lot of paper. You'll need it."

Wayne is only half listening as he scribbles his thoughts.

"It needs to be done. This is insane. I need a record of this. Who knows how long these memories will stay accurate for? What if they fade or get distorted over time? I want them fresh and recorded."

"Do you think that will happen?" Alejandro looks alarmed.

"Mine haven't changed," I say. "I wouldn't worry too much."

"You only think they haven't changed," says Wayne absently, still jotting down notes. "You wouldn't know if they had changed if you don't have a record of the first occurrence."

"There's a sobering thought," I say, vaguely disquieted. "Memories are all I have, so I hope they're correct. So sobering, in fact, that I think we need more beer. Hold on."

I walk toward the kitchen but am distracted by the sound of the door clicking open. Minnie wanders in, shrugging off her coat, her hair windswept and her cheeks pink. I change direction and sweep her into a close embrace.

She responds to my kisses with arms entwined around my neck until Alejandro coughs behind me. Minnie peeks over my shoulder.

"Merry." She wriggles out of my arms and swats my side. "I didn't know we had company. You're bad."

"I know," I say. "Want to meet an old friend?"

She searches my face but doesn't get any answers.

"Who?"

"We told Wayne about the effects of the grail, and he wanted to give the past-lives ride a whirl." I gesture grandly to Wayne, who places his papers to the side and stands to greet Minnie. "Minnie, meet—well, Wayne, it's your surprise."

"Merry said you were Nimue?" Wayne says slowly. When Minnie nods, he says, "I'm getting memories of Gawaine."

At Minnie's delighted squeal and clap of her hands, Wayne grins. Minnie squeezes my elbow, then runs across to fling her arms around Wayne.

"I can't believe all this," she says when she releases Wayne. "I hope you're feeling okay. It's a big shock, isn't it? Maybe you should sit down. If you want to talk about it, I'm here to listen."

"He's too busy committing his past lives to the longest memoir in history to be bothered by the revelations," I say. "He's probably the best prepared and the least bothered of all of us. Typical Gawaine, really."

Minnie rolls her eyes at me and turns to Wayne.

"My offer stands."

"Thanks, Minnie," Wayne says. "But I feel great, like my eyes are finally open. I'll keep you in mind if I find myself having an existential crisis, though. You're probably the only therapist qualified to handle past-life regression."

Minnie laughs and steps back to my side. She swats something in front of her face and sways. I catch her shoulders and hold her steady with a frown. The few lauvan left covering her eyes wriggle and writhe, and Minnie looks faint.

"Are you all right?" I lead her to the couch, and she sinks heavily onto it.

"I'm fine." She tries to smile but it looks forced. "Really, Merry, I promise."

"I should head out," Wayne says with a worried glance at Minnie. "Early class tomorrow. And I want to get a start on hunting March."

"You think I don't know you're going home to write more memory notes?" I raise an eyebrow at Wayne, who laughs. "See you tomorrow. And call if it gets too much—we understand."

Alejandro follows Wayne out the door, and their chatter about memories filters through the hallway until the door closes. When I turn, Minnie has her eyes closed with a look of concentration on her face.

"What's wrong?" I ask.

"It's nothing." She pats the couch beside her. "Just a little dizzy, that's all. Come sit with me."

I lower myself onto the couch and Minnie cuddles into my side with my arm around her shoulders. I wish I could believe her assertions, but something is wrong. What isn't Minnie telling me?

CHAPTER XI
Dreaming

This year for Lúnasa, Uther, Arthur, and I have traveled to the villa of Gawaine's father, Lot. The Saxons are quiet after our latest push, and Uther was confident enough to order a return to his villa for a brief respite. When Lot invited us for the festival, Uther was quick to agree. Lot's villa is closer to the borderlands than is Uther's. If the Saxons grow restless, we will be well situated to respond quickly.

Arthur is overjoyed. He looks up to Gawaine, and the older boy is clearly fond of Arthur. Arthur looks forward to the tests of skill that always feature at Lúnasa, horse racing and sword work and the like. It will be a small gathering this year, as everyone waits for the Saxons to make their next move, but I'm confident it will be an enjoyable one.

When we arrive at the villa, the celebrations are well underway.

"You will play for us, won't you, Merlin?" says Lot in the great hall, who has clearly already enjoyed the fruits of his brewer's labor. At my side, Gawaine greets Arthur with a hearty slap on the back that causes Arthur to stumble and grin.

"Of course," I say. "If my throat is loosened with the right libation."

"Someone bring this man some ale!" Lot roars. Gawaine rolls his eyes and passes me a mug.

"Any requests, since you're providing the drinks?" I ask Gawaine. He pauses in thought.

"Anything about Boudica, the warrior queen?" he asks. His lauvan, the color of fresh salmon, wriggle with enthusiasm. "I love stories from the past."

"I know just the song." I give him a wink and find a nearby bench to settle on. By the time my harp is out of its case and I've tuned it, an audience has gathered around me.

Without introduction, I launch into a song about Boudica's last stand on the Icknield Way against the Roman army.

"Boudica, her tawny hair like a raging lioness…"

Arthur listens with his shoulders swaying to the beat, as he often does, and the rest of the audience looks relaxed and happy as I play. Gawaine, however, is enthralled. When Arthur leans over to whisper something to him, Gawaine waves him away and continues to listen intently.

"Her hand rose, and her people rose behind her…"

After a few songs, I plead thirst and the audience disperses. Someone calls for a contest, and half the crowd leaves the great hall for the yard outside. Arthur attempts to drag Gawaine out, but the older boy approaches me instead.

"That was fantastic, Merlin," he says with enthusiasm. "Where did you learn that tale of Boudica?"

I place my harp back in its case, cover it carefully with a cloth, and close the lid.

"An old bard I used to travel with," I say. "It was one of the earliest songs I ever learned, but it's still a good one. Worth bringing out and polishing from time to time."

"Do you think it actually happened that way?" he asks. "The battle, I mean. Boudica's defeat to the Romans."

I shrug.

"Something like that. I imagine the part with the *sidhe* prince might be embellished, though."

Arthur laughs. Gawaine grins but glances at my harp case again.

"Do you want to learn?" I ask. He is so fascinated by my playing, that I can't help but wonder.

"No, no." Gawaine's eyes widen as if he had never given the matter any thought. "No, I like the stories. That's all."

"I'll be sure to play more later, then. We can't leave you wanting."

Birds twitter, tweet, cheep, flutter.

Light in my eyes—gone—back—gone

The forest is deafening. Rustling leaves. Wind. The damned birds.

I can't focus

Water in the stream, more noise, always more noise

Never enough to stop the faces.

No names only faces. Blink and they're gone, then back.

They torture me and I don't know why—I don't know anything. Only that the forest is so loud—

Wind cold on my naked skin, so cold but I don't feel anything

A new noise to torment me. A voice?

Words, words, words—meaningless words. I understand the damned birds better.

Boudica, her tawny hair like a raging lioness…

More meaningless words, but I can focus on them.

Wind fades, leaves quiet.

The damned birds finally stop.

Her golden torc gleaming in Lugh's light…

My heart beats to the words.

Do I know this? Do I know anything?

The feet like thunder marching along Icknield Way…

My mouth opens, sounds come out.

Hoarse and terrible, but something to focus on. Words come out. Where do they come from?

I know this.

"Her hand rose, and her people rose behind her…"

More words come, and a tune. My voice finds notes. I sing?

This would sound better with a harp.

The words end. I blink and the trees come into focus. The stream twinkles. The damned birds twitter again, but I can ignore them for the first time in a long while.

Was there another voice, or was it in my head?

A sigh from beside me. My head creaks as I turn to look. A man sits on the dead leaves. His hair is gray and bushy, and his wide shoulders are wrapped in a warm woolen cloak. I could use a cloak. It's cold being naked.

I reach out to his lauvan, the color of salmon flesh, and twist one around my finger in wonder. I haven't seen human strands in a very long time. My own brown threads are too similar to the forest's that I simply blend in, like some mossy tree. His strands look familiar, and I study the one in my grasp. How do I know him?

The man stares at me steadily. His eyes are sad.

I stare back. A breeze within my mind blows away my inner fog. When only wisps of it are left, the man's name emerges from the depths of memory.

"Gawaine," I whisper.

He smiles, but his eyes remain sorrowful.

"Merlin," he says. "You remember."

I look away, across the stream at the sweeping branches of a willow. More memories bombard me, each one piercing my soul with their poignancy. My jaw tightens.

"The battle. Arthur. Then Nimue." I swallow past the lump in my throat. "Was it all real?"

"Yes," Gawaine says softly. "I'm sorry."

We sit in silence and allow the stream to burble in place of words. Memories fill my mind, but whether through the passage of time or madness, they are not as sharp as the painful knowledge that drove me to run wild in this forest. I wonder if perhaps I can bear them. I think I would like to try.

"Will you come back with me?" Gawaine says finally.

I nod slowly.

93

"Yes."

CHAPTER XII

I don't know what to do about Xenia except wait for the next time she approaches me. Hopefully, her current body will give her a day or two of use before she strikes again. Wayne and Alejandro are on the task, but searching takes time, and they haven't uncovered anything yet.

Minnie is still understandably horrified by the prospect of the successor wandering the city looking for new bodies, but when she checks our empty fridge, she agrees to go to the grocery store before we visit Wayne's house for dinner once more. I did offer to host this time, but Wayne scoffed at my lack of yard to spar in, so I buy ingredients for spaghetti instead.

"It's hard to feel anxious with an evening with friends to look forward to," she says in contentment while we walk down the road to my van. "Let's do a lap around the park."

"As my lady desires," I say and guide her toward a row of trees with our linked arms.

The street is moderately busy, with customers spilling out of restaurants onto the sidewalk and cars meandering past. Minnie's hand tightens on my arm, and I tense instinctively at her alarm.

"Is that guy watching us?" she hisses. "On the patio, ten o'clock. Don't look now!"

I give it a moment, then I sweep my eyes past the spot Minnie indicated. No one looks at us with anything more than a passing disinterest.

"It's fine," I say. "No one's looking. We're all right."

Minnie heaves a deep breath.

"Sorry, getting paranoid there. I just hate the thought of Xenia sneaking up on us. We wouldn't even know until it was too late."

She rubs her eyes with an expression of distress, and I clutch her closer.

"Are you all right?" I ask. She's been doing that more, lately, and she won't tell me what's wrong. True to form, she stops rubbing and smiles at me.

"A long day, that's all. Head back to the van? I think I've had enough phantom eyes tracking me today. My nerves are shot."

I dutifully turn us back to where we parked the van, but a prickling sensation crawls up my neck. Is Minnie paranoid, or are we being watched? I casually glance at the surrounding passersby, but no one obviously watches us. A shiver tingles my shoulders and I quicken our pace. I have no proof that the successor is here, but that doesn't stop me from wanting to get Minnie off the streets as soon as I can.

We drive the short distance to Wayne's house with no misadventures. When Alejandro spies me, his eyes light up.

"Did you bring the sword, Merlo? We forgot to show Wayne yesterday."

"What sword?" Wayne asks with interest. I give Minnie a guilty glance, and she narrows her eyes.

"Why do you have that look? What did you do?"

Alejandro looks contrite.

"Sorry, Merlo, I didn't know it was supposed to be a secret."

"Oh, it's not." I sigh and heave myself up from my chair. "I try not to keep secrets these days. Alejandro and I were bad boys on Friday and stole a priceless artifact from the museum." At Minnie and Wayne's gasps, I hold up my hand. "In my defense, it was my sword to begin with. You explain, Alejandro. I'll grab it from the van."

By the time I return with the sword wrapped in my coat, the others are caught up on Friday's events. Wayne still looks flabbergasted at our audacity, although inclined to laugh at it. Minnie has her arms crossed with disapproval, but she wears a resigned expression.

"If this is what you get up to when I'm around," she says. "I'd hate to know what you do when my law-abiding influence is not present."

"You'd have to get comfortable." I lay the sword carefully on the table and unwrap it from my coat. "It's a long list."

Wayne's eyes are riveted on the sword. He reaches out with yearning fingers but hesitates before touching it.

"Go on," I say. "Perhaps it will help you remember."

He holds the grip and lifts the sword off the table. His muscles tighten at the weight, but he carries it like he's familiar with swinging a sword.

"Such a little thing," he says. "You were always odd to disadvantage yourself with a short sword, Merry."

Wayne's eyes are distant as he gazes at the weapon. Alejandro glances at me with shining eyes.

"He had to have one hand free for the lauvan," Alejandro says quietly.

Wayne steps back and rotates his wrist experimentally. The sword whooshes through the air with a familiar sound, and I sigh wistfully.

"It has been a long time since I've heard that." I turn to a pot bubbling on the stove. "Pasta's ready to go in."

"Come on, Wayne." Alejandro jumps up. "Let's practice."

It's drizzling out, but that doesn't stop Alejandro and Wayne from gleefully taking over the backyard with their antics.

"Go on," Minnie says when she sees me looking out the window as we prepare dinner. "You want to be out there. I've got this."

I kiss her swiftly on the cheek and squeeze her bottom. She swats me with a tea towel on my way out. Minnie is a keeper, that's for sure, and I've unconsciously known that forever.

I'd like to use my own sword, the one I cut my teeth on, that held me in good stead for many years at the sides of my first friends. Although it's terribly dull—nothing a good grinding stone wouldn't fix—I would still dent the others' wooden weapons into bits. I pick up my wooden sword and push the door open.

By the time the gate creaks open on the side of the house, announcing a new arrival, the three of us are wet with sweat and rain. I bat away Alejandro's loose attempt at a slice and hold up my sword to his neck.

"Dead, again," I say in triumph. "And I didn't even use lauvan."

"I can't believe you're gloating when you have years of experience on us." Alejandro shakes water out of his hair. "Sore winner."

"And yet, still a winner." I grin at him then turn to see who has arrived.

Jen stands at the fence, looking small and unsure. Cecil hovers behind her, holding an umbrella over them both.

"I brought back your umbrella, Merry." She holds out the folded black accessory. "I borrowed it the other day, remember? And you said you were coming here tonight, so…"

She tries not to look Alejandro's way, although her gaze flickers toward him once or twice in an involuntary motion. I try to hide my smile. Alejandro, although his cheerful, round face is unlikely to grace a fashion magazine, nevertheless shows his physique to his advantage in a sodden tee shirt. His form has only been improved by visits to Wayne's gym and our new sparring classes.

"Thanks, Jen." I move forward to grab the offered umbrella.

"Want to stay for dinner?" Wayne says from his perch on the stairs. "Merry brought a ton of food."

"Don't tell me you don't get hungry after this," I say in my defense.

"Thanks, but we have plans," Jen says with an apologetic look at Wayne. Cecil waves at my wooden sword.

98

"That's pretty awesome that you do this," he says. "Totally vintage. Where did you learn?"

"Oh, here and there." I wave in the air dismissively. A thought traipses into my mind, and I tilt my head in question. "You want to try?"

"Oh!" Cecil looks at the sword again then at Jen, as if asking for permission. She shrugs tightly and grabs the umbrella when he hands it to her.

"Wayne, this one's yours," I say with a grin.

"Me? You're the teacher," he says, but he heaves himself off the stairs and grabs his sword. Alejandro silently passes Cecil the other sword and stations himself on the stair that Wayne vacated.

"What better way to learn than to teach for yourself?" I say. "Show him a few blocks, then have at it. Best way to learn is to try."

Cecil looks nervous but eager as Wayne demonstrates some basic defensive blocks. I stand beside Jen.

"Really, Merry? Swordplay?" she says quietly, for my ears only.

I glance sidelong at her, but she resolutely stares at Cecil's attempts to swing his practice sword.

"Just because you don't want to embrace your past, doesn't mean others don't," I reply softly. She stiffens, but she needs to hear this, so I plow on. "It helps them to remember, to connect with their past selves, to discover what skills they know now and what they knew before. You can do what you see fit, but don't deny them the joy of finding themselves."

"Don't talk about this sort of stuff around Cecil, remember," she says by way of reply. "He doesn't know anything."

"I should think not."

Jen sighs.

"Do whatever you want with your time, it doesn't matter to me," she says. I don't know if she meant it to sound as uncaring as it did, but I wince anyway. What happened to my friend?

She notices the gesture and has the grace to look chagrined, but she doesn't take it back. Instead, she says at her regular volume, "Have you heard about the latest disappearance on the news? Parvati Singh, thirty-three-year-old accountant, missing since yesterday."

"Parvati Singh?" Alejandro says from the stairs. "She was on the Potestas list. We've been trying to contact everyone on the list, and a few aren't answering their messages."

My shoulders slump, and I pass a hand over my eyes.

"Another one," I say. "Damn it."

"We'll find her," Alejandro says with force. "We'll get there."

"Text me a page of that list, Alejandro." Jen's eyes flash with anger at the situation. "Divide and conquer, right? This madness has to stop."

Alejandro nods. Only I can see his lauvan perk up at Jen saying his name.

A clattering brings my attention to the sparring pair. Cecil, somehow, has managed to swat away Wayne's attack and now presses his sword to Wayne's chest. Both men pant for breath. Then, Wayne's face breaks into an open smile.

"A natural," Wayne says, patting Cecil on the shoulder after the other man drops his sword tip. Cecil looks astonished but pleased.

"Thanks," he says. "That was way more fun than I thought."

"Come by anytime," Wayne says. Alejandro's lauvan bristle beside me but he says nothing aloud. He doesn't harbor welcoming feelings toward Cecil, that's certain. However, he's wise enough to know that making his animosity too evident won't win him any points with Jen. And, despite Jen's clear distaste for Alejandro's advances and his sense of destiny, that's still his goal. I don't know how that triangle will work out in the end, but I predict heartache for someone.

Alejandro stands and claps his hands together once. We all look at him in surprise.

"Xenia needs to be stopped," he says loudly. "And we're the only ones who know about the successor, so the responsibility falls to us. Let's divide the Potestas list up, like Jen suggested, and track down every single member. Either confirm that they know nothing or follow the suspicious ones. We need to do whatever it takes to stop this madman. Madwoman—mad elemental," he corrects himself, then he points to Wayne and me. "You two follow up with the list that I'll text you. I'll grab Liam and work on another third, and Jen and Cecil can be the last team." His lauvan twitch at calling Jen and Cecil a team, but he maintains an impressively calm face. "Anything you can't handle, call me or Merry. Okay? Let's stop Xenia from killing any more innocent people."

I find it hard to keep a straight face during Alejandro's speech, but out of respect for my friend, I avoid chuckling. He's falling into old habits, which warms my heart to see. Arthur was never an unparalleled fighter, but his skills at directing his followers and getting them to do what needed to be done saved us more than a few times. These memories must be molding Alejandro into a hybrid of all the men who came before him. He's metamorphosizing before my eyes, and I can't wait to see what happens next.

"Pick you up at nine tomorrow?" I say to Wayne. He nods and swings his wooden sword onto his shoulder.

"Let's find this murderous bastard. It's time to show her that this is our world."

CHAPTER XIII

Dreaming

It has been two years since Uther's death, and Arthur has grown into his role as warlord. It wasn't easy for him—the uncertainty of a young man when confronted with more experienced warriors took much practice to overcome—but with enough victories, he has earned the others' respect. Now, as the men gather in the damp spring weather to scout for Saxon advances, he has their ears. They travel to Arthur's villa to confer and receive advice on where to patrol, and he usually has excellent ideas. Most are his own, but he insists on my input.

I stayed at the villa this winter at Arthur's pleading. He tried not to show it, but the lauvan don't lie. He was truly terrified that I would die on my travels in the south and leave him without counsel. Although I chafed at the confinement, I couldn't leave Arthur in that state. Only I know that he's still a frightened young man trying to live up to his father's reputation. He puts on a good front for others.

I itch to jump on my horse and ride to the borderlands. We are preparing to do just that when a horse gallops toward the palisade. I peer at the rider, who wears a finely woven tunic and an expensive-looking leather vest that has seen a few battles, but I don't recognize his dusty orange lauvan. His sandy brown hair sways in thick locks over a well-proportioned face, which sports an expression of hesitation and determination.

I stride to greet the newcomer. Unfamiliar faces are welcome after a winter within the villa's walls.

"Who might you be?" I call out in a friendly tone. The young man's head snaps toward me. He can't be more than a few years older than Arthur.

"Good day," he says in a light and pleasant voice with a

slight accent. He dismounts and leads his horse close enough to speak at a comfortable volume. "My name is Lancelot, son of Ban. I've recently come home after many years away, and reports of Saxon villainy prompted me to seek out the leaders resisting their advance. My father is unwell and unable to come to Arthur Pendragon's aid, but he sends me in his stead."

I raise my arm and reach to pat him on the shoulder.

"You are most welcome, Lancelot. My name is Merlin, and I advise Arthur. How is your sword arm?"

"I have been in many battles," he says stiffly, as if concerned that I attack his honor.

"And survived to tell the tale. That speaks for itself. We never turn away willing blades, for the Saxons grow ever more numerous." I lead Lancelot into the stable, where Arthur checks his saddle. "Arthur, meet our newest recruit, Lancelot."

Arthur turns with an expression of warmth.

"Ban's son? I didn't know you had returned from Gallia. Welcome back."

"You know each other?" I ask.

"We met once or twice as boys," Lancelot says. "But I was fostered at my uncle's house in Gallia at a young age and haven't returned since."

"We're happy to have you," says Arthur. "Every good sword counts against the Saxons. We ride for our first patrol shortly. Will you join us?"

"Of course," Lancelot says. "That is why I came."

"Perhaps a mug of ale, first." I point him to the door and lead the way. "You must be thirsty."

We leave Arthur adjusting his saddle in the stable. Lancelot strides at my side while we cross the yard to the main hall. Three serving women carrying large baskets of linens meander past, and Lancelot's eyes follow them with a hungry gleam.

"Not many pretty faces where we're going," I say with a pat on his shoulder. "Ale I can provide before we leave, but that's all."

Lancelot blinks his confusion.

"What do you mean?"

I frown. It seemed obvious to me. Is Lancelot pretending to be naïve, or did he truly not notice his own ogling? I don't answer him and instead open the door to the hall to usher him inside.

Our first skirmish happens three days later. We startle a troop of a dozen Saxon warriors. When one man spots us exiting the forest near the meadow where they camp, he sends up a great bellowing call to arms. Round shields swing up from the ground and shining blades rise to meet our patrol group of eight riders.

They have the advantage of numbers, but we have the element of surprise and the height of horses. I leap off my mount as soon as we are near, as I always do, so that my opponents' strands are close enough for me to grab. Arthur fights efficiently, as always, and I'm proud of his skills. The others swing their swords with gusto and pick off the Saxons one by one.

Lancelot, however, is a force by himself. The speed of his blade is astounding, and the whistling noise it makes as it slices through the air travels to my ears from across the meadow. He easily takes down three opponents by the time most of us have handled one.

When the Saxons left alive are trussed up together, awaiting judgement, Arthur walks over to Lancelot, who cleans his sword on the grass.

"You are an incredible swordsman," he says, respect in his voice.

"I'm glad you're on our side," I call out.

Lancelot smiles then glances at Arthur's sword, still smeared with blood and dirt.

"Better clean that," he says. "It's too fine of a weapon to leave dirty. I wish I had a sword like that. Who made it for you?"

"It was my father's," Arthur replies, his voice sad. He bends to wipe the blade against a large tuft of grass.

Lancelot runs his eyes over the now-gleaming edge of Arthur's sword. His gaze is hungry again, and I wonder if this covetous streak will be a problem in the future.

CHAPTER XIV

I pull myself away from a sleepy, satisfied Minnie with regret early Sunday morning, but my mission can't wait. I want Parvati Singh to be the last person hurt by the successor, not the next in a long line. We need to find Xenia.

I keep kicking myself for my weakness. Xenia has been within my grasp twice, and while I can forgive myself for the shock of our first meeting, not attempting capture the second time was inexcusable. My thirst for knowledge cost Parvati Singh her life, and I must live with that. The least I can do is try my hardest to stop Xenia before she hurts anyone else.

The next time Xenia approaches me, I'll be ready. I can't let her touch me—I have no desire to be a host body—but I have a few tricks up my sleeve. With any luck, Xenia still hasn't figured out how to manipulate lauvan as well as I can, and I'll have the upper hand.

In the meantime, I can follow Alejandro's directions and investigate Potestas members. Wayne waits for me on his front porch, and his face breaks open in a wide smile when he spots my van.

"Sweet ride." He chuckles when he slams the passenger door shut behind him. "You going to get yourself a Great Dane while you're at it?"

I sigh dramatically and pull away from the curb.

"The ridicule I endure for love. The vehicle was Minnie's idea. Some women want flowers, my woman wanted a VW van. Well, her previous incarnation did, and the desire held over into this life."

"It's something else, your history," Wayne says. "Epic love story, really. You two keep finding each other, century after century. Makes the rest of us wonder if there's someone out there for everyone."

I glance at Wayne, but he maintains his gaze through the

106

windshield. His rust-colored strands swirl slowly, matching his thoughtful tone.

"Hard to know, unless we start pushing the grail on everyone we meet." I don't know what to say—what Minnie and I have is amazing, no doubt about it, but I don't know if everyone has something similar—so I try to lighten the mood. "But it's probably just me. I am extraordinary."

Wayne laughs and his strands relax.

"In your own mind, I have no doubt. What's our first target?"

"Tawnie Reagan. She's on Sixteenth Avenue, not far from here. Let's see if we can see anything at her house."

Tawnie's address is a three-story character house, split into apartments like Wayne's. She's on the bottom floor, but before we knock and find out more, Wayne and I look at pictures of her that he scoured from the Internet.

She's in her fifties with a snub nose below laughing eyes and a wild mane of graying hair. She looks friendly, and I wonder what drew her to Potestas. Pictures can be deceiving, I suppose.

"Wait, who's that?" Wayne points at the house.

The lower door opens, and a woman with black hair wearing scrubs backs out of the suite. She hauls a wheelchair, and when it turns, I recognize Tawnie with a sinking sensation in my stomach.

Tawnie's once-laughing eyes are vacant and wander restlessly from gate to bush to waving branch without seeing any of it. Her hands tremble in her lap, and her mane of hair is short and contained with a clip.

The aide pushes the wheelchair down the sidewalk, taking her charge for a morning walk. Wayne sighs beside me.

"Looks like we can cross Tawnie off the list," he says heavily. I don't reply, and he peers into my face. "Are you okay?"

"That was me," I say quietly. "I did that."

It was me, fiddling with her lauvan after the debacle at the cave, that addled her mind. I erased her memories of elementals and Potestas to protect Minnie, and I'd do it again without hesitation, but the cost still weighs on me, despite my justifications. It was me who turned Tawnie Reagan into a wheelchair-bound husk of her former self.

"Yeah," says Wayne. "You did. You turned her brain to mush. But." He holds up a finger. "You did it for a good reason. Don't forget, she was willing to kill Minnie for her own ends."

"I know. And I don't regret it. But it's still hard to know that I irrevocably changed this woman's life."

"And that's why I still have faith in you." Wayne claps a hand on my shoulder with a comforting weight. "If you didn't feel sorry, that would be a bad sign. Come on, let's find the next on the list."

Wayne's words make me feel marginally better, and I approach the next residence with greater composure. It's a four-story apartment block, but the name on the buzzer doesn't match the name on our list, Lela McClellan. When I speak to the grumpy man who finally answers my insistent ringing, he informs me that he moved in two days ago.

"Did Lela move, or is she missing?" I ask Wayne. He frowns and makes a note on our list.

"It's suspicious. I'll look into her more at home."

Wayne directs me to the next former Potestas member but doesn't mention a name.

"She works in a coffee shop over on Broadway. I scoped her out before, when Alejandro and I were looking into people." Quickly enough that I glance at Wayne in suspicion, he changes the subject. "Did I tell you that Alejandro wants to take me trail riding on a horse?"

I laugh with delight.

"He wants to trigger memories as fast as possible, doesn't he? Will you take your practice sword with you?"

108

"Don't you dare mention that to Alejandro. He'll make it happen, for sure. I doubt the old nags they'd have us ride would be warhorses."

When I pull the van over into a free parking spot—a legal one, for once—Wayne looks nervous.

"Who's this one?" I say.

"It's Anna Green," he says in a rush.

My breath hitches as memories of Anna flood my mind. We had a complicated connection, from a two-night stand in the little town of Wallerton, to various interactions within Potestas, to the final mind-wipe after her attempted murder of Minnie. After messing with her brain, I'm torn between hoping she's all right and not caring.

I exhale explosively and tuck my keys in my pocket.

"Let's get this over with."

"Why don't you let me do the talking?" Wayne says. "Since you have history with her. Not that she remembers, but still."

"Sounds good. Grab me a coffee, will you?" I could turn on the charm and find out what we need to know, but if Wayne is willing to do the work, I'm happy to let him. I don't know if I could easily hide the bitter taste in my mouth at the thought of Anna's treachery.

Wayne pulls the door of the shop open for me and a warm blast of coffee-scented air hits me in the face. I breathe in deeply, enjoying the smells and the sounds of chattering people that fill the shop. Wayne steps beside me, then he turns to the counter and his lauvan freeze.

I look in the same direction, on high alert for danger, but there are only two baristas behind the counter. One is a weedy-looking young man with a morose face at the till. The other is Anna.

She looks younger, somehow, happy in a way that I've never seen her. Her long, curly hair is pulled back in a high ponytail and her face is calm and content as she pours flavored syrup into a mug. For the first time since seeing Tawnie Reagan in

109

her wheelchair, I feel that perhaps altering Potestas members' minds wasn't such a bad thing.

I don't know what I would say to Anna, this new Anna that I don't know, so I give Wayne my order and he wanders to the counter while I seat myself at a bar stool to watch.

Anna greets Wayne with a smile of recognition, which surprises me. Has he spoken to her before? My suspicions are only heightened by the rusty strands that swirl around Wayne and reach toward Anna. They chat for some minutes, my long-completed coffee cooling on the counter between them. I tap my fingers on my lap with growing impatience.

Finally, Wayne bids Anna farewell and turns my way. I hop off the stool and grab my offered drink on the way out.

"You two seem quite friendly." I try to keep the accusation out of my voice, but Wayne looks guilty anyway.

"Alejandro and I looked into her last week, remember?"

"And what do you conclude? Is she working with March, bringing elementals to Earth, all of that?"

Wayne shakes his head slowly.

"I mean, maybe, but if so, she's an excellent liar. I just can't see it. And she says she works extra shifts, so when would she have the time? We can mark her down as a maybe, but my guess is no."

I nod with satisfaction. Despite Wayne's attraction for Anna, he's not letting it get in the way of his evaluation. I didn't see any signs of deceit during their chat, so I'm inclined to agree with Wayne.

"Good. I'd hate to bring her to justice yet again. I'm tired of dealing with Anna Green." I shoot Wayne a sideways glance. "You'd like to deal with her a little more, though, wouldn't you?"

Wayne colors, something I've never seen my calm friend do before.

"I don't know what you're talking about."

"Good luck with that one. She's a firecracker. She might spit you out at the end, but it'll be worth it."

"I did not need to hear that," Wayne says, half-aghast, half-laughing. "Now I have terrible visions of you and her, and what I really wanted were sexy visions of her and me." He sobers. "But I don't know—if she doesn't remember things, and I do? And I know what she has done—and it's not good—but if she doesn't remember doing them, did she really do them at all? Is this a second chance for her?"

"Questions you'll have to answer for yourself." I climb into the van and Wayne follows with a creased brow. "There's no right answer, just what you can live with. Come on, let's whittle down our list some more."

By the time I pull up to Wayne's house, we're both tired and dejected. Of the twelve people on our list, three are unaccounted for. The rest don't appear to be hiding deep, dark secrets. I wince at the memory of Tawnie Reagan and another unfortunate, David Holt, who was clearly not his old self. I suppose I should be thankful that the rest were fine, but it's hard to look past my failures.

Alejandro sits on Wayne's porch, waiting for us.

"What news?" he asks. Wayne shoves the annotated list at him before collapsing in a wicker chair beside the door.

"The crossed-out names all check out," he says with a sigh. "I doubt they're harboring Xenia. The circled ones we couldn't find. They're candidates for helping Xenia, either by releasing her into the world or donating their bodies. But I don't know, Alejandro. How is this helping? How is this getting us closer to stopping a killer? It feels futile."

I lean against a pillar without speaking, but I agree with Wayne. This whole endeavor reeks of fruitlessness. Even if we know who might be helping Xenia, what can we do with that information if we can't find them? I'm tempted to walk around, shouting Xenia's name. It might get results faster than this.

"This is crucial work," Alejandro says to Wayne firmly. "We now know the names of people who might be helping Xenia. We can check them against the missing persons list, we can ask your police friend for help tracking them down, and we can follow their trails, work, home, wherever. Don't forget, Xenia is new here, and she's bound to slip up soon." Alejandro turns to me. "Merry, you need to talk to your elemental friend, Ailu, see what he knows. We'll get Xenia, don't worry."

Alejandro's pep talk lifts Wayne's slumped shoulders and brightens his tired eyes. I straighten my back. Alejandro has always been good at boosting morale.

"You're right," I say. "We'll get Xenia."

Minnie is at the beach, again, so I drive there once I leave Wayne's house. It's cold with threatening clouds above—a few drops of rain even touch my cheek—so I text Minnie my location and wander into a nearby restaurant. It's steamy and filled with bustling noise and happy chatter. I'm not the only one in search of a pre-dinner appetizer. By the time I order and find a seat with a view of choppy seas and gray skies, a pair of soft lips kisses the back of my neck.

"Hey, you," Minnie says. She slides into the seat next to mine. Her hair is still wet, but her cheeks are pink from exertion and her eyes bright. "What a beautiful day. It's lovely to come from the water and see your handsome face waiting for me."

I understand the words, but it takes me a moment to realize that she speaks in a Middle Mongol dialect, the language of my eighth wife, Khutulun. She grins widely when comprehension lights my eyes.

"Feeling better?" I reply in the same language and squeeze her thigh in greeting.

"So much better," she says in English. "The water grounds me, somehow. I went windsurfing and got some great air on the waves. My arms will be sore tomorrow, but it was worth it."

I sigh in mock-exasperation.

"You know you're never sore when I'm around. If you want a massage and a lauvan-detangling, you need only ask."

Minnie flutters her eyelashes at me then bursts out laughing.

"Sorry, I can't manage pouty. You'll have to make do with me."

"That's all I ever wanted." I lean forward and kiss her lips.

"Excuse me," an embarrassed server says behind us. "Your nachos are here."

"You brilliant man," Minnie says. Her eyes are ravenous at the sight of the platter of nachos. "This is just what I wanted."

"I aim to please."

Minnie chatters more about her time on the water, and I tell her about our lack of progress in the hunt for Xenia. Her eyes darken at the subject.

"I'm sorry I couldn't help today," she says. "I just felt so crummy that all I could manage was getting out on the water. I hope you're being careful. This elemental needs to be stopped, but we have no idea how dangerous she is. What will you do if you see her again?"

"I can't grab her." The thought of being possessed turns my stomach, and I place the chip in my fingers back on my plate. "I don't want her to take over my body. Same goes for you— you can't get anywhere near her. I think I'll have to summon some winds to blow her down, grab something heavy and knock her out, perhaps. Then what? I don't know. Solitary confinement? What happens if I kill the body, where does the elemental go? I just don't know enough."

"Talk to your wind elemental," Minnie says. "Get some answers. Let's be as prepared as we can be."

"Yes." I tap my fingers on the table. There's a decent wind today. "Let's go outside, see if I can speak with Ailu. Are you done eating?"

Minnie slaps her napkin on the table and stands with determination.

"I'm ready."

We find an exposed park bench on the shoreline. Minnie shivers, and I pull the water lauvan out of her hair before she gets too cold. She covers her now-dry hair with her hood.

"How do we do this?" she asks. "Do you need me to do anything?"

"Pretend you're chatting with me," I say. "I'll be talking, but seemingly to no one. You'll hear the elemental but won't see him. From a distance, it will look like we're speaking together."

"Got it."

I turn to face Minnie then snatch a few air strands that fly past my face with a speed born of the coming storm. I send my intention through the silvery threads, then release them and wait. It isn't long before an air cable descends into my waiting hands. Minnie's eyes flicker over the cable, and I wonder if she can see a disturbance in the air. I don't have time to ponder long, for Ailu's form rises from the cable.

"Greetings, Merry," he says hoarsely. Minnie stifles a gasp but stays still. "I enjoy our frequent talks. Tell me, are you liking my wind? I've recruited a few other air elementals for today's storm."

"It's ramping up nicely," I offer, unsure what Ailu hopes I'll say. He appears satisfied, so I plow on. "The earth fundamental, Xenia, is on Earth, as you know. Since she is too much for a human body to handle, she switches bodies every few days. She leaves the bodies for dead."

"This displeases you?" Ailu says with a tilt to the lauvan that

114

comprise his head. His words are said without malice, as if he truly doesn't understand and wants to know my opinion.

"Yes, very much so. I need to stop Xenia, but I don't know how. She can transfer to a new body at a single touch. If I go after her, she might possess me or my friends. If I kill her, what will happen? Will the elemental be sent back to your realm, or will it be free to possess another body?"

"I don't know," Ailu says, his tone musing. "Either is possible. None of the stories mentions such an occurrence. I can ask around, if you like."

"So, I can't kill her, just in case." My heart sinks. Even if I capture her, what will I do with her? Minnie's face behind Ailu is torn between horror at the thought of killing Xenia's body and disappointment that it's not an option.

"I wouldn't worry about the earth fundamental possessing you," Ailu says. "Your own earth elemental strands wouldn't allow it, at least not easily. You would fight back, unlike the human strands of other bodies. You could be possessed, but it would take more effort and preparation."

"Well, that's something." If I can rely on my own strength as well as my lauvan, I stand a much better chance at overtaking Xenia. I've spent centuries honing my fighting prowess.

"Yours would be the perfect body to possess, though," Ailu continues. "Your nature—half elemental, half human—gives your body a complimentary strength that would support even a fundamental. It would take the right conditions to transfer, but the fundamental could stay in your body for a long, long time."

My eyes meet Minnie's, and we share a flash of fear.

"Xenia doesn't know that, though," I say to comfort her. "She still wants me to show her around Earth."

Minnie's eyes snap to something behind me and narrow in confusion.

"I didn't know," a rough voice says in my ear. "But I do

115

now. You've been very helpful, Merry."

CHAPTER XV

I draw my hands out of the air cable and Ailu disappears. My head whips around to see the speaker. A heavyset man in pale jeans and a red raincoat gives me a salute as he walks away.

It's Xenia, now in the body of a man. Fear and rage war in my gut, and I vault over the bench to follow her—him, now, I suppose. It's hard to keep up with Xenia's changes.

He breaks into a sprint, his gravelly laughter flowing past my ears with the wind. He reaches down and yanks at a few earth lauvan that lie on the ground. The path below my feet buckles, and I sprawl headlong. The gravel moves in rolling waves, making it impossible to gain my footing. It takes me too long to crawl past the patch of heaving ground and rise to my feet.

"He went inside!" Minnie shouts behind me. I spring forward and race through the doors of the sailing club.

It's pandemonium in the building. People are shrieking and yelling, and a few frantically gesture as they talk on their phones. A girl cries at the edge of a crowd surrounding a figure lying on the floor. An arm encased in a red raincoat lies lifelessly among the legs, and my heart sinks. Is Xenia's newest body dead?

But that must mean—I look frantically at every person's lauvan, desperately searching for slender chestnut brown threads among the human strands present. Xenia must have jumped to another body. It only takes one touch.

"What's going on?" Minnie grabs my hand. My eyes dart from one person to another, and I drag her around the crowd.

"Xenia's body is dead, and I think the elemental lauvan jumped ship. I'm trying to find them. Damn it!" I say once we circle back to the door. "Nothing. Come on, let's check outside."

We run out the door, still hand-in-hand, but the parking lot is sparsely populated, and those few present have no earth lauvan among their own. A throaty engine roar draws my eyes to the road in time to watch the tail end of a motorcycle disappear behind a building.

My shoulders slump and I run a hand through my hair in distraction.

"Gone," I whisper. "We were so close."

We stare after the vanished motorcycle for a moment of heavy silence. Minnie eventually pulls me around to look at her.

"He's after you, now," she whispers. Her eyes are full of pain and worry. "What will he do? How can we keep you safe?"

"I'll be all right. I've survived this long," I say automatically, but the words sound hollow even to my ears. I don't know how to fight someone who can switch bodies at a whim, someone who has full control over the elements, someone who wants to take over my body for their own use. How do I fight that?

"Wait here," Minnie says, and she darts into the building. Before I can follow her, I'm distracted by the sound of sirens. The ambulance must be here, but there's nothing they can do. That body, whoever it was, is dead. Xenia leaves no survivors.

Minnie returns and tucks her phone into her pocket.

"I got a picture of his face," she says. "We can see who Xenia picked this time. Maybe it will help us narrow down who he chooses as his victims."

My attention is only half on the road. The other half tries to imagine what Xenia will do next. He doesn't know what he needs to do to transfer himself into my body—Ailu said it would take more effort than usual—but that won't stop him from trying. If he can capture me, he can experiment as much as he needs to.

His new goal, even if he hasn't formulated it yet, must be to capture me alive. Plenty try, but very few succeed, at least not for long. None ever had the power of lauvan at their fingertips, and Xenia has an advantage there.

The only saving grace is that I know he's coming for me, and I can take steps to safeguard myself. It shouldn't be difficult, especially since I can watch for anyone with brown lauvan and give them a wide berth. Xenia's elemental strands are visible to me.

But what of my friends? Would Xenia harm one of them to get to me? How much does he understand of relationships and the lengths I would go to preserve them?

Minnie taps her phone in the passenger's seat beside me, and I glance at it distractedly.

"What are you doing?" I ask. She shakes her head, finishes tapping, then lays the phone in her lap.

"Texting Wayne and Alejandro the picture of the dead man," she says. "Maybe they can find out who he is, see if there's a missing person report for him. We need information if we're going to keep you safe."

"It's not only me I'm worried about. What if he comes after you, or any of the others?"

"He doesn't know any of the others," she says reasonably.

"He saw Jen."

"Oh." Minnie's face scrunches with worry. "I don't know what to do about that. Would Jen be willing to lie low until we figure this out?"

"I don't know." I drum my fingers on the steering wheel. "And what about you?"

"We'll both hide at home tomorrow. That will give us a day to come up with a better plan. Surely, there's something in your notebook or your memory that will help us out. Let's get creative."

I nod slowly. Minnie's practical suggestions calm the churning in my gut that started at the park bench when Xenia confronted us.

"You mean some kind of lauvan protection."

"Maybe," she says. "Or something that can show us who to look for. Is there any way for ordinary people to see lauvan?"

"You're always extraordinary to me." My words are rewarded by a squeeze on my thigh. "We dabbled with that, once, but not very successfully. I can give it another stab, though."

"Do that," Minnie says. "Anything to give us an advantage."

Minnie's strands are agitated but move in deliberate motions with her determination to follow through on our plans. I pull the van into our parking spot and kill the engine. On our walk to the elevator, someone across the garage drops his keys.

Minnie leaps into the air, and her lauvan buzz outward with such force that I can feel them against my own, like a static shock.

"It's only a neighbor," I say quickly to calm her. "It's not Xenia."

Her body droops in relief, but her strands remain restless, growing more active with each passing second. Her breath comes in short pants, and she clutches my arm.

"Every shock I've ever had," she gasps through her heavy breathing. "Every single one, coming at me right now. It's too much, Merry. I can't handle it. No one should have this much memory."

She's having another episode. I lower her to the cement floor, where she lands on her hands and knees. Her lauvan fizzle around her, and I grab a handful. She groans.

"You'll be all right," I say softly and begin to pour intention into the strands. Brythonic words float to the surface, my default when trying to soothe. No matter how far I go, my native tongue never leaves me. "Breathe, love, just breathe.

You'll be all right. I'm here. Hold on."

Slowly, so slowly, the strands buzzing around Minnie's body quiet into a natural swirl, and her breath returns to normal. She sits back on her heels and sighs deeply with her eyes closed. When I'm sure she has recovered, I release her lauvan. She sighs again.

"Let's get you upstairs," I say quietly. "The couch is much more comfortable than this cement floor."

Minnie chuckles and opens her eyes.

"That's not a high bar."

She holds out her arms and I pull her upright. She tucks her arm around my chest, and I hug her close with my own arm as we shuffle to the elevator.

I don't know how to help her through this overload of memories that she endures. All I can do is be there for her when she has an episode and hope that her mind will get used to the sensation soon. I hate to see her suffer like this, but I don't have any answers. She might have been happier not knowing her true self, but there's no way I could ever wish for that. I'm far too selfish. We'll simply have to muddle through and hope for the best.

In the meantime, since there is little I can do for Minnie besides making her comfortable, I can spend the whole of tomorrow figuring out how to protect us from Xenia. There must be something. Before bed tonight, I'll consult my old friend Braulio's notebook that he left me when he died. It's full of information about spirits and lauvan. If that comes up empty, perhaps Ailu will have some ideas. One way or another, I will find a way to stop Xenia from claiming any more lives, including my own.

CHAPTER XVI

Dreaming

Snow threatens in the heavy clouds this morning. I know I must leave shortly if I wish to be back at Arthur's villa before the way is impassable, but it's hard to leave Nimue.

My horse is fed, and its bridle tightened, my bag is packed with a skin of ale and loaf of bread in case I must spend the night hunkered in the shelter of a hollow tree, and my cloak is on. Still, I dither.

"Do you have any more oatcakes?" I say with a winning smile. Nimue's mouth twists as she tries not to grin.

"You know you have to leave soon."

"Not on an empty stomach, I hope."

She sighs dramatically but rises to collect the frying pan from the fireplace. I lean forward and pull a few of the fire's sparking orange lauvan to make the flames rise higher. Nimue glances at my movements.

"I wish I could see through your eyes," she says. She flips the cakes into my waiting hands, and I pass them back and forth to cool.

"Then you would see a beautiful woman with the most exquisite eyes and oatcakes surpassing description."

Nimue crosses her arms but can't hide her smile.

"You know what I mean. The lauvan. I wish I could see the world the way you do."

I chew slowly, my mind wandering over her words.

"I wonder if there is a way," I say. Nimue stiffens and stares at me.

"How?"

"I don't know," I admit. "But we could try. What if I push my strands into yours, make them mix? Do you think that might do something?"

"I don't know." She looks crestfallen. I'll be the first to

admit it's not a great suggestion, but I don't have any better ideas.

I stand and gesture for Nimue to do the same. When she steps close to me, I turn her around by the shoulders and press myself against her back.

"I thought you wanted to help me see the lauvan," she says. "This feels like you're trying something else."

I kiss her dark hair and wrap my arms around her torso.

"Perhaps we have time for both?" When she bumps her shoulder against mine in protest, I laugh. "Fine, fine. I'll get to work."

My fingers comb through my strands. If I can get them to mix with Nimue's, perhaps whatever in them that allows me to see lauvan will let Nimue do the same. It's a weak supposition, but worthy of trial.

My brown strands resist leaving my form, but I coax them out of their tight swirling over my skin. They skitter and coil around Nimue. When I tease Nimue's light blue strands together with mine, she gasps.

"What is it?" I whisper in her ear.

"It feels strange. Wrong."

My eyes track our intertwined strands. Nimue's squirm and writhe, clearly desperate to get away from mine. She clutches her stomach in a quick motion, and I release her. My strands slither back to their rightful place next to my body.

"That was horrible," she wheezes. "Wrong. I felt ill until you stepped away. And I didn't see any lauvan."

"Our first trial was not a success," I say lightly, although a part of me shrivels at the incompatibility of our strands. Why do hers recoil from mine? What does it mean?

My concern must be apparent from my expression, because Nimue wraps me in an embrace.

"It doesn't mean anything," she answers my unspoken question. "And it doesn't matter if I can never see the lauvan."

"It would be nice to have someone understand what my

world looks like." I stroke her hair with slow fingers. My mind leaps to the reason I am different in the first place. "One day, I'll find my father's people. I would like that."

Nimue squeezes me more tightly, and I belatedly realize how my words might make her feel.

"But, right now, I have everything I want." I lift her chin, so she looks in my face. "My search can wait for another day."

CHAPTER XVII

My text must be sufficiently concerning, for Jen promises to call in sick to work the next day. I do the same, and for most of the day, I pour over Braulio's extensive notebook, desperately searching for any hint of a protection spell against someone like me—useless for myself, but at least Minnie and Jen would be protected—or a way to reveal lauvan to a regular pair of eyes. I have my doubts that this is possible if the person has no elemental lauvan to transition between worlds, but I continue to search.

By dinnertime, I throw the notebook on my coffee table in disgust. Not for the first time, I wish that I had access to the library at Potestas headquarters. There was so much knowledge there, and I hardly mined the top surface. Now, it's gone, and I'm left scrambling in the dark. Minnie looks up from her book.

"Nothing?" she says, her face sympathetic and worried.

"I don't know. Perhaps? There's one spell that increases a person's ability to see 'auras,' which may or may not be lauvan. It requires a rare psychotropic herb from South America, so that's out. The notebook also reminded me that any elemental ceremony works best within its own element—remember the cave—"

"Not likely to forget," Minnie mutters.

"It was perfect for bringing out the current earth fundamental, because it was deep underground and at the confluence of multiple earth cables. My point is, if Xenia needs somewhere special to transfer his lauvan into my body, I'd expect it to happen somewhere very earthbound."

"Like where?"

"Near a cable, I'd guess, but that doesn't narrow it down

very much." I blow air through tight lips. "I don't feel any farther ahead than I was this morning."

Minnie stands and walks to my bookshelf. She slides out a folder and lays it on the coffee table.

"Where's your local cable map?" she says.

I rifle through the pages, some old enough to be inked on parchment, until I find a piece of paper with a rough sketch of the surrounding area. Lines bisect the land, indicating where earth cables travel across the globe.

"Here." I push the map toward her.

"Good. We should keep this handy. You might be able to see the cables, but the rest of us can't. If you go missing, how would we ever find you?"

"Let's not get to that point." I stand and walk to the balcony. Minnie is being practical, but it gives me a sick feeling to think of her trying to find me. That would mean I'd been captured. I don't want to put Minnie through that. "I'm going to talk to Ailu."

Minnie is quiet behind me. I slide the balcony door open and step outside. A few lazy cables loop through the air, slow and stately after the windstorm of yesterday. When one snakes toward me in a smooth spiral, I plunge my hands into it and hold on.

Within moments, Ailu emerges.

"Ailu, do you have any news on how to take Xenia down?" I say by way of greeting. Ailu's lauvan-face looks affronted.

"I thought humans enjoyed small talk before jumping into business," he says. "Good evening. How are you? Not that I particularly care how you are. Is that one of those human niceties that you wanted the earth fundamental to exhibit?"

"Sorry." I squeeze my eyes shut tightly for a moment to regain my composure. "Thank you for coming to speak with me. I'm on edge after learning that Xenia wants to possess my body. I've been searching all day for answers, but I have nothing."

126

Ailu sways like a flag in the breeze.

"It was a good storm yesterday. It's hard to work up the energy for feeling concerned. I gathered dozens of dormant elementals for the show. It was one of my better orchestrated ones, if I do say so myself."

"Yes, it was magnificent," I say with thinly veiled patience. If Ailu hears my tone, he doesn't let on. I'm grateful, because I need his advice. "Do your allies have anything to say about containing Xenia?"

"We only spoke yesterday, and I was very busy," he says. "I'll ask soon. Stay vigilant in the meantime. Xenia could be anywhere. Speaking of vigilance, have you met the other half-human elemental?"

CHAPTER XVIII

A moment of silence passes while I digest Ailu's change of topic.

"What are you talking about?" I say sharply. My heart pounds with excitement and fear that I've misunderstood Ailu. "Do you mean someone like me?"

"Exactly. I sensed the person a few days ago. Their strands joined with mine briefly, when I was sneaking around your realm. Nobody's watching over here, it's both liberating and worrisome. But, now that I know what I'm looking for, the person is easy enough to spot. Let me take you there."

I can barely push words through my dry throat. Fifteen centuries, and this is the first I've ever heard of someone like me. Can it be true?

I don't know of any reason why Ailu would lie, and I'm willing to follow him to see the lauvan of this person. My eyes close, and my elemental strands dive into the air cable. Ailu's presence surrounds me, along with a host of less sentient air elementals that bustle along next to us as Ailu draws my conscious forward.

It's a turbulent ride, unlike the smooth rolling I experience in an earth cable. I'm jostled up and around, barely catching a sense of where we are going or my surroundings. It's such a jumble that I rely exclusively on Ailu's guidance, and I hope I can trust him. Silver threads whisk past my senses, some brighter than others.

Despite the tumult, part of me exhilarates at this glimpse into Ailu's world. What would it feel like to be fully immersed?

Perhaps we descend, because colors other than silver flash past me. Brown earth lauvan appear solidly below, and assorted colors of strand clusters dot my mindscape. One particularly active grouping at head-height dances with fire threads.

"Human energy gathered around a fire of sorts," Ailu says within my mind. To me, it looks like a group of people warming themselves with a heat lamp. "Look at this one."

We swirl around one cluster floating above the group. Perhaps it sleeps in an apartment above a patio. Instead of a singular color, as all the other human clusters are, this one contains three different shades. The flickering orange of fire strands twist among wispy air threads, cemented together by human lauvan of a pale peach. This person, whoever he or she is, has not one, but two elemental associations.

"Two," I say softly to Ailu with my mind. "What does that even mean? How did that happen?"

"It's strange, certainly," Ailu says. "But intriguing. The person isn't aware enough to contact me, unfortunately, or else I would know more."

"I can find the person," I say, my mind buzzing with excitement. For centuries, I've looked and hoped for someone like me, only to be disappointed again and again. Could I have explored like this ages ago, and found someone? My eyes have been opened so many times since I discovered the elemental world. It's exhilarating. "I'll find them."

"Introduce me, will you?" Ailu says. The air lauvan surrounding me dance eagerly. "You human-elemental crosses are fascinating. And the person has a bit of air element, which is obviously more interesting to me than your dull earth strands."

"Hey," I say, but without animosity. I'm too exhilarated to take offense. "Thanks for showing me. I'll introduce you as soon as I'm able, but I don't know what to expect."

Ailu gathers my conscious in air lauvan and whisks me back to my body in a rush of silver and motion. Soon enough, my chocolate brown human strands glow quietly before us.

"Good luck, Merry," Ailu says. "We'll talk soon."

He pushes me into my body. Once my eyes open, a thick cord of air threads leaps into the sky and out of sight.

My head spins, and my stomach lurches alarmingly. The motion of my trip through the air, although only experienced by my mind, now affects my body. Terrible vertigo overwhelms me, and my stomach protests again. I stumble inside and race past a surprised Minnie to the bathroom just in time.

Dull earth strands, indeed. There's a reason I'm better on solid ground.

Thinking of my earth lauvan reminds me of the unknown person who has two elemental associations. My heart, now that it is connected to my mind, pounds in my chest. I will find out who it is. I will finally meet someone like me. I have a solid goal, something I want desperately to achieve, and it fills me with purpose. This meeting can't come soon enough.

I can't wait for the morning to find this half-elemental. I need to find him or her right now. Once Minnie hears the news, she doesn't try to dissuade me from my search.

"Come back soon," she says from the balcony doorway, her silhouette dark against the lit living room. I rub my thumb over her cheek.

"Just a quick flyover. Warm up the bed for me?"

She grins, and I pull my lauvan until my body dissolves into a merlin falcon. With a shriek and a flap of my powerful wings, I soar into the night.

I don't fly for long. I have no idea where the person is—my journey through the air strands with Ailu gave me no sense of direction—but I might now know how to look.

Above the lawn of my apartment complex, I let go of my twisted strands and transform from a spread-winged bird to a kneeling human. My knees grow damp on the grass, but I ignore the discomfort and close my eyes. My strands spread out from me, questing for their earth lauvan compatriots. I've never experimented with sending my conscious among earth lauvan without using a cable, but Ailu's antics make me think that it's possible. I don't know how else I can explore as thoroughly as I need without straying from the cables, which would be too limiting.

It's difficult, and slippery to manage, but I persevere. My threads twist and link with silvery-brown lauvan that lie along the ground like spiderwebs and rivers of glimmering light. When they connect, I send myself along the nearest strands.

A few presences touch me in question, but they don't feel as intelligent as Ailu—perhaps they are like the less sentient elementals that accompanied him—and I think soothing thoughts at them until they are reassured. It's a much different sensation from flying with Ailu. There is no sense of tumbling and soaring, for one, and my conscious is pleasantly grounded. The lauvan that I explore are tiny compared to the great rivers of cabling that I normally travel through, but once I get used to it, it's a similar sensation.

My mind connects with a trickle of strands and I follow it, gaining speed with every moment of confidence. My thoughts spread out until I'm exploring multiple directions at once, over hills and between buildings, along streams and vast networks of threads. Human lauvan flicker by me, hundreds of them, thousands, every color of the rainbow until I can barely keep up. There is only one that I care about, only one that is three, orange and silver and peach...

There.

Clear as a diamond, the triple-lauvan cluster hovers high in the air above the fire strands. I've found the person, but where? I pull all my disparate parts together—a strange, yet natural process—and try to remember how I got to this place. There are no landmarks in this world of threads and nothing to orient myself in the physical world.

But I'm no slouch, now that I'm in my element. I send some

tendrils of myself back toward my body. It's not difficult. My body exerts a force on my conscious, as if the two yearn to be together. While I watch the triple-lauvan cluster, unwilling to take my thoughts off it, I carefully feel the path back to my body. A few more tendrils travel the same way until I'm confident in my directions, then I let go with regret and come back to my body.

Once in my bird form again, I soar in the direction of the person's lauvan cluster. Now that I have my directions from the earth strands, I am unerring in my path. A few minutes later, I circle a small apartment building on a busy road. As I suspected, a ground-floor patio houses a heat lamp and six people loudly enjoying their evening.

The window, behind which lies the triple-color cluster, is covered with a curtain. I droop with disappointment then rally myself. Tomorrow morning, I can arrive here early and watch for the lauvan. With a plan, I swoop toward home.

My sleep is fitful, and when the sun fills my bedroom with pale autumn light, I leap out of bed and dress. When I walk toward the kitchen to make breakfast, Minnie moans behind me.

"Why are you up so early? Where are you going?"

"I want to catch this half-elemental before he or she goes to work for the day."

"Are you going to work, too?" Minnie stares at me in fear.

"I can't stay in the apartment another day. I'll keep my eyes open, and if Xenia tries any stunts, I'll be ready for him. I do have an advantage—I've been using lauvan in this body for centuries. He is new at it."

"He's also one of the most powerful elementals." Minnie strands twist in agitation. "Don't underestimate him."

I slide back onto the bed and stroke Minnie's hair away from her cheek with tender fingers.

"If fight or flight are the usual responses to danger, well, I've never been one for running. I can't stay inside forever. Best that there is a confrontation, one way or another." I kiss her forehead and stand again. "Besides, we don't know if he's even ready for the transfer. Today might not be the day. But, you should stay put. I have no way of protecting you from afar."

"I'm not much use to him," Minnie says. "And would he even know that we're important to each other? You say they don't have relationships like we do."

"Ailu talks about allies, not friends or family," I say. "It's true, Xenia might not recognize how to exploit our relationship. But still, don't take any chances. Take my van today, and stay at work, all right? I'll fly to the university. Make sure your clients today are all ones you've seen before. No new faces."

"I can do that." Minnie frowns and grabs my hand. "Wait, what if Xenia does take over your body then pretends to be you?"

"Ask me something when I see you at home. We have plenty of memories to choose from. Think of something that no one could guess."

Minnie nods. Her face creases in worry, but she knows better than to talk me out of it. She has spent enough years badgering me that she knows when my mind is made up.

"Don't forget your classes this morning," she says with a stern look. "You skipped out on yesterday, don't forget."

"There is plenty of time to stake out this person before class. I can do it all."

"There is also plenty of time afterward to search."

I make a face.

"Most of the students sleep through class anyway. I have someone like me to find. Surely, that takes precedence?"

"Merry."

I deflate.

"Fine. Duty calls. I'll try my best to be there. I hate September, far too many courses offered. Next time I reinvent myself, I'm not being a low-paid instructor. Too limiting with my time."

"You love it, don't try to fool me." Minnie kisses my cheek. Her citrus scent wafts in a delicious trail past my nose. "Text me when you find this person." She narrows her eyes at me. "After work, if need be. And check everyone for brown lauvan, remember."

I do enjoy teaching—it was one of my earliest professions, after all—but my work is falling flat lately. It's difficult to muster enthusiasm. Something is missing, and I can't put my finger on it. Perhaps there is too much else going on.

I transform on my balcony and fly to the apartment building over top of the morning rush and turn back into myself behind a tree one block over. My feet take me down the sidewalk with enthusiastic strides until I face the apartment. It's drab in the morning light, its stucco in need of a wash and the single-pane windows moist with condensation. For the first time, I wonder what sort of person this half-elemental is.

I wait for five minutes in the front. Three decidedly ordinary people exit the building before I walk to the back. My heart leaps at the sight of the curtains open, but it falls when there is no movement inside. A dumpster sits at a haphazard angle in a parking spot. I scramble on its lid and peer into the apartment.

Nothing. The person with the intriguing strands must have left for work already.

"What the hell are you doing?" A woman yells from another balcony.

CHAPTER XIX

After I escape from the irate neighbor, I duck into a bush in the front yard and close my eyes. Entering the earth lauvan is even easier than last night—practice makes perfect, after all—and after a few minutes of scanning the strands, I am rewarded. The triple-lauvan cluster shines brightly in my mind's eye. With a gasp, I remove myself from the strands. Before I can lose my sense of direction, my fingers search for the threads to transform, and I speed to the university. The person is this way.

I release my lauvan in a dim alley and continue on foot. When I reach a construction site, I stop. This is almost where I saw the cluster. Unless the person has run off, they must be near.

My eyes scan the construction workers. Lauvan of blue, green, brown, yellow, and pink swirl around each worker. I narrow my eyes and keep searching. The person must be here. I could check the earth lauvan again, but I'd rather not do that out in the open. According to Jen, my body goes unnaturally still when I leave it, and I don't want to be vulnerable to attack.

A flash of color grabs my attention. Was it peach? The man disappears behind a pillar on the third floor of a new building, which is scarcely more than a concrete frame, and reappears in a glassless window. I squint until I'm sure.

Peach, orange, silver. That's him.

I stare at his face until I have it memorized, then I stroll to the gate of the construction site. When a worker walks by, I hail him.

"My buddy's working here today," I call out. "What time do I need to swing by to catch him for lunch?"

"Come back at eleven," he shouts back with a wave.

I check my watch. There are hours still to go. How will I concentrate on my work when my appointment with destiny awaits?

It's a terribly long morning, not hastened by the lectures that I power through with a maniacal edge that has my students glancing at each other with bemusement. Rain patters the lecture hall windows by ten o'clock, and by ten to eleven, it's a downpour. I shake an umbrella open over my head and stride with glad steps toward the construction site. The wet gloom turns the corners of everyone's mouths downward, but I can't help the pep in my walk. My nerves jangle with anticipation while construction workers trail out of the site, soaked and disgruntled.

My target is near the end of the pack, and I'm tapping my toe with impatience by the time his eye-catching lauvan hove into view. I debate with myself how best to approach him. Without even knowing his name, any tactic will unnerve him. I'll have to spill a few secrets to get him interested enough to come with me for a greater unveiling.

"Hi," I say when I fall into step beside him. His brown hair is dark with condensation, and the stubble of a three-day beard on his square chin is beaded with raindrops. He glances down at me with suspicion, and I remember regretfully the days when I was considered a tall man.

"Yeah?"

"We should talk," I say. "You don't know me, but I recently discovered that we have something in common."

"If this is a religious thing, I'm not interested." His eyes dart around as if searching for an out, his shoulders hunch deeper against the rain, and he quickens his footsteps. I'm losing him, so I'd better talk fast.

"You look about my age, but how old are you really?"

These words cause him to stumble and glare at me, fear in his eyes. He appears about thirty, but I know better than most that looks can be deceiving.

"What do you mean?"

In reply, I swiftly gather a handful of water lauvan that trail from each raindrop as it falls. Within seconds, a sphere of water the size of a golf ball hovers below my hand, dangling from blue threads. His eyes widen until the irises are surrounded by white.

I drop the water and it splats on the ground. He follows the motion with unblinking eyes.

"Can I buy you lunch?" I say. "I think we have a few things to talk about. My name is Merry, by the way. My current name, that is."

He finally drags his gaze back to my face and searches it for a long moment before he grasps my outstretched hand. I shake it firmly.

"I'm Todd," he says in a dazed manner. "I've never thought of changing it."

"Best way to disappear and start fresh somewhere else. Come on, we can talk more out of the rain."

I lead the way to a nearby pub on campus where the drinks are overpriced, and the chatter is overloud but perfect for covering a conversation from interested ears. Todd doesn't protest when I order beers on tap and a burger for him from the smiling server in her tight black miniskirt that matches the other women's. I take a moment to appreciate the beauty of the human form before turning to Todd.

"Perhaps I might volunteer some information about myself, as a show of trust." I lean my elbows on the table and fold my arms against each other. Todd stares at me, still looking bewildered. I wonder how I would have reacted if he had approached me first. "I've called Vancouver my home for

137

more than three years, but before that I've lived all over. And I do mean that—on average, every five to twenty years I change location so that no one notices that I don't age. I've been doing that for the past fifteen hundred years."

Todd's eyes bug out, and he sputters incoherently. I allow him to gather himself while the server returns with our drinks, and I gratefully wet my throat.

"Fifteen hundred years?" he hisses then passes a shaking hand over his eyes. "That's insane. I had no idea. So, we just keep going? We're invincible?"

"Immortal, not invincible," I say. "There's a big difference. If someone shot me in the heart, point blank, I expect I would be dead. I have never proven my theory, but the necessity for healing from other wounds would indicate as such. So, if you're careful and expedite the healing process with your natural talents, I assume you can enjoy an extended life."

"You can heal yourself?" Todd says after a moment digesting my words. I frown.

"How have you managed to stay intact? How old are you, anyway?"

"Eighty-one." Todd gazes at his hands, as strong and unblemished as a young man's. "I figured something was up by the time I was in my forties. People were getting suspicious, joking about finding the fountain of youth, prying into my life. I had to skip town. The healing thing would have been handy a few times, I can tell you. Recovering from my appendix removal wasn't fun."

"What have you tried to do with your powers?" I'm curious. Even as a child, I experimented with manipulating the lauvan in every way I could to learn what was possible. The knots of illness are so easy to see. Why would he never play with them to find out what he can do?

"I don't know." He shrugs. "A few things. I can light a fire anywhere, that's easy. I've tried things at work—I can make something lighter if I want, it's like a cushion of air lifts it—

but I can't always control it, and it's backfired on me once or twice. There was an explosion that I was lucky to escape from without damage."

"I wonder if your fire lauvan helped protect you," I say quietly. Todd frowns in question.

"What did you call it?"

"Lauvan, that's what I call the strands of energy around everything. You can see them, I presume?" At Todd's nod, I say, "You have an affinity with two elements, fire and air. I have one with earth. See the thinner brown strands among my thicker, human ones?"

Todd looks obediently at my strands, but his face is still bewildered.

"Element?"

I forgot how much Todd doesn't know. Briefly, I sketch an outline of the elemental realm, the four elements they control, and how we came to be.

"My dear old Dad was an earth elemental possessing a human body." I point to myself. "Yours truly was the product. I have no idea how you came about, though. What do you know about your parents?"

"They weren't great parents," Todd says with his eyes narrowed. "I remember some good times when I was a tiny kid, but everything changed when I was four. They both changed. Mum split, never saw her again." His face tightens at the memory. "Dad was a jerk, no other way to slice it. Didn't really care about me, told me to never talk about the—lauvan, you called it—so that I would fit in better, not that it worked. I guess I should be grateful he fed me and bought me clothes to wear, but that was as far as the fatherly love went. When I was old enough to leave, I did, and he didn't try to get me back."

"I'm sorry to hear that," I say quietly.

He shrugs again with a wry smile.

"Water under the bridge, right? Dead now. And I'll never have to deal with his shit again. I won't even have to deal with death." He shakes his head with a growing smile. "That's insane. I might have lost the parent lottery, but I won the genetic one."

"I wonder how you ended up with two elements," I say. Two color signatures must mean that two elementals were involved. Two elementals might have possessed one body, but since both his parents were changed—one leaving, one dissociating from his son—I suppose that both parents were possessed. If they survived their possession, does that mean they were weaker elementals than Xenia, who leaves bodies for dead? And what happened four years after Todd's birth to make the elementals leave their hosts? I'll have to follow up with Ailu for more details of this fascinating story.

Todd clearly isn't as interested in the source of his powers as he is about using them.

"It sounds like you're full of tricks," he says with a grin. "You've had a lot of time to think about it, I guess. Care to share?"

I return his smile. It's exhilarating to meet someone like me and to find out he's a decent man wanting to learn what I can offer.

"Of course." I check my watch. "It's late. I'd better get back to work, but let's meet soon. Here's my card." I hand him my calling card, inscribed with my name and phone number. "Are you available in the evenings?"

"Anytime. I don't get out much, never really played well with others. Anyway, this is way better than anything I would do otherwise. Name your day."

"Let's meet Wednesday night. I'll be in touch." I stand and offer him my hand. He joins me and grasps it firmly, his eyes bright with the same excitement that fills my chest. "I'm glad we could meet, Todd."

CHAPTER XX
Dreaming

I stand in a tiny biplane, a parachute on my back and a question in my mind.

What the hell am I doing?

Skydiving has been a recreational activity for ten years, at least, but I haven't yet tried it. I never let an opportunity to experience something new pass me by, but the last few years have been busy. Josephine thinks I'm crazy, although she's waiting for me in the field below with a picnic lunch.

I didn't think it was crazy when I was on firm ground, but now that my jump is imminent, I'm less certain. The ground is ridiculously far away, and cars driving between fields look like fleas on the back of a patchwork dog.

"Jump in one minute," the instructor shouts at me over the scream of wind past the open door. I jerk my head in a semblance of a nod.

I didn't realize how attached I am to Earth until I am so far away from it. I've flown in hot air balloons, dirigible airships, and planes without problem. Perhaps there were enough grounding lauvan of the aircraft themselves to tether me.

My flights as a merlin falcon never bother me, either, but that could be due to the tight windings of my strands around me when they are knotted in my temporary form. Now, the open door fills the plane's fuselage with swirling threads of air, and they filter through the spaces between my own strands in a highly unsettling way. My brown lauvan twitch and writhe with the unfamiliar contact.

"Countdown starts now," the instructor shouts. "Five, four, three, two, one, jump!"

It's now or never, if I want to greet Josephine at the appointed field. I take as deep a breath as my constricted lungs will hold and step out of the plane.

141

The air wallops me with a force that leaves me gasping. There is nothing below my feet, and I spin wildly as I fall, faster and faster. I don't know what's worse: that the ground is still so far away, or that it is rapidly growing closer.

Great coils of air lauvan pummel me as I crash by them. Each hit pricks me with thousands of needle-sharp prods. My own strands twist and coil in an instinctual attempt to protect me, but I feel the force despite it. A few desperate strands reach out, searching vainly for earth lauvan to tether to, but there is nothing but empty space and the painful air threads rushing past.

My hands hunt for my rip cord. It takes a few panicked seconds of fumbling, but I finally locate it and pull. With a tugging, slithering motion at my back, the parachute releases and unfurls like a massive red flower. My body jolts when the parachute takes my weight and stops my headlong rush toward certain death.

Now that there is relative quiet, without the incessant roar of wind in my ears, my heart thunders loudly in my chest. I gasp for air and wish for this jump to be over. I signed up to skydive in my quest to experience everything novel. Now that it is done, I can check it off my list and never attempt it again.

I belong on Earth.

CHAPTER XXI

Calls to Wayne and Alejandro the previous night reveal no sign of Xenia or any suspicious-looking former Potestas members. Now that the euphoria of meeting Todd has worn off, I'm in a terrible stasis of uncertainty. What am I supposed to do? I can't wait around for Xenia to grab me at his leisure. I need to be proactive, but in what direction should I turn? I can't stand waiting for an ambush I know is coming.

Not knowing what else to do, I drop Minnie off at her work an hour after waking and glide into my usual parking spot at the university soon after. I stride into the lecture room one minute before the starting time, and most of my students are there, yawning and bleary-eyed. I clap loudly to wake them up, and half of them jump.

"Good morning, all. I have papers to return to you. Some were abysmal, lacking originality and deeper thought. Others were passable, if you're willing to squeak by with a poor grade. A few contained gems of brilliance amid the roughage. Take note of my comments and improve for next time." I grab the stack of papers from my satchel and call out the top name. "Roshni Rao."

I pass out papers in this fashion until three remain. Students look cautiously optimistic, resigned, or downcast, depending on their grades. I read out the names of the absent students.

"Does anyone know where Afsun Darzi, Kami Hashimoto, or Carson Barends is?"

"Afsun is sick," a young woman with too much eye makeup pipes up from the side.

"Kami didn't read the material for today, I bet," says a young man in the back. The class titters, and I nod sagely.

"Smart woman. If you're not ready to discuss the literature, you're not welcome here. And Carson? Any guesses?"

"I haven't seen him for a few days," a student in the middle says with a frown. "He's usually here. It's not like him to miss class."

"All right, they can get their papers next class." I shove them into my satchel. "Bring out your textbooks. I need someone to read today's passage. Su-Jin?"

I might feign nonchalance, but Carson's truancy disturbs me in a way I can't pin my finger on. I push the matter aside during my lecture, but once the students depart, I wind my way through crowded halls to the departmental office.

My favorite admin assistant is at his usual desk. He looks up with his features carefully schooled into an expression of disinterest, but his lauvan sharpen at my presence. He has never liked me much. I can't say it bothers me.

"Strange question," I say. "But is there any news about a student named Carson Berends? He hasn't shown up to my last few classes, and I'm concerned."

The admin's eyes widen.

"Actually, yes." He points to a flyer taped to the wall that I hadn't noticed. It's a grainy photo of Carson. It must have been taken on a camping trip, because he sits in front of a tent, smiling and holding a water bottle aloft. The notice says that he has been missing since the Friday before last. The admin continues in a grave voice, "His friends posted this. They haven't seen him for days."

I swallow. Days ago, Xenia came to find me in my classroom, the first time we met. Is it a coincidence that Carson disappeared around the same time? Did Xenia need a fresh body, and Carson was nearby?

"I'm sorry to hear that," I say. "I hope he turns up soon. If I see him, I'll be sure to alert the authorities."

At lunch, I knock on Wayne's office door. Wayne answers

with his mouth full and a sandwich in one hand. He waves me in.

"What's up?" he says after swallowing. His rusty lauvan are clear of brown strands and show no signs of possession by Xenia.

"One of my students is missing," I say flatly. "No one has seen him lately, possibly since Xenia first came to my class."

"You think Xenia snatched this kid's body?" Wayne's face is horrified. I nod, and my mouth tightens.

"It could be a coincidence, but I find it hard to believe."

"Damn." Wayne thinks for a moment. "Any sign of the bastard today?"

"Nothing." I push aside Wayne's papers and sink onto the corner of his desk. Wayne reclaims his office chair and leans back. "It's so much worse waiting for an ax to fall than to face one in battle. I am always more effective in the heat of the moment."

"Remember when we knew about the ambush at the Iolyn pass? It was such a long journey, knowing that the enemy could descend on us at any moment."

"Yes, and remember how I dealt with it? I set fire to the woods to smoke them out."

"You're not always the most subtle, are you?" Wayne says with a chuckle, then he sobers. "How do we smoke out Xenia?"

"We can't," I say with a sigh. "We can only try to find him before another victim falls prey to his needs. Trust me, if I had any sort of leverage, I would have used it by now. But if he doesn't care about anyone, and his only concern is staying on Earth, what do we have against him?"

"What if we follow you around until Xenia tries to nab you, then we can ambush him ourselves?" Wayne sits up straight. "He wouldn't suspect it."

"It's impractical. What about your classes? Who knows how long it will take Xenia to capture me? And it's too dangerous.

At least with me, something bigger must happen to make the transfer successful. With you, he need only touch you and you're possessed, then dead. It's too risky."

"And there's no way to protect against possession?" Wayne says.

"There are a few vague hints, but nothing concrete. Nothing I'm willing to bet your life on."

"Do them anyway," Wayne says. "Better to have something than nothing. We won't rely on their protection, but if the worst should come to pass, at least we'll have something to fall back on."

"All right," I say, but it's without much hope. Some of Braulio's notes are worth their weight in gold, but others are simply fables. It's impossible to tell the difference until it's too late. "On a cheerier topic, I met someone like me."

"Someone very full of himself?" Wayne shoots back with a grin. "Or someone who thinks he knows everything?"

"Enough, enough," I say with my hands up. "Someone with an elemental for a parent. He's the first one I've ever met. His name is Todd, and he's eighty-one years old but looks thirty. I met him yesterday, and we had a good talk."

"That's great, Merry," Wayne says. "Centuries of nothing, then here he is."

"I said I'd show him some tricks with the lauvan. He hasn't played with them much, if you can believe it. By his age, I'd run the gamut, had been shapeshifting for decades, could do most things, really."

"Maybe he doesn't have much imagination," Wayne says. He frowns in thought and turns to his computer. "Oh, I wanted to tell you. I found a match for that photo of the body that Minnie sent me. My contact in the police force is very helpful. Here." He turns the monitor toward me and points. The picture of the dead body is beside a mug shot. They are clearly the same man, heavyset with wavy brown hair.

"Who's this character?"

"Marcel Devine. Put away a few years ago for rape. Released last year, but all sex offenders must be registered, so I found out that he is living in Vancouver. Was living," Wayne corrects himself. "And that's not all. The most recent missing person, other than this guy, is also a registered sex offender, now out of custody."

"Isn't that interesting." I stare at the mug shot, my mind whirling. "That is no coincidence. Why would Xenia target sex offenders now, after the Potestas members? As far as I'm aware, elementals have no regard for human social conventions. Why would he zero in on these two men?"

"Someone else is helping him," Wayne says. "It must be."

"March," I say quietly. "It's March. There's no doubt. First, the bodies are Potestas members, then Xenia visits me at work—where March knows I go—then these carefully chosen victims? And March told me she donates money to a women's crisis support service. It all fits."

Wayne heaves a long sigh.

"We need to change tactics," he says. "We've been looking at Potestas members, but we need to cut the head off the beast. I'll double-down on finding March. We have a few promising leads, so I'll see what I can do."

"Thanks, Wayne." I stand and clap him on the back before moving to the door. "I'll do what I can on my end. If there is protection to be had, I'll figure it out."

I like the thought of ambushing Xenia, but I don't want to risk Wayne or Alejandro in the process. Although they've proved themselves time and again as valiant warriors, they have nothing to protect them from an elemental. I will have to think of the best way to trap Xenia. Surely, my greater experience on Earth must count for something.

And why are we still talking about March Feynman? I thought I'd plucked out that thorn in my side. Why does she keep cropping up like a pernicious weed?

I finish my marking before Minnie's day is done, so I decide to visit Jen at her work. I want her opinion on all of this. I know she doesn't want to see me, but perhaps over time she'll get used to my presence and the past won't bother her as much. Minnie chatted with her on the phone on Saturday, but she didn't get very far. Jen was not interested in talking.

For the past few years, Jen has been a fixture in my life, and I miss her. She used to be in my court, and now she's not even a spectator. Even more, I miss Guinevere and all the women that Jen might have been, but I know that is too much to ask for. I would be content with my modern friend back.

The campus is quiet between classes, and I stroll through piles of fallen leaves. The day is bright and clear, the sun low on the horizon at this latitude, and the crisp air that fill my lungs energizes me. My feet direct me to an alley between two buildings that provides a shortcut to my usual parking lot. It is dim and cool, but the brilliant sun beyond beckons me.

It isn't until I'm halfway through the dark corridor with stone walls on either side of me that I notice a mat of earth lauvan at my feet. It's thick enough to reach my ankles and so dense that I can scarcely see my shoes. This isn't normal.

A huge cracking noise makes my head snap up. With a whoosh and a tremendous thud that shivers the ground under my feet, a mighty tree topples across my path at the end of the alley. Its branches waver from their final journey through the air and block my way forward with dense foliage.

I can't go forward, so I spin on my heel and race to the other end. The earth groans, then cracking and grating emerges from a rapidly spreading hole in front of me. I skid to a stop and backpedal furiously as the sinkhole gets wider and longer with every passing second. The buildings on either side shudder from the damage to their foundations.

This is not natural. I'm under attack, and I don't know who to fight. My head spins wildly to find the source of the attack, but no one is in sight.

It's clearly Xenia. I clamp down firmly on my mounting panic and try to think rationally as I back away from the sinkhole. Xenia is an earth fundamental, first and foremost, and earth is his forte. Despite now inhabiting a body and being able to manipulate other elements the way I can, I doubt he has experimented. The tree and the sinkhole are perfect examples of earth lauvan capabilities.

How can I escape earth, when it is everywhere?

A smile tweaks my mouth, despite the circumstances. My fingers comb through my strands, searching for the correct ones. The sinkhole gapes open like a hungry maw, closer and closer to my now stationary feet, but I focus on placing my lauvan just so. Below my shoes, the ground shudders, cracks, and gives way…

The final strand slots into place, and I fly upward with strong wingbeats of my bird form, the merlin falcon. Wings were an early and much-needed addition to my arsenal of tricks. I can't count how many times they've wrangled me out of tight spots.

When I'm a safe distance up, I glance down at the extensive devastation. The sinkhole reaches from one end of the alley to the downed tree at the other. The buildings are standing, for now, but they'll need expensive renovations to make them safe once more. Already, the few people in the area are running toward the alley, yelling about earthquakes. I scan the new arrivals carefully with my keen falcon's eyes, but none has the characteristic two-toned lauvan that I would expect to see for the successor. There is one woman with brown lauvan, but when I swoop closer, the color is not close enough to hide Xenia's strands.

He must be somewhere close. I consider transforming back into a human and searching the nearby buildings, but I wonder. As the earth fundamental, what is his reach? Could he be sitting beside a cable on the other side of the city, manipulating lauvan from afar? I can certainly travel great distances through the cables, and I know little about it.

Is there anywhere that is safe? Perhaps I should travel everywhere by wing. I shake my head and dip down to my van. That won't work for Minnie, nor for Jen. Xenia isn't omniscient, otherwise I'd be captured already. He must have known where I'd be and planned an ambush accordingly. Perhaps my escape gave him pause, and he will come closer next time to be sure of his prize. If he approaches, I'll be ready. In the meantime, I will keep my hands free to transform into a bird with ease.

CHAPTER XXII

I speed through the city streets, anxious and jittery from my close encounter. My mind races through ways I could have combated the sinkhole, but the truth is that there was no one to fight. Since Xenia wasn't physically there, how should have I attacked? Belatedly, I think of sending my conscious into the lauvan to find him, but I'm so inexperienced at that. Who knows if I would even find him? And there, Xenia would most certainly have the upper hand. That is his domain, after all.

No, I need to draw Xenia out in person. I need to see the vessel he currently possesses. Only then will I have a chance to overpower him. The physical world is my domain, and I'm reasonably certain that we are on equal footing here. I might even have the advantage.

After the attack, my body buzzes with anger toward Xenia. I'm spoiling for a fight, but there's no one to attack. I want him to come at me again. I want to show him what he's up against. I want him to fear me.

But there's only me, sitting in a tiny blue van at a red traffic light. I slam my fist against the wheel in frustration. Attacking from afar is like shooting arrows at the enemy. It's effective, no doubt there, but hand-to-hand combat lets you look into your enemy's eyes. You know them, in that split second before you attack, in a way that an archer or sharpshooter will never understand. It's easier to respect your opponent when you're face to face. A coward can stomach shooting at a distance but rarely at close quarters.

I want Xenia to award me that respect. I don't want to be hunted like a stag for meat. If he is my enemy, I want to look in his eyes as he attacks. I want a fighting chance. If I best him, I want to see it happen. If he takes me, I want to see him do it.

The traffic finally unsnarls, and I pull in front of Jen's office building. My text is short and to the point.

I'm downstairs. Please come?

Ten minutes pass before Jen pushes the glass doors open. She ties her hair back in a ponytail as she walks, and her face is set in a tight frown. Her golden lauvan are clear of brown strands, and I breathe a sigh of relief.

"What's going on, Merry?" she asks when I open the passenger's door for her and she slides in. "If it's not urgent, I have lots of work I need to do."

"Xenia attacked me just now. And I miss you, Jen," I say with bald honesty. I'm too old to be embarrassed by the truth. "I miss what we used to have."

"I don't want to talk about that." Jen crosses her arms. Her lauvan turn sharp.

"Not the past." I wave my hand to disregard her past lives that she won't talk about. "I miss Jen, my friend of the past few years. I miss movie nights, and discussions about obscure literature, and trips to the fair. I miss us."

Jen's face melts before she turns away from me to hide it. When she speaks, there is a slight wobble in her voice.

"I do, too. But every time I see you, it forces me to think about more than just the present. I can't handle that right now, and I don't know how to separate you from the past." She turns to me. Unshed tears fill her eyes with liquid brightness. "I'm sorry, Merry. I can try."

She leans over to hug me, and I wrap my arms around her, pleased and grateful for our breakthrough. I didn't expect it today, but it's a weight off my chest. I have missed Jen. Minnie fills the largest hole in my heart, and Alejandro and Wayne are important pieces, but the loss of Jen was significant. I'm glad she's back, even if she's only willing to be her present self. I can wait for Guinevere.

Jen pushes back and wipes underneath her eyes with her fingers, careful not to smudge her work-day makeup. She fixes me with a stern look, not undermined at all by her still-watery eyes.

152

"What's this about Xenia attacking you? What happened?"

I recount the ambush. Jen's eyes grow as round as coins.

"And he wasn't even there?" She looks around fearfully. "Should you even be here?"

"Where should I be? There's earth everywhere. I can't hide."

"What about your apartment? Aren't there fewer earth lauvan there?"

"Yes," I admit. "But I refuse to stay cooped up in my nest for longer than a day, and Sunday was that day. No, I need him to find me, fight it out face to face, none of this dancing around from a distance. I need to draw him out, somehow. Any ideas?"

Jen's brow furrows as she thinks.

"What about your lauvan cable thing? When you travel through them? Could you search for him there?"

"I could. Honestly, I'm nervous meeting him in there. It's his world, and I know very little about how it works. I fear he would have the advantage in a fight."

"Not fight," says Jen with exasperation. "Draw him out. Find him, let him know where you are, and race back to your body as quick as you can."

"And when he uses my now-known location to attack me from afar?"

"As soon as you're back in your body, fly into the air." Jen warms up to her idea, and her strands wave around her with excitement. I've missed her enthusiasm. "That's it! You'll be out of lauvan reach, and he'll have to come in person to find out what's going on. Then you can trap him."

I nod slowly. That might just work.

"Brilliant. I will try that first thing tomorrow, when Minnie isn't watching. She'll say it's too risky, but I'm out of options. But, please, stay safe, all right? Ask probing questions of everyone you meet. You never know what body Xenia might sneak around in. Be careful, in case tomorrow doesn't go well."

"You're going to win," Jen says firmly, but her eyes are

153

fearful.

"Of course I am," I say calmly. "But contingencies are never a bad idea."

I told Todd that we could meet Wednesday evening. Minnie is strongly opposed to the risk of Xenia, but when I call Todd about canceling, he sounds so despondent that I relent. Meeting another half-elemental is an experience I've waited centuries for, and I don't want to ruin this chance by misplaced timidity. Besides, Wayne is still searching for March, and I'm only a nuisance in his way. Tomorrow morning, assuming Wayne's search does not bear fruit, I will draw Xenia out and stop her once and for all.

After a quick supper with Minnie, who goes over my plans for safety with a fine-toothed comb, I hop in my van and drive back to the university. The sun has almost reached the horizon by the time I park, but there will be enough streetlights to get around by the time we're through.

Every sense I possess is on high alert during my walk across campus. My eyes constantly scan my surroundings, my ears are tuned for deep groans of the earth, and my lauvan swirl around me, touching every strand in their path with heightened sensitivity. There are few people about, and most of those walk with determined strides to their destinations.

My department's building is not a far walk, and Todd is already waiting for me at the door. I greet him with a wave, and he nods back stiffly, although his eyes are bright with interest.

"Todd, good to see you." I shake his hand and usher him inside. "Up to the roof. It's quiet there, and no one will see us waving our hands around like lunatics."

"Is that how it's done?" Todd looks at me askance. I grin.

"When you're learning, it is."

The roof access is locked, but Wayne stole a key ages ago, and I made myself a copy last month. We mainly use it as a peaceful lunch spot, but tonight's endeavor is a perfect candidate for rooftop undertakings. Todd wants to learn more about his abilities, and I'm happy to teach. When I wasn't pondering the mysteries of Xenia yesterday, I was concocting lesson plans in my head in preparation for tonight. I don't know who's more eager, Todd or me.

The roof has the bonus of being off the ground. Given recent circumstances, removing myself from the reaches of earth lauvan is advisable. Short of toppling the building, which is empty at this hour, there isn't much an earth elemental can do.

I hope. Should Xenia feel like some earth shaking is in order, I can transform myself and Todd into birds and we can fly away. Always have a plan B, and plan C doesn't hurt, either.

"Where do we start?" Todd asks when the door to the staircase swishes shut behind us. His lauvan are jittery with anticipation.

"I thought we could play with fire, first." I produce a candle from my pocket then light the wick with my trusty flint. When enough wax has melted, I drip a little onto the roof's concrete pad and squish the candle into the wax puddle. "You might get burned, but I doubt it. Your fire affinity sounds like it will protect you, if your story about the explosion has any merit."

We squat next to the candle. Todd's face glows in the warm light, and his eyes flicker between my face and the sparking lauvan above the flame.

"Fire lauvan are ephemeral." I adopt my teaching voice. "They are quick, and they don't last long. You'll need to hold the strands with steady fingers and put a fair bit of intention into it. Intention is key to all lauvan manipulation, by the way. If you don't try to touch them, you won't. Your hands will pass through and touch the physical world instead."

"How do I 'intend' to touch them?" Todd says with a hint of

anxiety.

"Want to," I say. "It's as simple as that. Watch this."

I lean forward and hold my finger and thumb at the ready a handspan above the flame. When an orange strand leaps up, I push my hand forward like a darting snake and snatch the lauvan from the air. It writhes between my fingers, but I pour intention into my motion and pull up.

The flame rises, higher and higher, until it is three times taller than it was. When I let go of the strand, it flickers into nothing and the flame snaps back into its usual size. I look at Todd, who gazes at the flame with wide eyes.

"Go on, reach to the top, right where the fire lauvan peter off into nothing. It's not very hot up there, you should be fine. Really want to hold it, then pull slowly up."

With hesitant fingers, Todd reaches toward the candle. He holds his hand like I did and waits for a spark-like lauvan to fly up. When it does, he darts forward.

He misses the first one, but the second he grasps tightly between forefinger and thumb.

"Good," I say. "Now, pull up."

Todd drops it at the sound of my voice. His face scrunches in annoyance.

"Hold on," he says. "Let me try again."

The second strand he clenches tightly in his fingers and immediately draws it upward. Higher and higher the flame rises, until it's the height of the candle itself, then twice the height. Heat from the once-tiny flame pushes me backward.

At my movement, Todd drops the lauvan, and the flame shrinks once more. He beams at me.

"How's that, professor?"

I laugh in delight.

"If all my students were so talented, I'd be out of a job. Well done, Todd. Let's see it again."

Todd repeats our exercise twice more before I pronounce myself satisfied. While Todd stands and stretches, Alejandro texts me to let him up to the roof. I told him earlier we would be here, and he was keen to meet the only other half-elemental we know of. He professed a desire to keep an eye on me in case Xenia showed up, but I suspect his lack of girlfriend played a larger part in wanting to fill this free evening. When Alejandro emerges from the stairwell, his green lauvan mercifully free of brown, Todd looks discomposed. Alejandro soon puts him at ease.

"Nice to meet you, Todd," he says, offering his hand. Todd takes it reluctantly and is rewarded by a firm shake. "I've been friends with Merry for a long time, and I know he hoped to meet someone like him forever. Please don't let me get in the way of your lesson. I'm just here to help."

"Now, there's a thought," I say with mischief in my voice. "Since Alejandro is here, why don't we use him as our test subject? There are so many things we can do with human lauvan, after all."

Alejandro grins.

"I've always wanted to be taller. Or maybe a beard, a long one."

Todd raises his eyebrows and looks at me.

"You can do that?"

"We can do that," I correct him with a smile. "Watch and learn."

We have fun turning Alejandro into wild versions of himself. Todd lets out a huge guffaw of laughter when I first change Alejandro's hair into a rainbow clown wig. Soon, Todd suggests his own changes, and I help him feel out for the correct lauvan. It's not easy, and often his vision isn't realized, but Todd enjoys himself despite the mishaps. It's a tremendous icebreaker for the two, and by the time Alejandro collapses on the rooftop, breathless with laughter, he and Todd are on their way to becoming friends.

"This is amazing," Todd says after a pause in which we collect ourselves. "I can't believe I haven't done this before.

Think of the possibilities. I can do anything."

"You can certainly do a lot, with practice and patience," I say with a smile. It's invigorating to see his enthusiasm and satisfying to teach what I've been perfecting all my long life. I enjoy teaching literature at the university, no matter how I might gripe about it to Minnie, but this is pure joy.

"What about me?" Todd says finally. "Can you show me how to change myself?"

"Of course. Let's start with your hand. We'll turn it green. It will be difficult one-handed, but easier because you can feel what you're doing. Here, let me show you."

I take his offered hand in my own and reach into the layer of strands above his skin. Todd hisses at the contact and pulls away.

"Ugh, what was that?" he says. "Way too close. Creepy. You're a nice guy, Merry, but we'll never be tight like that, I can promise you. Did we make Alejandro go through that? Poor guy." He eyes Alejandro with curiosity. "Unless you're into that, buddy. Then, you're welcome."

Alejandro looks at me in bewilderment. My mouth opens when I realize what happened.

"The sensation is heightened when someone touches your lauvan, just like it is for me. I've only ever had one person do that to me, so I forgot. Never mind, I'll show you on myself, and you can try on your own."

We practice for a little longer, but eventually I check my watch.

"Sorry to break up the party, but my—" Girlfriend? Partner? Wife? "Minnie is probably getting frantic. I should head out."

"You up for another session soon?" Todd looks so hopeful that I couldn't say no even if I wanted to, which I don't.

"Of course. We can bring the practice dummy along, too." I jab my thumb at Alejandro. He pretends to look offended but can't hold the expression for long.

Chuckling, I lead the way down the stairs, through the

deserted department, and outside. Streetlights bathe the sidewalk in an orange glow that only serves to highlight deep shadows behind bushes and railings. A quick look around convinces me that we are alone. Xenia surely wouldn't suspect that I was at the university so late—it's not my normal pattern of behavior, that's certain—and with nobody in sight, I can relax.

We meander toward the parking lots with jovial ease. Alejandro draws Todd out of his shell, and I pitch in from time to time. Todd tells us about his upbringing in rural British Columbia in the nineteen forties, which sounds rather cheerless under a distant father and absent mother. I may not have had long with my own mother, who died when I was fourteen, but I was well loved until then.

"I remember better times," says Todd. "When I was a tiny kid, before my mother left. Lots of laughing, silly games, hugs. We had a special candle that we never let burn out, Dad called it the life candle. Strange, huh? I guess every family has weird rituals. Anyway, the life candle went out when she left." He shrugs, but his lauvan are tight with his remembrance. "Ah, well, I'm not alone having a dysfunctional family. Life isn't a Norman Rockwell painting."

"True," I say. "My mother and I lived with my uncle until she died, then he threw me out of the house. We soldier on, right?"

"These powers are a nice consolation prize," Todd says, his eyes crinkling at the corners. "I can't believe I've been looking at them as a liability for so long. Dad always told me to keep a lid on them. Wasted years."

"The future is yours," Alejandro says with a pat on Todd's shoulder. "Look forward, now."

A figure walks toward us. A hoodie hides his face in the darkness, but his wide shoulders and oversized height make him stand out. The hairs on my neck prickle with foreboding, and I look at him more closely.

His lauvan glow faintly with an otherworldly light. Dark purple strands swirl around his torso and head, with a few tendrils trailing down his limbs. What makes my eyes widen are thin brown threads intertwined among the purple.

"That's Xenia," I hiss. "Alejandro, behind me."

Alejandro's head whips around until he sees the figure, who closes in on us with quick strides of his long legs. Todd looks at me with puzzlement.

"Who is Xenia?" he says.

"That would be me," the figure says with a deep growl of satisfaction. "Well met, Merry. Wait, what is this?" Xenia stops and looks Todd up and down with interest. "You found another half-elemental. Is this a present for me? You are too kind, Merry. This way, I can have a stable body and we can join forces. What a clever mind you have."

Quick as a bolt of lightning, Xenia's hand darts toward Todd.

"No!" Alejandro shouts, and he tackles Todd out of the way. They land in a heap on the ground, and Todd's face is astonished and angry.

"What the hell, man?" he yells. "What was that for?"

While they scuffle, I am not idle. Xenia bends to hold out his hand to Todd, but I harness the air lauvan surrounding me and direct it into a howling wind that blows Xenia off his feet.

"Stay away from him," I shout. "He's a friend. His body is not for you."

Xenia looks hurt. He stands and brushes dirt off his clothes with swift strokes.

"You wound me, Merry. I thought we had an understanding."

"You understand nothing," I snarl. "Stay away from this man, do you hear?"

Xenia regards me for a long moment. Alejandro and Todd rise to their feet. Alejandro must have explained enough to Todd for him to recognize the danger, for he remains silent, standing slightly behind Alejandro. Alejandro's face is set in a determined scowl, ready to defend his friends.

"You know I can't transfer to a half-elemental right away," Xenia says finally. "This man was in no danger. And, now that I look at him, I don't think he would be compatible. I could make it work, but he is fire and air. Your body would be much more comfortable. I was willing to endure the other elements to preserve you as an ally, but now I see that you are no ally of mine. Your friend here is safe, but I will have you, Merry. Will you come willingly now, or will I have to force you?"

"You can try," I spit out. Fury rises like heat in my chest, fury and fear. "Alejandro, Todd, get back."

They waste no time stumbling out of the way. Xenia raises an eyebrow.

"If you insist," he says. "You may have lived on Earth for many years, but I *am* earth. Your body will be mine."

Without warning, a crack appears below my feet. I haven't lived so long without developing superb reflexes, however, and I leap forward with a cry of rage. Mid-air, I grab the gently swinging lauvan of a dangling tree branch and yank it down with me. There's a resounding crack, and the branch breaks. Xenia looks up in surprise, but he dodges the limb before it lands on his skull.

The branch might have missed him, but it was only a distraction. I'm on him, now, and I don't pull my punches. I pull hard at every lauvan I can reach, and Xenia screams in pain. He's a quick learner, and soon enough my own strands are yanked to excruciating effect on my own body.

I yell and roll to the side then leap up to face him once more. We circle each other, both taking measure. Xenia doesn't look quite as smug anymore, but there's a calculating gleam in his eyes that I don't like.

The ground shivers. I look down in consternation, but the whole path shakes and there's nowhere to run. The sidewalk splits, and a jagged pillar of rock dripping brown soil shoots

161

up from under my left foot.

I yelp and dive to the right, but another pillar rises with frightening speed from the ground. It bashes my side with an unforgiving punch, and my hip explodes in agony. I drag myself forward, through the pain, and my watering eyes see Xenia's gloating face inches from mine.

"That wasn't so hard, was it?" he says. "I guess you don't know as many tricks as I hoped you did. Just as well I'll be using your body. You don't have anything to teach me, after all."

A blur to my right flies into Xenia and shoves him to the ground. Alejandro pins Xenia down with his legs and swings at his face with punches designed to knock him unconscious, or worse. Alejandro's face contorts with fury.

"Alejandro, no!" I yell. My heart thunders in my chest, and I drag myself forward with grunts of pain. I must get him off Xenia. Every second that Alejandro touches Xenia is another chance that he will be possessed by the earth fundamental.

Alejandro ignores me and continues to punch whatever part of Xenia he can reach. Xenia is not idle, however, and already thin threads of chestnut brown curl among Alejandro's green strands as well as through the purple lauvan of the other man.

"No!" I scream, and I plunge my hands into Alejandro's strands. It's easy enough to differentiate between Xenia's and Alejandro's lauvan, and I comb with my fingers to remove the brown strands. But the more I pull, the more the brown leaks into the green.

I pour my intention into the strands, desperately forcing them back. A will as strong as my own greets my mind and pushes back, hard. Mental wrestling is a new sport for me, but I give it everything I have. One part of my mind is locked on the inner battle with Xenia's will, but the other watches the progress of brown lauvan. They pulse with their effort and creep forward despite my laboring.

Alejandro has stopped pummeling Xenia's body, and he

locks eyes with me, finally understanding what's happening.

"Don't let him take me," he whispers. "Please."

A fresh wave of resolve washes over me, and I close my eyes. Every fiber of my being sets itself to the task. There is a moment of struggle—Xenia fights back with all his might— but I can't let anything happen to my oldest friend, and in this contest of wills, I have the advantage of determination.

With a release, Xenia slithers back into the other man's body. I open my eyes with a gasp and push Alejandro out of touching distance of Xenia.

The earth fundamental climbs unsteadily to his feet, stumbles briefly, then stands tall.

"We're not done," he says to me. "I will have you."

He ducks into an alley and is lost to my sight.

"Are we going to chase him?" Alejandro says in a wobbly voice. I shake my head, and pain rises until it's all I can think about.

"I can't even walk. I'm in no condition to chase anyone. My hip is shattered."

CHAPTER XXIII

I don't want to heal myself while lying on broken pavement in the dark. It will take a good half-hour to properly untangle the lauvan, and I could do that much more comfortably on my bed at home with Minnie administering to my whims. I tie off a few strands to reduce the pain while Todd watches with wide eyes, and the two of them carry me to my van. Alejandro gives Todd a brief introduction to my history with Xenia. Todd listens with endless questions on his lips and only leaves when I promise to call him later to explain everything.

Alejandro drives to my apartment while I lie in the back of the van, where I'm intensely grateful for the room. A quick examination at my hip makes my stomach turn. It's the wrong shape, and already bruises darken the skin under the shifting glow of passing streetlights.

Minnie's mouth opens with horror when we stumble through the door, Alejandro half-carrying me beside him.

"What happened?" She wraps my free arm around her shoulder and the two of them drag me to my bedroom and lower me to the bed. Despite my numbing knots, fiery spears of pain lance through my hip.

"Xenia caught up with us," I say through gritted teeth. "Almost got Alejandro. We beat him, and he slunk away to lick his wounds."

"You'd better start licking yours," Minnie says. She pulls down my waistband and pales at the sight. "That's hideous, Merry."

"Thanks. That really helps."

Minnie shoots me a withering glare that I would take offense to if I couldn't see the love and concern behind it.

"Start unknotting," she says. "I'll get some wet towels for you two to clean up with."

Alejandro disappears with Minnie while I prop myself up on

pillows and get to work. There is plenty to do before I set the bones, so I procrastinate by unknotting every strand I can before the painful reshaping of my hipbone. That part is necessary, but never fun.

Alejandro wanders in with Braulio's notebook, of all things, and sits on the edge of the bed, immersed in the words. When Minnie returns with warm cloths, she hands one to Alejandro, who takes it absently. With the other, she wipes tenderly at a few scuffs on my face. I doubt there's much in the way of dirt there, but she wants to help, and there isn't much else she can do. I smile at her between grimaces of effort and pain.

"I think I know how we can protect ourselves," Alejandro says after a while. I squint at him through eyes watering with my most recent jab of pain.

"The aura-sensing spell?"

"No, this one." Alejandro points a finger on the page. "It's to prevent spirit possession. It was meant to protect against the ghosts of people who had died, but grandfather wrote that spirits were spirits, and there is no reason that it couldn't work against an elemental."

"So, an educated guess from Braulio." I hiss as a shard of bone snaps into place, then I slump into the pillows for a brief respite. "Granted, his educated guesses are uncannily correct, but I'm only saying that because he can't hear me now."

Alejandro smiles, but his mirth is tempered by the reminder that Braulio is dead. Braulio lived a full, long life, but Alejandro knows that I was good friends with him.

"It's worth a try," he says. "There's not much to it. We need something of the dead, mainly, so the spell knows what we're protecting against. There's an incantation, too."

"But no one is dead." I get back to work with a sigh. I really thought Alejandro had pulled a solution out of the book. "We don't have the key ingredient."

"What about something from the body he's possessing?" Minnie says.

165

"It's not the body that's coming into people, though," I say. "It's his spirit, his lauvan. We need to protect against that, and it's not dead."

"But Xenia is the earth fundamental," says Alejandro, with an air of patience. "If we use something of earth in the incantation, it might work. What about the lauvan from a dead tree?"

I turn Alejandro's words over in my mind. There is merit in them, but also a huge hole in his plan.

"It's a wild shot in the dark," I say. "Better to try something than nothing, I suppose, but I wouldn't want you to feel overconfident and take risks because you think you're protected, when we simply don't know."

"But we can find out," Alejandro says. "You have as much earth lauvan as he does. I could put the protection on me, and then you could try to possess me."

"What?" I stare at Alejandro. "I don't even know how to do that."

"Is it any different from when you transferred your lauvan to me, back in the cave?" Alejandro says with a raised brow. "You gave me all your human strands then. I bet, if the protection works, you wouldn't be able to do that with your elemental strands."

I lean my head back and study the ceiling in thought. He might be right. If it works, this could be our way of protecting the people I care about. If Xenia is feeling vindictive after tonight, he might come for my friends.

"There's a question," I say finally. "Why didn't you die after I left you?"

"Todd's parents didn't die when their elemental parasites left them," Alejandro says after a moment's thought. "Maybe you're not as powerful as Xenia. He's the earth fundamental, after all. And it was your human lauvan. Maybe they are different."

"Interesting," I say and ponder the plan for a moment longer.

"If your idea works, it will be brilliant. But I'll reserve judgement until then."

"But it won't protect you," Minnie says quietly. When I look at her, her eyes glint with tears. I stroke her fingers.

"It will be easier to protect myself if I don't have to worry about you. We'll figure something out."

She frowns but doesn't contradict me. I glance at my hip and sigh heavily.

"Now for the fun part. Minnie, could you grab me something to bite down on?"

Minnie blanches but runs to the closet. She comes back with an old belt and I nod.

"That will do nicely." I heave a deep breath. "Okay, here I go."

Minnie tucks the belt into my mouth. I look down at my hip. I've set it up so one tug will unravel the final knot and push all the disparate pieces of my hipbone into place. I've done it in steps in the past, which always ends badly—me passing out halfway through, needing to redo my tedious, painful work— so when I can, I do it this way.

I dither for another moment, but the lauvan won't pull itself. My teeth clench on the belt, then I swiftly pull the strand.

My hip explodes with agony. A grunting scream rips from my throat, and my teeth cut into the belt. Although this is certainly not the first occasion I have healed myself from terrible injuries, the pain is fresh and raw every single time.

The pain dissipates in a matter of seconds, but the ordeal leaves me sweating and shaky. Minnie smooths my hair with trembling fingers.

"Is it over?" Alejandro whispers. I nod then carefully roll over and spit out the belt.

"I hate that," I say weakly. Minnie takes my hand and holds it firmly. "If I didn't have enough reason to take out Xenia already, that would clinch it."

Alejandro waits a beat.

"Are you ready to try the spell?" he says. Minnie glares at him.

"Give him a minute, for pity's sake. That was rough."

"Yes, I'm fine now." I sit up and groan as my hip creaks. When I stand and experiment lifting my leg up and around, the joint holds steady. "Good as new. I'll do the spell, and you can take it home with you."

I hobble to the living room on my newly healed leg while Minnie hovers.

"What do you need?" she asks when I lower myself onto the couch with a sigh.

"A cutting board from the kitchen. Hey, and a beer would be good." This is why I didn't heal myself on the cold sidewalk. Who would be looking out for me then?

Minnie gives me a look, but I must have scared her more than she lets on with my antics, because when she returns from the kitchen with the cutting board, there's a beer in her hand. I give her a winning smile, and she snorts.

"You're lucky I love you," she says.

Alejandro isn't listening. Instead, he places the cutting board on the coffee table and holds the notebook in his lap.

"Okay, I need to recite these words with my hand on the board." He places his palm on the wood and reads a few words aloud in Latin.

"Is that it?" I say then look at the cutting board. "Oh, never mind. Keep your hand there, Alejandro."

The wooden board holds a few wisps of pale lauvan the color of dying leaves. It's the remnants of once strong strands that used to swirl around a living tree. It has been dead for years, but a few tenacious threads remain. That can also happen for human belongings, if the objects were dear to the dead person. Most strands will dissipate, but a few cling for years afterward.

The dead tree's strands wiggle limply toward Alejandro's hand, which is lightly covered in his dark green lauvan. Slowly, they rise, questing in the air like inchworms finding a

168

place to walk, and grasp onto the green strands that swirl around them. It takes half a minute, but three brownish threads fully incorporate into Alejandro's own.

"I think it's done," I whisper. "Something definitely happened."

"Now, the test," says Alejandro. He holds his hand out to me. "Try to give me your elemental lauvan."

I exchange a glance with Minnie, who looks curious but excited. If this works, she and the others will be safe from Xenia's machinations. My fingers comb through the strands on my torso, and I filter through them with my fingers. It's tricky to separate the elemental threads from the human ones, since they are the same color, but I've grown better at distinguishing them by feel in the past month. When I have enough for a test, I bring them forward and place them on Alejandro's hand.

At least, I try to. Every time I come near his skin, my elemental lauvan skitter away. Even when I press them firmly to his palm, they move to the other side of my hand, and Alejandro's strands give them a wide berth.

My astonishment must show in my face, because Alejandro lights up.

"It's working?" he asks.

"It's working," I say softly. "Amazing. I don't know how long for, but it's working right now." I look up at his shining eyes. "I'd repeat the spell every time you leave the house, just in case it doesn't last."

"Yes!" he shouts. "We did it."

"Not for you, though," Minnie says to me with worried eyes.

"At least I have time to fight back," I remind her. "He could possess you two with a single touch. He has to work harder for me, which gives me a fighting chance."

"I'll call Wayne tonight," Alejandro says. "Make sure you let Jen know, okay? Xenia saw her."

Alejandro's strands quickly twist themselves into anxious spirals. I give him a reassuring nod.

"Of course. I'll call her shortly."

"I forgot to tell you," Minnie says. "There was a lot going on, I can be forgiven. On the news, they said that the most recent body found was of Herschel Berne, a registered sex offender."

"That's a different name from our other offender," I say. "That's no coincidence."

"No," Minnie says. "They're definitely being targeted."

I pull out my phone—luckily in the opposite pocket of my pants from the smashed hip—and text Wayne.

Any news on March?

The answer is swift and disappointing.

Not yet.

"No sign of March," I say with disappointment. "I'm sure it's her, though."

"We'll keep looking tomorrow, Merry." Alejandro gets up from the couch and heads to the door. Before he leaves, he says, "Don't give up yet."

CHAPTER XXIV
Dreaming

Torches are few and far between this late at night on the streets of fifteenth century Zaragoza, Aragon. I have only recently arrived in town, and I won't be staying long. My Aragonese, while similar enough to the Castilian Spanish I learned last century, is rusty. I have no interest in picking it up currently. I have a desire to explore Portugal, and this town is only a stop along the way.

I was longer than I expected at the tavern, but the ale was surprisingly good, and the company as well, despite our linguistic differences. I made a tidy sum at dice and taught the other men a vulgar drinking song which they heartily appreciated, judging from the bellows of laughter and ale pressed upon me. I'm feeling at peace and a little unsteady as I weave my way to my lodgings.

I narrowly avoid stepping in a heap of refuse, barely visible in the dark, and my overcompensation slams my hip into an abandoned cart. I curse and wobble away. How many drinks did I have? I can't recall, now.

Shouting breaks the silence along with raucous laughter. Someone else is carousing tonight, by the sound of it. I toddle toward the noise on my way down the street, now eager to find my bed of straw. I hope there aren't too many fleas in this guesthouse. I was bitten raw at my last lodging and had to construct a barrier of lauvan around my body to prevent the little bloodsuckers from eating me alive. Sometimes it's preferable to sleep in the open air next to my horse, but tonight I needed human interaction and a tall mug of ale.

A woman's scream pierces the shouts. I stiffen, and all the fuzzy warmth of the ale drains from my body and leaves only cold anger. What I thought was innocent fun might be at the expense of another.

As a child, I was raised under the watchful gaze of a mother goddess. Although my beliefs are necessarily agnostic after so many years of religions passing by with no explanation for my immortality or abilities, my respect for women endured. My shapeshifting also gives me interesting insight into the female experience and the perils that sometimes occur.

So, when a woman screams while men laugh, there is only one direction to run.

It's a stumbling run, to be sure. The scream sobered me like a bucket of cold water over my head, but nothing will purge the alcohol from my system except time. But I doubt the men are any more sober than I am, and I'm more than a match for a couple of drunken louts.

I skid around a darkened house into a narrow passageway between buildings and stop short. I can manage a couple of louts, but there are six men silhouetted against a torch held by one. A young woman, her headscarf askew and her dark skin bloodless with fear, scrabbles backward on the ground. One of the men crawls forward on his knees, reaching for her legs and laughing.

"Where are you going, pretty?" he growls. "Don't run away. I'll make a woman out of you."

"If you don't, I will," another calls out.

I don't need to see more. With silent precision despite my inebriation, I lunge for my nearest target. It's unfortunate that I left my sword in my room, and all I have is a dagger. Luckily, I don't need much else.

My dagger slices through the man's neck with ease, and the others barely register my movement in the dark when I reach into the next man's center and squeeze hard. He collapses without a sound, and I whirl to my next opponent.

This one is prepared, but sloppy with inexperience or ale. I swat away his knife with my own dagger and reach to pull his center. He bends over, vomiting with stinking abundance, and I push him aside.

There are two men left standing, and they face me with their blades out. One has a sword which gives him a longer reach, but the other only has a dagger. The torch burns from its position on the ground where it was carelessly tossed. The third man is still on the ground adjusting his tunic. My nose wrinkles in disgust.

"You lost your right to be dignified in death," I yell at him, then I hit the sword with my dagger without warning and swing my leg around to buckle the wielder's knee. Dagger man thrusts wildly, but I duck and pull his lauvan. I can only reach his legs, but it causes him enough pain to fall to the ground.

Sword man swings at me again and narrowly misses my arm.

"Too close," I tell him after I dive to the ground near his feet. "I would have been really displeased had you drawn blood."

Sword man sidesteps away from my grasping fingers, but he can't see the trailing strands that follow him. With a mighty pull from my horizontal position, I yank the strands with both hands.

The man falls headlong and knocks his head against a wooden cartwheel. He hits hard enough that he slumps to the ground, unmoving.

The last man finally has his tunic in place, but he has no weapon handy. His eyes dart around to search for something to attack me with. I laugh coldly.

"You really think you stand a chance?"

He lunges for me, hoping to catch me off guard, but his strands told me his plans long before he moved. I step to the side with ease and reach into his center. With a gasp, he collapses and doesn't move.

It's finally quiet. No one has looked out their door, despite the ruckus. In this part of town, people are sensible enough to stay safe from whatever the darkness conceals.

The woman has regained her feet and is plastered against the nearest wall. Surprisingly, she is not shaking with fear, but instead looks around for an escape, or perhaps a weapon. I put

173

my hands up.

"I won't hurt you," I say softly. "My name is Merlo. I heard you scream and came to help."

Her eyes rake my face, searching for sincerity. She must find it, for she eventually answers.

"I am Mirela."

"Gypsy?" I ask. Her name sounds like she is one of the Roma.

"Yes," she replies with a defiant tilt of her head. "You want your fortune told?" She says this in a self-mocking way, but then her eyes travel over my hands and the bodies behind me. She looks at me again, appraisingly. "You are different. Those men didn't fall only from your dagger."

I stare at her for a moment. I don't normally tell everyone I meet about my abilities, but she did see me use them. Anyway, I'll only be here for one night. Even if she does cause trouble, I'll be long gone before she can organize a witch hunt.

"I am."

Mirela's eyes light up.

"How? Will you teach me?" She looks again at the dead and unconscious men, and her face darkens. "Then I would never be helpless like that again."

My heart squeezes for this plucky young woman. She has spirit, but I can't give her what she wants.

"I'm sorry," I say. "I was born like this. I don't know how to teach it. I wish I could."

Her expression closes with disappointment.

"It is hard when hope is crushed," she says finally. "Even if it was a brief, faint hope. But I thank you for saving me."

CHAPTER XXV

Jen insists on stopping by my apartment in the morning so I can check that the spell works. I don't want to leave it to chance, either, so I'm ready for her when she knocks on the door.

"Did you do it yet?" I say by way of a greeting.

"Good morning, Merry. How are you? I'm good," she says. At my exasperated huff, she grins cheekily. "Yes, but I want to do it again while you're watching."

"Come in."

Once seated on the couch, Jen opens her voluminous purse and slides out a long wooden spoon.

"How did you fit that in there?" I say in disbelief. "Magic carpet bag?"

"It's not that big," she says. "Honestly. Here, watch."

Jen recites the incantation with her hand over the spoon. Minnie comes out of the kitchen to watch, coffee cup in hand. Her eyes follow the spoon intently.

"Well?" Jen whispers after a minute. "Did it work?"

"Yes, indeed." With my finger, I trace the movement of the pale brown lauvan that twine sluggishly through her golden strands. "Repeat it every few hours, just to be certain. Take no chances, all right?"

"Got it." Jen nods firmly. She tucks the spoon into her purse again, then says, "Have you asked your elemental friend, the wind one, about banishing the successor from our world?"

"Not in so many words."

"Okay, do it right now." Jen stands quickly. "We need answers, and we need them before more people die. Come on. I need to get to work, but I'll see you off. Do we have to go somewhere special?"

"The balcony will do."

"Then, go." Jen points to the sliding glass door with an

imperious gesture. She waits until I walk toward it before heaving her purse to one shoulder and heading out the front door.

I follow Jen's directions, bemused by her taking charge but happy to let her do so. It means she's back in my life, and I can only rejoice.

Minnie follows me silently outside and stands to my right on the small outdoor area. A chill breeze billows my shirt around my torso. I take a deep breath and raise my hands.

Air lauvan sift through my fingers. I let them tickle my skin for a moment before my hands close around a few. I send out my intention to meet Ailu then release the silvery threads.

Within a few seconds, an air cable whooshes down from the morning sky and lands with a gust in my outstretched hands. Minnie glances at me.

"Is he here?" she whispers.

"Greetings, Merry," Ailu says from his perch on my hands. Minnie can't see him, but from the intake of breath beside me, I know she can hear him. He peers at her with interest. "You brought your friend again."

"Hello, Ailu. I'm glad to see you. This is not a social call, unfortunately. We still need to stop Xenia, the earth fundamental. Have you spoken to your allies yet? Is there any way we can contain him, or, better yet, banish him to your realm?"

"You are distressed,' Ailu says, his voice puzzled. "These dead bodies upset you. I wish I had better news for my only part-human ally. The earth fundamental is far too strong to banish, even if we did know a way, which none of my allies do. I am sorry, Merry."

"There must be another way," I say, desperation roughening my voice. "I must stop him. Did you find out what would happen if I kill the host body? Would that stop the cycle?"

"I communicated with an ally of mine, and it suspects that Xenia would find the nearest available body and possess that.

He needs a stable body. That is the only way he will stop jumping from human to human. It must be tiresome, continually switching bodies. He will want to settle in a form, I am sure."

"Yes, I know he wants my body," I say with exasperation. "But I'm rather fond of it and not willing to donate it for the cause quite yet. What about his current body? Is there any way to stabilize that?"

"That's an interesting point." Ailu tilts his head-shaped lauvan in thought. "Possibly? It sounds feasible, but I don't know how."

I growl in frustration.

"Do you know anyone who would know? Time is not on our side."

"Perhaps. I can ask around. So much knowledge has been lost over the centuries, since last we were allowed to enter the physical realm. But there are three half-elementals you could use. Surely, one would suit your purposes?"

"Again, using my own body is a last resort," I say. "I'm sure Todd, the fire and air half-elemental, would say the same thing. We're not sacrificing someone for this. Who's the other half-elemental you're talking about? I thought it was only me and Todd."

"You found a water half-elemental, didn't you?" Ailu points to my right, then his lauvan freeze. "I must go, I'm being watched. Good luck, Merry."

Ailu's torso melts into the air cable, which leaps into the sky and disintegrates into a million glittering shards of silver that blow away with the wind.

I turn slowly to my right, where Minnie stands with a shocked expression on her face. She meets my gaze.

"What did he mean?" she whispers. I reach out with shaking fingers to touch the lauvan swirling around her center. She gasps and closes her eyes, and my heart stutters.

That's not a normal reaction to touching lauvan. Most people can't feel it. Todd can, and so can I, on the rare occasion that someone has been able to try. I always thought that Minnie was responding to my presence near her—touching her strands is often accompanied by other intimacies—so I've never considered her reaction a clue.

I ignore her gasp and run my fingers through her strands, searching for evidence. Her knees buckle and she clings to my arm.

There, I feel it. Although all her lauvan are a deep, navy blue, my experienced fingers sense two thicknesses of strands. The difference is tiny, but obvious enough when I look for it. My breath comes faster, and I pull my hand out so Minnie can concentrate.

"Did you know?" I whisper hoarsely.

Minnie shakes her head and opens her eyes, those beautiful blue eyes partly covered by a few strands. They've been that way since I've known her as Minnie Dilleck. I narrow my own eyes as a thought crosses my mind, and my fingers gently brush the strands away.

Minnie inhales sharply and clutches my arm so tightly it might leave bruises.

"Oh, no," she breathes.

"What do you see?"

"The squiggles," she says. "That's the psychosis I've suffered from since I was a child. It's what prompted my interest in psychology."

"You've known my secrets for over a month," I say in disbelief. "And you didn't realize that you've been seeing lauvan your whole life?"

Minnie's mouth drops open, and she glances all over my body, then at the swirling air lauvan around us.

"I haven't seen it like this since I was very small," she says in wonder. "It has been floaties and eyespots since then. I'd forgotten what it looked like. It's beautiful and terrifying all at once. My parents didn't know what to think of their hallucinating child, so I learned not to see the squiggles."

I wrap her in a crushing embrace, overwhelmed by sadness for Minnie as a small child, unable to accept her true nature for fear and misunderstanding.

"We'll make up for lost time," I promise. "I will show you everything."

"This is insane," Minnie says a few minutes later in the kitchen. "How did I not figure this out? Have I always been like this?"

"As Minnie Dilleck, yes," I say. "But in your other lives, I don't think so. For one, I don't believe that in all these centuries, we wouldn't have stumbled across the truth."

"You didn't know you were a half-elemental," she says.

"Yes, but I knew about lauvan. It stretches credulity that I wouldn't have noticed your reaction to me touching your lauvan, not even once, or that you would have hidden the truth from yourself every single life. Also, why did you die? Water elementals might be reborn more frequently than earth ones, but still, you showed very typical lifespans for a human."

"So, somehow, in this life I was born a half-elemental." Understanding crosses Minnie's face. "My biological father died before I was born. It wasn't a love match, anyway, just a passing fling. I was raised by my mother and stepdad."

I nod slowly.

"Yes, of course. That begs the question, why? And how was this water elemental allowed to cross the divide?" I run my hands through my hair. "The more I learn, the less I understand. Is there a connection between your birth and Todd's? The timing is strange."

"I don't know." Minnie frowns in thought. "How do you think it works? Did my spirit—soul, whatever makes me, me—did it find this half-water elemental body and choose it to be reborn into? Or was it just chance?"

"I believe in chance less and less, these days." I run my eyes over Minnie's blue lauvan. "Perhaps you were drawn to it. You must have had some trace elemental in your ancestry as Nimue—Ailu said that was more common back then—which gave you that insight into all things water. Lady of the Lake, remember?"

"Clearly." Minnie smiles, then sobers. "So, I was drawn into this body through some affinity, maybe. And now I have an elemental father on the other side."

"Do you think he's in dormancy, just like mine was?" I lean forward with my intense interest. "To keep the balance? And why, oh why, would he do that? For what purpose?"

Minnie shrugs helplessly.

"I don't know. I don't know anything. Although I do wonder if my memory dump is because I'm different. Wayne and Alejandro have been getting memories from their past lives at a manageable rate. I got everything at once."

"Interesting theory."

Minnie waves her hand in front of her face.

"Lauvan are very distracting. I don't know how you put up with it."

"I've never known anything else." I move to her side and put my arm around her shoulders. She leans into me. "It will be strange at first, but give it a chance. You'll come to love it, even rely on it, as the special sense you didn't know you needed."

"Do you think the fact that I'm half-water elemental is why I love being on the ocean so much?" Minnie asks. "And why you like to hike in the mountains?"

"You do seem to be part fish," I tease.

I'm in favor of calling in sick at work and spending the morning experimenting with Minnie's new vision, but she doesn't want to disappoint her clients. She almost agrees when

I run my fingers through the strands on her arm, but she pushes me away with a laugh.

"Nice try," she says. "But I'm onto your tricks now."

She turns and stumbles. I catch her mid-fall, but her eyes follow my cloud of swirling lauvan in distraction, and she has a hard time keeping her feet.

"Are you sure you should be going to work?" My excitement about Minnie's new skills is overshadowed by her reaction. If I suddenly discovered the ability to see lauvan, what would it be like? Chaotic, I'd imagine. Everything in motion everywhere, after a lifetime of static shapes. No wonder she's off-balance.

"I don't want to let my clients down," she says weakly. "I'll be fine."

"I'm driving," I say firmly. "There's no way you should get behind a wheel right now, not until you're used to this. And I'd recommend not looking at your clients much. Distracted glancing at their bodies will be disconcerting for them. Although, it will give you greater insight into their moods and trustworthiness, so it will be helpful in the future."

"Good point." She links her arm through mine. "I'll be discreet. Help me to the van?"

"Don't forget this." I hand her the cutting board from the coffee table. She accepts it with a nod and mutters the incantation. Halfway through, she stops.

"Will it work on me?" she says. "It doesn't on you."

"Of course." I clap my hand to my head. "You don't even need it. You're as safe as I am from immediate possession. That's a relief. And he'd rather my body, because of the earth thing. I don't have to worry about you."

"No, but I have to worry about you," Minnie says. She presses into my side and her lauvan curl around mine in a pleasantly intimate way. "Be careful today, okay?"

"I will. And at lunch, I'll check in with Ailu again. Perhaps he'll have heard of a way to stabilize a body for elemental possession. That's our best bet right now."

I wasn't lying about our need to find a way to stabilize Xenia's current body. We need to figure that out, but it's not the most pressing matter. Above all, I need to stop Xenia from possessing any more unfortunate victims. The only way to do that is to trap him away from others. I don't know what will happen when his current body can't handle his elemental nature—will his lauvan hang around the body until someone stumbles across the corpse, at which point Xenia will possess a new host? I don't know, and I don't care. I won't borrow problems from tomorrow when I have enough to keep me busy today.

I need to ambush Xenia, and the best way to do that is to call him out onto a battlefield of my choosing. I'll hunt him down in the lauvan cables as Ailu taught me—his brown strands should stand out among the human ones of whatever body he's currently possessing—and wait for his response. A quiet spot on the ground ought to do the trick, with a rooftop to fly to nearby. Anywhere rife with earth lauvan will enable me to call him out more easily. An abundance of earth strands might give Xenia an advantage, since he's the earth fundamental, but I'm no slouch myself. I may only be a half-elemental, but I've been playing with lauvan as a human for centuries before Xenia was born. Or reborn, whatever the terminology is. I give myself headaches trying to understand this other world.

I have a few lectures to give this morning, but Xenia needs my full attention. What are a few disappointed students against a cold-blooded killer? I'm looking forward to finally pinning the slippery bastard down. He's a loose cannon and an unpredictable thorn in my side. He needs to be stopped, and I want to be the one to stop him. It's only fitting, since it's my presence here on Earth that created this monster in the first place.

It's exhilarating to have a purpose. I feel clearheaded and in control. People are counting on me, even if they don't know it. Xenia must be stopped, and I can do it. I've been floundering since Arthur returned in the guise of Alejandro, and while it fulfilled all my deepest desires, I didn't know what to do with myself after.

Once Xenia is taken care of, I'll be in the same purposeless boat, but until then, I have a plan.

I pull my van into the parking lot with a flourish of my hands on the wheel and a contented smile on my face. I didn't tell any of this to Minnie, of course. She would try to talk me out of baiting Xenia, even though it's the sensible thing to do. She would want me to rely on my friends. Normally, I would agree with her, but there's little they can do against someone like me. I should know—I've had a singular advantage over my opponents for all my long life. Xenia needs to be taken down by someone with an elemental side. Minnie is far too new to rely on—she could barely walk straight this morning—and I can't ask Todd to fight alongside me when we've only just met. He needs some time to come to terms with this new world he's been introduced to.

I pass Wayne's office on my way to drop off my satchel, since I won't need it when I look for Xenia. Alejandro is there, peering at Wayne's monitor.

"There you are." Wayne greets me with a nod. "I thought you'd turn up soon. Grab yourself a coffee."

He waves at the takeout cup in a cardboard tray then turns back to his computer screen to point something out to Alejandro. I wander over and pick up the coffee then narrow my eyes at the company name on the side.

"Did you visit Anna Green again?" I say with suspicion. Wayne doesn't look at me, but his lauvan squirm.

"She was there when I picked up the coffee, yes."

"You just happened to stop by that coffeeshop, despite it not being on your way to work," I say with thinly veiled teasing.

Wayne ignores me and speaks to Alejandro.

"My police friend got me this list. It's all the sex offenders in the region, they have to be registered for legal reasons."

"Great." Alejandro's eyes scan the list. "We can choose the closest ones and follow them, hopefully catch Xenia in the act."

"And then what?" I say. "He's no match for you. I know you have the spell, but he can do other things besides possess you. Earth fundamental, remember?"

"Yes, yes, we know," says Alejandro with a bite of impatience. "As soon as we're sure he's there, we'll call you."

"This spirit mumbo-jumbo is annoying," Wayne mutters. "I feel like Xenia would benefit from a sword to the neck."

"No doubt, *Gawaine*," I say with emphasis. "But don't forget what century you're in. Trust me, the authorities don't take kindly to medieval weaponry."

"I sense a story," he says with eagerness. "Do tell."

I wave his request away.

"Another day. We have an elemental to catch. Give me a name from the list and I'll do some spying this afternoon."

"Me too," says Alejandro. He seems too eager, and I glance at him sharply.

"Be careful, Alejandro," I say. "No heroics, all right? Call me the moment you feel something suspicious. This is out of your league."

"Okay, okay," he says, but his lauvan show me that he doesn't really mean it. I'm worried that he'll try something foolish, but beyond locking him in my office, there isn't much I can do. At least he has the anti-possession spell. He might get hurt, but he has a smaller chance of ending up dead.

I don't know why I'm worrying. This is all a sham, something to keep the two of them busy. As soon as I leave here, I will call out Xenia and end this ridiculous cat-and-mouse game he's playing. There will be no need to stake out sex offenders, not when I can find him using the lauvan. This will all be over by mid-morning, and my friends will be safe.

They don't need to know my plan, because doubtless Alejandro would race to my side with Wayne at his heels. They can't help in this, so I might as well keep them out of harm's way. Alejandro is acting more reckless than usual, and I don't want to expose him to more danger than he can handle.

This morning, then, I will defeat my enemy, and wrap up the problem in time for lunch.

I pull on my coat and walk swiftly outside to find a quiet spot to enter the lauvan. Halfway down the boulevard, an uneasy feeling washes over me. The hairs on my neck prickle with tension. I can hardly explain it. It's as if my lauvan are mildly electrified, but it's not a sensation I remember ever having before.

Perhaps it's a side effect of Minnie touching my strands this morning. The thought puts a smile on my face. In all my long years, never has anyone been able to interact with my strands until recently. I'm thrilled to explore this unknown side of Minnie and experience something new with her. It has been centuries since I've encountered something novel, and I thought I'd seen everything. The past few months have taught me how wrong I am.

The prickling sensation persists, and I navigate the chaos of rushing students with difficulty in my distracted state. I draw in deep breaths while I stride to a bench along a quieter walkway. The sensation isn't reduced by my walk, and when I drop onto the bench and close my eyes, the feeling of tension is only heightened. Now that I think about it, it's clear that the source of my unease comes from below me, within the Earth itself.

My mind flashes back to the volcano at Wallerton, months ago. Elementals had disrupted the earth lauvan to create a catastrophe. This feels different. Where the lauvan at Wallerton made me feel ill with their sickliness, what I'm sensing now is tension. I don't understand.

I push the worry aside. I can figure out this new issue once I've dealt with Xenia. My eyes glance furtively around, but already the pedestrian traffic has slowed as students reach their intended classrooms. My pathway is secluded enough to afford me a little privacy. I can call out Xenia now and get this over with. With any luck, I can lure her to the university then knock her out with a powerful wind from a rooftop vantage, and no one on campus will notice my elemental antics.

I reach down and grasp handfuls of earth lauvan that swirl around my feet. With an effort that comes more easily every time I do it, I send my conscious into the lauvan in the same way I do with a cable. As Ailu taught me, I travel the paths of glowing strands, searching for the two-colored signature of Xenia.

Traveling the earth strands is far more natural than whirling along air lauvan with Ailu, due to my affinity with earth. I briefly wonder if Todd would enjoy traveling with Ailu, since he has his own air threads.

Strand after strand, lauvan whisk by me on my search. The network of earth strands spreads across the city, thick and solid, and interspersed human lauvan twinkle with a myriad of colors. It's dazzling, but I ignore the beauty in my quest to find Xenia. Every time I sense brown human strands, I focus my intent, but it's never him. It surprises me that Xenia hasn't found me like this, but I suppose I am not obviously a half-elemental, since both my strand types are the same color. Ailu had to look closely at Minnie to catch the difference.

I circle around and travel back to my body, intending to travel in the opposite direction. Before my conscious reaches my body, a cluster of brown strands mingled with red catches my attention.

It's Xenia. If I could feel my heart, it would be racing with the knowledge that I have him. I barrel toward the cluster. If I'm quick, and can catch him off guard, I will have the advantage. With a start, I realize that Xenia's chestnut cluster is right next to my own chocolate brown strands. A twinge of fear lances through my conscious. Did he find me? What is happening to my body while I'm traveling on elemental paths?

I collide with his strands with all my force. They yield then snap back and fling me into my body. My strands rush into my physical form and I open my eyes with a gasp.

Xenia, now a lanky man with floppy black hair in a knitted sweater, leers at me.

"Gotcha," he whispers. Before I can muster any defense, he shoves his hand into my center and squeezes. The world turns black.

CHAPTER XXVI

I come back to myself slowly, unable to do more than squeeze my eyes shut tightly and curl in a ball on a hard floor. My stomach clenches spasmodically as it recovers from Xenia's treatment of my center. Xenia pulled the same move that I've used countless times to incapacitate my opponents. How did he figure it out so quickly? It took me years and a lucky coincidence to realize that it would work. Did his knowledge of the lauvan help him understand the weak point of a human?

However he discovered it, it rankles that he used my signature move. I wince when my muscles spasm once more. Recovery is more uncomfortable than I'd expected. Perhaps I should use it more judiciously in the future.

If I have a future. A shiver travels down my back. Xenia captured me. He has me, and I'm at his mercy, to be used as a vessel for his own strands.

I try to push myself off the cold floor, but my hands are tied behind my back with painful rope, and my feet are likewise bound. I thrash for a moment of panic but quickly calm. I've been in tighter scrapes than this before. Houdini had nothing on me. I was sorely tempted to compete with him for audiences after seeing a show of his, but I resisted. Fame is a tricky beast to contain, especially when keeping a low profile is more advantageous for me.

I open my eyes and blink until they focus. I'm in a basement room that does double duty as prison and laundry room, if the washing machine and sink in the corner are any indication. There are no windows, but someone kindly left the overhead lights on. The floor is covered with cheap linoleum but is cold from the cement foundation underneath. As my limbs start to shiver, I wonder how long I've been unconscious.

I heave myself to a seated position—not an easy feat with

arms tied—and prop myself against a cupboard door to allow my stomach to cease its distracting clenching. It's time to unbind myself from these ropes. With any luck, it will be the work of a minute. I haven't yet met a rope that wasn't able to be broken using lauvan.

My fingers reach up and fumble for the rope coiled tightly around my wrists, but they slide off. Bemused, I try again, with the same result. What is going on? I feel around more carefully, and the sensation is too familiar to ignore. Somehow, Xenia has wrapped lauvan around the ropes to create an impenetrable-to-me barrier. A quick glance at my bound ankles illustrates my fears. A thick layer of silvery brown strands covers the ropes entirely.

With much twisting and stretching, my hands touch the strands surrounding my ankles. It's no use—they're as untouchable as the ones on my wrists. It's strange that I can't manipulate them, but clearly Xenia knows a few tricks that I don't. If I make it out of here intact, I plan to learn them.

I look around, but there is nothing sharp in sight to saw off the ropes manually. I clench my teeth over the cupboard doorknob, but the cavity behind is empty.

I lean back against the cupboard, trying to stay calm. I can't tear off my bonds, but there must be something else I can do. I'm more than a physical body. Can I send my elemental lauvan away from here to find help? Minnie can see lauvan, and so can Todd. I could even contact Ailu through the air threads, if need be.

My heart pounds from excitement. I might not be able to escape on my own, but I have friends and a way of contacting them. They can get me out of this. I am not alone.

My eyes dart around, and it's only then I realize that I am surrounded by a blank circle devoid of earth lauvan. When I shuffle forward, the circle follows me.

What devilry is this? How is Xenia so powerful that he can change the flow of earth strands to avoid me? With a sinking heart, I start to comprehend the power of my enemy. He is the earth fundamental, after all, first among equals, longest lasting of the earth elementals. I've treated him as a newcomer to this world, when he is vastly more powerful than I've given him credit for.

Now, I have no way to break free of my bonds and no way to send for help. I am truly on my own.

I wait for ages before the outer door finally clicks open. Xenia, in his most recent body that I glimpsed before I passed out, enters my prison.

"Merry," he says with a broad smile. "You're awake. I wasn't sure how long the effects would last for. Humans are quite fragile, aren't they? Even you."

"Fuck off," I say eloquently. At the sight of Xenia's grin, anger heats my chest and fills my head with hot blood. I want to leap up and punch the smirk off his face, but I'm trussed up like a side of venison.

"Now, now, Merry," he says in disappointment. "There's no need for that sort of talk. It's your own fault you're here. We could have been allies. You were the one who pushed me away. If we had been allies, I would have used a different half-elemental body despite the incompatibility. It would have been worth the discomfort to have you by my side. What heights could we have risen together?" Xenia shakes his head at his vision. "It's unfortunate you are stubbornly against me. I can't fault you too much, though. Stubbornness is an inborn trait of all earth elementals."

"What are you going to do?" I know he wants my body, but I don't know the details. I need to understand his plans in case there is anything to help me escape.

"Your body is so perfect for my purposes," Xenia says.

190

"Your human and elemental parts have been intertwined for centuries. When I rip away your elemental strands and replace them with my own, your physical side won't even notice the difference. You'll fit like a glove. And so strong." He waves with disgust at his current body. "After these weak vessels that fall apart as soon as I enter them, I look forward to a body that can easily hold all my power."

"So? Why haven't you done it yet?" I say with distaste. "Rip my lauvan away from my body?"

Xenia shakes his head with a patronizing air.

"This is special, Merry. It needs to be done right. While I can enter a human body without a fuss, yours will be considerably more difficult. I'll need to remove your elemental side before there is room for mine, and I sense that I won't do that without a fight. Not that you'll be a match for me—I am the earth fundamental, after all—but still, I want the process to go as smoothly as possible. Why gamble with such an important procedure? I'll wait until night falls and the humans go indoors then take you to a location well rooted in earth. I'll have the strength of my element to sustain my efforts." Xenia opens the door behind him and steps outside.

"How long?" I shout hoarsely after him. He pokes his head back through the door.

"Hours yet," he says. "Relax and treat my body well. I look forward to inhabiting it."

The door closes. To my ears, the gentle snick of the lock sounds more like the thunderous closing of a portcullis.

The clenching of my stomach finally subsides, but the lack of connection to earth lauvan disorients me. I didn't realize how connected I've always been until I wasn't. Waves of dizziness engulf me, and I can only control it by closing my eyes and swallowing hard.

It's over an hour before my door swings open again. A familiar face gazes at me intently over a tray of food.

"March?" I say, although I'm not surprised. I knew she was involved. "You're a hard woman to pin down. We've been trying to track you for ages."

"Merry." She walks over and places the tray on the floor, then eases herself down to kneel beside me. "With enough money, records can be overlooked, and itineraries rewritten."

"Well, you did a good job." I eye the plate of food, and my stomach rumbles. It's simple fare—a grilled cheese sandwich and a glass of water—but it looks delectable after my imposed fast. I hope my dizziness will hold itself at bay until after I've eaten. "Are you going to untie me so I can eat?"

"Nice try," March says with a sniff. "I'm here to handfeed you."

"That's a bit of a comedown for the leader I know. Handfeeding the prisoner, when you used to run Potestas with a benevolent fist? Where are your lackeys? Why are you doing the grunt work?"

"You put a stop to all that at the cave," March says with tight lips. "I make do with what I have. I've never been afraid of getting my hands dirty, and I do what I need to do to get what I want."

"Speaking of getting your hands dirty, I desperately need the little boys' room. What do you suggest?"

March sighs, and her lips tighten to white lines.

"I have a spare cup. It will have to do."

March reaches for the zipper on my jeans and I roll my eyes.

"Truly? Xenia must not think much of you, if he makes you do this. This is hardly the least dignified thing I've done in my life, but I can't imagine you're used to this sort of humiliation."

She yanks down my underwear and holds the cup in place.

"Just get on with it," she growls.

When I'm finished, March places the cup outside the room,

washes her hands in the sink with an expression of distaste, and kneels beside me again. I nod toward the sandwich.

"All right, Warden Feynman, feed me that sandwich. I'm starving."

Her mouth twists, but she raises a half sandwich to my waiting mouth. The cheese has cooled and congealed, but it tastes divine to my hungry tongue. I don't speak while I inhale the sandwich, but after March holds the glass of water to my lips and I drink deeply from the cup, I'm ready to ask questions.

"What's your stance on Xenia murdering your former acolytes?" I say casually. March winces.

"He didn't explain until later that regular humans were not compatible with his power," she answers quickly. "I never wanted them to get hurt. That's why I gave him the sex offender list."

"They are people, too," I say.

"A lot less precious than the innocents from Potestas," she says with heat. I frown at her.

"The Potestas members were all willing accessories to ritual murder. Their innocence is open to debate. And the sex offenders have done their time and paid their price. Do you have the right to decide guilt and innocence better than the courts?"

"Sex offenders are five percent likely to reoffend once they're released," March spits. I've clearly struck a nerve.

"And ninety-five percent are not," I say calmly. "Do you know which are which? From what you've let slip in the past, I guess you have a history of abuse." March grimaces and her lauvan flare, but she doesn't deny my words and merely straightens her spine. "But at the end of the day, you are sanctioning murder, no matter who it is. Is that justifiable?"

March doesn't respond, but she avoids my gaze as she offers me another sip of water. Her burgundy strands squirm. My words clearly bother her, but she doesn't want to admit it.

193

"What happened in your past?" I say quietly. "Who hurt you?"

To my surprise, March throws back her head and laughs loudly. When her laughter subsides after a long moment of mirth, she looks at me with a shake of her head.

"Can you guess who I was in my past?" She stares at me, deep into my eyes. "Can you guess, Merlin?"

The revelation hits me like a slap to the face, and I close my eyes in defeat.

"Morgan," I whisper. In a past life, March was Arthur's sister, my friend, my brief lover, then my enemy. Our relationship was complicated, to put it mildly. Details of March's life and decisions slot into place with what I know of Morgan's personality, and I nod involuntarily. I open my eyes. March's own pierce my gaze.

"You got it," she says.

"Of course. Your quest for elemental power, it makes so much sense now. You've always envied my abilities. You found out about your past on the boat, didn't you? After we dived to retrieve the grail?"

"I was so confused," she says. "Memories of my history bombarded me. You were in so many of them, and I couldn't figure out why, until enough of the memories clicked into place. And Anna had her own memories, and we pieced it together."

"Who was she?" I lean forward in my curiosity.

"Vivienne," March says with a gleam in her eye. "But now that you have stripped her of her Potestas memories, she doesn't know who she is. And since I don't have the grail anymore, thanks to you, I can't have my oldest friend back with me."

I lean back to digest that news. Anna was Vivienne, yet another complicated relationship from my past. How many of my previous acquaintances wander this Earth? Is everyone whose life I touched now fated to repeat themselves, over and over again?

March's strands twist with her emotion. I pity her. Although I couldn't have left Anna's mind intact and kept Minnie safe, I know the pain of having friends ripped away. Vivienne was Morgan's closest confidante, and to have found that again must have brought March almost as much joy as I felt when Alejandro discovered his past.

To tear my mind away from somber thoughts, I focus on the situation at hand. After all, I'm still a prisoner here, no matter how many revelations I might be granted.

"What are you doing with Xenia?" I say. "Truly, what do you hope to gain? What has he promised you?"

"He offered me a spirit traveler," she says quietly, but her heart isn't in the words. A spirit traveler is what the Potestas members called possession by an elemental. "He said it would give me great powers. I declined."

"After you saw what actually happened to those possessed?"

"Yes. But there are other ways to gain power. Xenia promised to teach me, once he was in a stable body."

"He can't teach you anything," I say flatly. "He is trying to be me. Part elemental, part human. And there is nothing he can teach you. Trust me, I would have passed on my knowledge ages ago if I knew how, if I thought it would make my friends and lovers more like me. I never wanted to be alone for so long. I would have done anything to change that. But, unless you have some elemental lauvan within you, you will never have the powers you seek. And if you do become a host to an elemental, you won't be yourself anymore."

March stares at me for a long while after this speech. Her strands swirl in thought.

"There might still be a way," she says finally, but her lauvan don't match her words. Is she talking about finding a way to gain power for herself, or something else? "From what I've read, possession is not set in stone. There are ways to strengthen a host, to prepare it for possession, in a way that will enable the body to maintain itself. If the body is prepared, especially with the element needed, success is possible."

She shakes her head and pushes herself to her feet, using the counter for leverage. She bends to pick up the tray.

"I don't suppose you'd let me go," I say without hope. March smiles grimly.

"No. I've gone too far, now. And this will stop the murder spree. At least you've had a long, full life, far longer than most. I don't feel bad about ending it now. Take heart that you will be saving the lives of your precious sex offenders. I'll send Minnie a condolence card."

With those hurtful words hanging in the air between us, March spins on her heel and exits the room, leaving me to contemplate the depths to which a person will descend for a taste of power.

March and Xenia leave me to stew for hours. My thoughts are disjoint, disturbed every few minutes by waves of dizziness caused from my separation from the earth lauvan. I never realized how dependent I was on that connection. Even in an airplane, I can still sense the cables far below me. Perhaps, my elemental side is a larger part of me than I thought. Now, with whatever Xenia has done, all strands are masked from me. I'm untethered, and more alone than I've ever been. My friends, Minnie, and now my powers are out of reach.

It is time to face the truth: there may be no way to stop Xenia. He will take me to a location full of the power of earth, and he will take over my body. If I fight him, chances are I will lose. I could fight him, but should I? With his strands possessing my body, Xenia would finally stop killing people. The murders would stop. He would go on to experience life in the physical world, but without the expense of innocent lives. Perhaps that is a worthwhile sacrifice. I'm not the martyr type, but this time it might make sense. Perhaps this is my new purpose.

As March said, I've lived for far longer than most. Perhaps it's time to try something new. My human lauvan would stay behind in my body, to support Xenia's schemes, but my elemental lauvan would be free to leave. I experience my consciousness through them, so what stops me from joining the elemental realm? It would be a new chapter, one that I've been searching for my whole life. My mother, centuries ago, wanted me to find the land my father came from. She had no idea, of course, that he was from another plane of existence, but I finally found it.

And that world is my birthright, the same as Earth is. Why shouldn't I live in it? I've experienced everything that the physical world has to offer, a thousand times over. I've always been a wanderer, but what's the point of wandering if you've seen everything? The elemental realm is a new frontier, and my heart quickens at the thought.

Despite my interest, I wouldn't think twice about it, except for Minnie's recent revelation that she is also part-elemental. It's the perfect solution. If I give up my body to Xenia, she can live out her life for as long as she wishes, then her elemental nature can join me on a new adventure. We can still be together, forever, simply in a new form. Would that mean that Minnie would never die, and I would never suffer the pangs of her loss again? My heart thrills at the notion. Alejandro and Wayne, while I am overjoyed to be reunited with them once more, don't truly need me.

I stare at the wall across from me and contemplate how tired I am. I've been alive for so long, that the thought of passing over into a new way of existing is a peaceful one. I will miss being human, being alive, but if this is my time to go, then I'm ready. I hope Minnie will understand and follow me when she's ready. I think she will.

The door clicks open, and Xenia enters with March

following.

"You look rough," I say to Xenia. His skin is gray and dry, his eyes are bloodshot, and some of his hair is falling out. He grimaces.

"I didn't have time to grab another body before the ritual. Besides, it only needs to last for another hour, then I get your fresh body. Come on, let's move."

I glance at March, but she keeps her eyes away from mine and her strands tightly coiled. I still don't know how she can contain her lauvan's reactions so that I rarely see them, but if she has Morgan's memories, I don't doubt that she figured out a way to hide her thoughts from me. Morgan always knew about my abilities, and she hated any advantage I had over her.

"Come on," Xenia repeats with more force. I look at him with a raised brow.

"I'm sorry I didn't leap up at once," I say with as much sarcasm as I can pack into the few words. "Only, it's a tad difficult with bound legs and arms."

"Help him up," Xenia says to March. "And cut the ropes around his legs. If he runs, I'll grab him."

"Sarcasm is wasted here," I mutter. March hears me, and the ghost of a smile passes her lips before she controls herself.

CHAPTER XXVII

I stumble after Xenia, my legs wobbly after hours of inaction. March brings up the rear with a shovel on her shoulder, but her hand is ready at my elbow every time I falter. Xenia leads us up a set of rickety wooden stairs and through a kitchen last updated in the eighties.

"Whose house is this?" I ask March.

"Rose Dwight's," she says. "The first body Xenia took. She doesn't have any family in town, so it was a good base for us."

In the hall, dizziness overwhelms me, and I stagger into the wall.

"What's wrong with you?" Xenia says, concern for my wellbeing absent in his voice. "It had better not be permanent. I want your body in full working order."

"You cut me off from my connection to earth," I gasp while the room slows its spinning around me. "It gives me vertigo."

"So, it won't last. Good." Satisfied, Xenia exits the front door. March grips my upper arm and supports me over the threshold and to a waiting car. The silver sedan is inexpensive and nondescript, certainly nothing I would have expected March to drive. She hid her presence in the city well.

Xenia slides into the back seat and beckons me to sit beside him. After March straps me in, she climbs into the driver's side and starts the engine. My hands dig uncomfortably into my back, but I console myself with the thought that bodily hurt won't be an issue for much longer. A moment of panic engulfs me—I don't know if I am ready to give up my human life— but the thought of new horizons steadies me. I can do this, for the people that Xenia won't kill in the future and for myself. With Minnie by my side, we will explore those new shores together.

Rose Dwight's house is near Commercial Drive, and it's no more than fifteen minutes before Stanley Park rises ahead of us from our downtown vantage.

"Are we going to the North Shore?" I ask March. The mountains seem like prime candidates for an earth-based ritual.

"There's a convergence up ahead," Xenia answers for her. "In these trees. It will do."

"To the west of the aquarium," March adds.

"I know the place," I say. Two lauvan cables cross each other within Stanley Park. I often wonder if those in charge of delineating park boundaries during the development of Vancouver somehow felt the presence of the cables, because the park conveniently surrounds their convergence.

The sky is clear, and Cassiopeia is faintly visible on the horizon above the northern mountains, despite a haze from city lights. Years of navigating and telling time without modern aids left me with a keen sense of the natural world that hasn't faded despite the watch on my wrist. Given the placement of the stars, I suppose it's a little before midnight.

There is plenty of parking on this dark night. March pulls into a spot close to the aquarium and walks around to help me unbuckle and exit the car. Xenia sets a brisk pace through the trees, and I stumble after him as best as I can. I stop once when another wave of vertigo spins the trees around me. March holds my arm and I concentrate on her firm hands around my elbow to ease the dizziness.

Xenia doubles back when he realizes that we aren't behind him.

"What are you waiting for?" he barks. When I don't answer, he reaches forward and grabs a handful of my lauvan. With a yank, he pulls hard.

Pain explodes in my chest and abdomen, so strongly that my already queasy stomach revolts. Vomit pours out of my mouth and sprays onto the ground. Xenia leaps back with a look of disgust.

"That's repulsive," he says. "Clean it up, March. I don't

200

want my new body covered with that mess. And hurry up, both of you. This body is close to done. I want to make the switch now."

He snaps his fingers then whirls around and strides off. I breathe deeply to control the fading pain and wooziness and try to ignore the stench of my own sick.

"Why don't you clean up your own mess?" March mutters after Xenia, but not loudly enough that he can hear her. She pulls me around the mess and leads me forward while rummaging in her pocket. A moment later, a tissue wipes my chin gently.

"Thanks," I rasp. "I have to say, I'm feeling some pity for those I've bested in battle over the years. Pulling lauvan around is serious business."

March snorts but doesn't reply.

The next corner yields the glimmering beauty of two lauvan cables crisscrossed in a massive X in a small clearing. They shine softly with a silvery brown gleam that shimmers with movement of the thousands of strands that create them.

"Can you see it?" March whispers to me. I nod.

"I wish you could, too. The magnificence of cables is breathtaking every time."

"Set Merry down here," Xenia says to March. "And we'll get to work. Hurry up, I don't have long."

March nods and helps me to the ground. I watch in fascination as Xenia instructs March where to dig holes while he pulls lauvan from trees and weaves it into a circle around the convergence. I don't understand what they're doing, but they seem to know what they want to do. March does the heavy labor while Xenia winds strands around his hands and yells at her to be quicker. She's clearly fuming, but she takes the abuse without comment. Whatever he has promised her must be worthwhile in her mind. It's hard to comprehend powerful March or proud Morgan allowing this treatment.

It takes a good twenty minutes of March toiling and Xenia

twisting strands around the clearing, but they finally complete their task. Despite my seated position, waves of vertigo overwhelm me every few minutes and leave me sweating and shaking.

Xenia stalks toward me, a predatory gleam in his eye. March follows at a distance, distaste for her companion clear from her expression.

"It's time," Xenia says. He waves March forward. "Get him up and bring him to the convergence. Oh, right, I forgot you can't see. It must be terrible to be so blind." He grins at me. "How do you tolerate dealing with these sightless moles?"

I don't bother answering him, partly because he isn't worthy of an answer, and partly because my concentration focuses on calming my queasy stomach. March supports me around my waist and hauls me up. I avoid relying on the older woman's strength for long, but she's surprisingly sturdy, even when I stumble sideways as the trees spin around me.

Xenia plunges into the crossing of the cables with a gasp then plants himself in its midst. He beckons me forward. March gently pushes me toward him, and I catch my breath when the first strands collide with my own. The sensation only increases with every step, and my eyes close briefly with the momentary overwhelm. When they open again, March gazes at me with frustrated longing.

"You still want to trade places with me, even now?" I say to her. She looks away to hide her expression and doesn't answer.

Xenia pulls away the ropes and lauvan that bind my arms together. He keeps a careful hold on both of my hands and brings them to each side of my body so that we face each other. Even if I had wanted to pull away, I'm not certain my vertigo would have let me get very far.

"Heady, isn't it?" he says. His voice is clear, although I can hardly see his face through the swirling strands around us. "That feeling. The pull between spirit and body. I can see why elementals used to come through, just for this."

"You get used to it." I shrug, but Xenia looks at me with a raised eyebrow. I lie, and he knows it. That feeling is as astonishing now as it was the first time I touched a cable. Minnie hasn't experienced that yet, and a pang of regret hits me that I won't be by her side when it happens. She should experience a few more things as a human before she joins me. I'll find a way to help her do that, from the other side.

Since March's role is complete, she backs away and watches us from the edge of the clearing. Xenia squeezes my hands.

"Farewell, Merry," he says. "Too bad we couldn't be allies. I'll enjoy your body. You can console yourself with the thought that you've had far longer than most in a human form. Consider yourself passing the torch, like your father did to me. It's fitting, in a strange, circular way, that your father's reborn spirit will now inhabit his son's body. Hell, even I'm confused now."

He chuckles then closes his eyes. For a long moment, nothing happens. Then, a trickle of Xenia's chestnut brown strands slither down his arm and along my own. I watch with growing horror as more follow, causing a crawling sensation deep in my center. It's a disgusting feeling, like an insidious fungus creeping through a healthy tree, wrong and full of doom. Immediately, I regret my acceptance of this path I was made to choose and have to remind myself of the new life to come, even as every cell in my body screams at me to fight back.

My nausea worsens at the repulsive sensation, and I gulp reflexively to keep control of my body. There's a tug at my lauvan, ticklish and persistent, until the tug becomes a push and the push turns into a shove. My conscious is forced forward and down, through my arms, and the last thing I feel in my body is my heart hammering a panicked staccato.

Then, nothing. I feel nothing, only sense the world through lauvan. Xenia's strands glow chestnut brown all around me as they slither past, toward my body, away from the tomato red

203

strands of his old form. I am tether-less, unable to return to my physical home, and the feeling of rootlessness is hard to bear. I've been a vagrant wanderer my whole life, but the one thing I could always count on was myself. My mind and my body have always been mine. I never realized how dear I held that until it was taken away from me.

If I still had lungs, they would be gasping with anxiety and dread at my current state. My elemental lauvan begin to dissipate into the space around me, like those of a dying man. Am I dying? Why aren't my strands holding together? This is my great fear, my strands floating away from me until there is nothing left, and I cease to exist.

I thought I would become like the elementals, but now I realize I don't even know what that means. I'm not ready for this. I can't leave this physical world, not yet. Minnie's face passes before my mind's eye, her clear blue eyes gazing into mine. *I never left you*, she seems to say. *Don't you leave me now.*

My panic gives me mental strength. My intent pours into my strands, and I claw them back together through sheer willpower. What now? My own body is unavailable—the force that pushed me out is still in there—and I don't know where to go. The red strands of Xenia's old body catch my attention. They are puddled on the ground below me, fading into wisps but still present. The body must be dying, but it's not gone yet. With a jolt of fear, I rush toward the cluster. Will it work? Can I take over this body, the way Xenia did to the others?

Slowly, so slowly, physical sensations return to me. First is the feeling of grass on my cheek. Then, the smell of wet dirt and the flavor of whatever Xenia had for dinner. A greasy burger, by the taste of it.

Sound hits me next, but I'm too groggy to distinguish the noise. Shouting, perhaps. Thuds and cracks as well, but I can't understand what they are and why. Everything hurts, and I feel tight and out of place, like I'm squeezing my hand into the glove of a child. It occurs to me that I now have eyes, and my tired brain finally remembers how eyelids work. They rise heavily, and I blink a few times as the world comes into focus.

Everything is sideways from my prone position on the clearing floor. There are more people than Xenia and March, and I wonder whether I'm seeing double. I blink a little more and the fuzzy world grows clear, even though the cables prevent me from seeing everything plainly.

Wayne is here, swinging my sword around with practiced strokes and roaring his intent. He must have sharpened it tonight. Alejandro leaps toward Xenia in my body with fury in his face. And Minnie, my dear love, stands with a bottle full of water and her eyes narrowed in concentration. Her fingers pull blue strands out of the bottle and fling them forward.

They're here. My friends have come to save me. My unfamiliar heart swells with familiar feeling in my new chest. How did I ever think that leaving them was the right decision? I am clearly not suited for being strictly an elemental, as my experience minutes ago showed me. For better or for worse, I am half-elemental and half-human.

Xenia is now in my body, and it's a disquieting experience to watch myself from a distance. He rolls away from Wayne's sword thrusts, deflects Alejandro's well-placed kick, and throws up a wall of dirt that turns to mud from Minnie's water attack. He reaches down with my fingers, makes my eyes narrow in concentration, and yanks at the earth lauvan that writhe on the ground.

Cracks form in the soil below the others. Minnie shrieks and disappears into a sinkhole. Alejandro yells but manages to cling to the side of the pit. Wayne sidesteps with quick reflexes then sprawls on his stomach to retrieve Minnie from her hole.

Xenia smiles with satisfaction, and my chest heats from fiery anger. It's good to have a physical form again. Without the feedback of my body's reactions, emotions are too muted to be gratifying. Xenia is hurting my friends, and I can't leave them to suffer while I waste away on the forest floor.

Giving Xenia my body wasn't the answer. If I had the fortitude to become an elemental, what would it serve? Even now that Xenia has what he wants—a stable body—his mind still turns to the destruction and death of my friends. My sacrifice would have been for nothing, and others still would have been in danger from this treacherous fundamental.

I've been searching for a purpose, and perhaps this is it. My friends still need me, and the people of this world still need protection from Xenia. In a way, since I am the only one qualified to confront him, and since he is partly my own doing as the product of my strange birth, he is my responsibility. I need to do this.

But first, I must pull myself together. Do my limbs even work? I maneuver my hands under my body and push upward with a groan. Everything is shaky but functional, and with a lurch I stand on my new feet.

This body is taller than my old one, and I feel like a newborn giraffe with wobbly knees. I take a step forward and nearly lose my balance until my brain catches up with the shape and size of the unfamiliar form. I can do this. It's just like changing shape with my strands. At least I am once again connected to the earth lauvan around me. My main issue is the lingering effects of the transfer and the feeling of dissociation and ill-fit, but I can shake that off quickly, I hope. I'll have to. My friends need me.

Alejandro gives a strangled yell, and I squint through the cable to see what's happening. Alejandro's legs are stuck in a pile of muddy soil and he can't break free. Xenia stalks toward him with a maniacal leer. It's a horrible expression, and I hope I've never transformed my face like that in the past.

Wayne looks at Alejandro with a look of anguish, but he holds Minnie by the arms and clearly can't help Alejandro without dropping Minnie. It's up to me. I hope my new body is up to my old standards.

I charge through the cable, gritting my teeth against the painfully pleasurable sensation that ripples through me, and raise my hands to gather as many dangling strands from the surrounding trees as I can. With a mighty yank accompanied by a chorus of tremendous cracks, I send a dozen huge branches tumbling from the sky straight toward Xenia.

Belatedly, I recall that it's my body I'm attacking. If there's even a slight chance that I can get it back, I don't want to kill it first. I'm rather fond of my body. We've been through a lot together.

With mixed feelings, I watch Xenia twist and deftly pluck strands out of the air. The branches thunder to the ground in a neat circle around him.

"Merry?" Xenia's face smiles with a look of surprised glee. "You're tenacious, aren't you? Comes from your earth nature. You and your friends are a wrench thrown into my plans, but it's a detour I don't mind making. Let's see what you have for me. Come on, pit your half-elemental strength against the earth fundamental. I want to see this."

"Merry?" Alejandro gasps, but I ignore him. My focus is on my opponent and what he will do next.

Xenia doesn't waste time. Quick as a rolling landslide, he whips his hands out and grasps the nearest swaying earth strands. The ground beneath me shakes and I leap to the side to avoid a widening crack in the tortured Earth.

"Come and play, Merry," Xenia shouts. "You're dancing about. I want to see what you've got."

I pull the nearest earth lauvan upward, and the soil gapes open, the spilt traveling right toward Xenia. With a groan, the split stops expanding before it reaches Xenia. He looks at me with a wide smile and a condescending shake of his head.

"Too predictable. I thought this would be more interesting. Do you really think you're a match for me? I *am* earth. Good luck besting me with my own element."

He raises his hands, and a splitting crack rents the air. Too late, I look up. Whooshing toward me is a branch the width of my leg. With a jolt that slams my teeth together and sends an explosion of pain through my skull, it glances my head. I'm thrown to the ground in a daze, and my unfocused eyes watch Xenia turn his back on me. I am no longer a threat to him, and now he seeks to dispatch my friends.

CHAPTER XXVIII

Xenia was so preoccupied with me that he didn't notice Alejandro breaking free of his mud prison. Alejandro charges Xenia and bowls him over onto the grass. Xenia lets out a grunt of surprise. Alejandro presses his advantage by swinging his fists at Xenia's face.

"Don't hurt him too much!" Minnie screams from beside the pit that Wayne pulled her out of. "That's Merry's body!"

Alejandro's face contorts in confusion, and he aims his punches lower on Xenia's torso. I wince, which sends fresh waves of pain through my aching skull and makes my eyes cross. I have a concussion, and I won't be able to help much until it's gone. My fingers search my head and encounter wetness—head wounds bleed excessively—and a huge lauvan knot. Feverishly, I massage and untangle the knot while I watch the fight before me.

Wayne runs toward the grappling pair, but Xenia pushes Alejandro off before they can press their advantage and leaps to his feet. Blood trickles down his mouth, and he spits on the ground before grasping the nearest strands.

"Impudent human," he rasps out with my voice twisted in anger. "You have no idea who you're fighting. You are insects beneath my feet, and it's only my unfamiliarity with this human form that allows you to attack. Once I understand this world better, I will be unstoppable. Even today, you have no chance."

"Big words from the bleeding man," Wayne snarls. He runs toward Xenia, sword at the ready, and swings powerfully. Xenia ducks, but the sword grazes his arm, and he hisses in pain.

"Wayne!" Minnie screams. "Watch it!"

She grabs a handful of blue water strands, darts forward, and flings them at Xenia's face. It makes him pause and wipe his streaming eyes with a sleeve. Alejandro takes the opportunity to pounce on him again. He charges forth without any weapon but his determination, and I can't help but admire his boldness, even as I condemn his recklessness.

Despite their attacks, the ground shakes and tree limbs fall like deadly rain. Xenia wastes no time and grabs every strand he can reach, between grappling with Alejandro and avoiding Wayne's sword strokes.

I must get out there. My friends need me if we are to have any hope at defeating Xenia. My fingers work ceaselessly, and moment by moment, the pain lessens.

My view of the battle is obscured when March kneels before me.

"Merry," she says quietly but with urgency. "Listen to me. You need to force Xenia into my body."

"What?" I'm confused, and I don't think it's only from my concussion.

"I prepared my body, made myself an appropriate vessel for him." She glances around, but the battle continues to rage behind her.

"How? Why?"

"My library of spirit-related books holds a lot of knowledge—the answers were all there. As for why, I want what Xenia has, what you have." Her expression turns thoughtful. "You really have no idea what it feels like to be powerless, do you? For your entire, far-too-long life, you've always had the upper hand. I can't expect you to understand my motivations."

"But you'll die," I say. Surely, she has seen enough of her Potestas members fall prey to Xenia. "You know what happens to the bodies Xenia possesses."

"The library, Merry. It's all in there. I dug deep and found the answers I needed. My body is ready, and I'm certain that he won't take full possession. I can control him."

March is right—I don't understand her. How is this an

acceptable risk to her? My concussed brain tries to grasp the situation.

"If there's a way, why didn't you tell Xenia before now? Do you know how many people died to give him bodies?"

"Nine," she hisses, her eyes suddenly bright with unshed tears. "I know every single one. Too many were my compatriots from Potestas until I gave him the list of sex offenders. Trust me, I told Xenia about this—begged him to use me—but he was too stubborn." She dashes away the wetness in her eyes, and her face grows grim. "Once he realized that he could use you, and that you weren't going to be his ally, he wanted your body. He wouldn't even listen to alternatives. Your compatibility appealed to him and taking you out of the picture at the same time was a definite draw. But he needs to be stopped. I'm prepared, and it's the only way."

Her voice turns pleading.

"Please, Merry, no one else can do this but you. Once I have the power, I promise I will use it for good. Please believe me. I know it looks like I have dreams of grandeur, but all I ever wanted was to not feel powerless, and to help others feel that way too."

March may believe her own assertions, but power has a funny way of corrupting some. Still, if there's a way that someone can control Xenia—I grasp desperately at other options.

"Can't I prepare this body instead?" I wave at the body I currently inhabit then turn my fingers back to their task of unknotting my tangled strands.

"It's too far gone," March says. "Look at it. Xenia wore it ragged. Besides, the preparation takes too much time. For how long do you think your friends can hold Xenia off?" March glances to where Xenia sends tendrils of vines toward Wayne, who chops at them raggedly with my sword. She turns back to me and presses a small package wrapped in a handkerchief onto my lap. "Use this to ease the transfer. You'll have to figure out the rest with your lauvan tricks."

"What is it?" I glance at the package on my lap while my fingers continue to work at the knots. I've almost untangled enough for me to be useful once more.

"It's earth," she whispers in Brythonic. "Use it as a conduit to bring the earth fully into me."

I stare into March's eyes that flicker with Morgan's stubborn intelligence and hunger.

"I have to try preparing this body," I say doggedly. "I don't want to be party to your demise."

"You don't even know how, you idiot," she hisses.

"I can try."

Enough of my lauvan are untangled to clear my head, and my fingers dive eagerly to the bundle on my lap. I'm still not certain what March meant by an earth conduit, but when I see the item, my mind clicks over until all the clues I've received slot together into an answer.

It's a tiny statue of a woman carved from striped sandstone. Her features are indistinct, and her body rounded in a symbolic interpretation of the female form. Surrounding it are many faded strands of all colors, but among them are the slender threads of earth.

Long ago, this was a statue of a mother goddess, perhaps an earth deity. Likely, it was kept near the hearth and prayed to daily. It hasn't been used in this capacity for many years, given the dull colors of the lauvan swirling around it, but it was revered strongly enough to create a lasting bond with inanimate stone. March must have found it on her travels.

March called it a conduit, and I think I understand why. If the body is prepared with the element needed, and the host strengthened to prepare it for possession, success might be possible.

How can I prepare this body for possession by Xenia? It is overwhelmed by the presence of such a strong earth elemental. Why is my own body different?

My body is intimately connected to my element and has been from my birth. Is there a way to bring that connection to a body not born to it? If I bring the element of earth a little bit at a time into this body instead of slamming Xenia into it all at once, will it better handle the earth fundamental?

And I can do that by using this tiny goddess from a different era, when the elements were worshipped. I hope it works, because I am out of ideas.

My presence in this body likely started the process already, but I need to bring it up to Xenia's speed. I slam the little statue to the ground and send my intent into my borrowed hand. My elemental strands pour through my arm and into the goddess, my conscious with it.

My current body shudders then shakes in a spasm. March grabs my wrist.

"Stop it," she says. "That body is too weak. You're killing yourself. Who will do the transfer then? We need to stop Xenia *now*."

"Fine," I say between clenched teeth. "But I'm getting Xenia into this body, one way or other."

I push the goddess into my pocket then lurch to my feet and sway until my brain adjusts to the difference in height. This body is failing, but I have experience in pushing myself past my limits. When one can heal from almost all ills, the boundaries of endurance shift.

Minnie is trussed up with vines against the trunk of a tree, unable to move. Alejandro is slumped on the ground, covered in dirt and fallen branches. Wayne roars loudly but ineffectively, his legs trapped in a mound of dried mud. He swings the sword at Xenia, who stands just out of reach with a smile on his face.

I can't fight against Xenia with lauvan. He is literally the embodiment of the power of earth, and all earth is under his dominion. Even with my abilities and heritage, my tricks pale in comparison to the sheer might of Xenia's power. I can't stand against that.

But human battles are my domain. I've been fighting in this physical world for centuries. Xenia may have the jump on me with the elements, but I know how to move my body. Even this fading, unfamiliar one is more natural to me than my body is to him. This is my world, and he is the usurper. It's time to show him who has mastery here.

My feet pound on the uneven ground, and I shout wordlessly at Wayne. He stops swinging the sword with a look of surprise at my reappearance, and I grab it from his unresisting hands and swing it at Xenia's astonished face.

Xenia pulls up a wall of gravel to stop the blow, but it was only a feint. My real slice nicks his leg and draws blood. He yells at the unexpected pain, and I pull the strands of gravel to open a hole large enough to swing my fist through. The smarting ache in my knuckles eases at the sight of his bloodied nose.

Once more, my sword thrusts. This time, I slide it into Xenia's outer thigh. I don't want to nick an important artery along the inner leg, but a flesh wound is easy to heal. He shrieks and lands on his bottom in the dirt, but his hands clench the strands that surround him. Branches fall and soil fills my face so I can't see or breathe, but I merely close my eyes and mouth and press my advantage. I drop my sword and grab Xenia's forearms in a crushing grip. He struggles, but I kneel on his wounded legs and he thrashes in pain. It's an asshole move, but a very human one. I bet Xenia would never have thought of it.

I send my conscious down my arms. His strands are bright before me, horribly intertwined with my body's thick chocolate brown threads. That should be me in there, and I use that anger to fuel my attack. My elemental strands flow into my old body and surround Xenia's, plucking and tearing at the threads to make them let go.

He's as tenacious as I am, and his strands glue themselves to my body's. I tug and yank, trying desperately to extricate the infection of his strands among mine, but he won't budge. What am I doing wrong? Why is he stuck here?

A glimmer catches my eye. It's one of the cables, glowing brightly in the otherwise dark landscape of threads. The other cable crosses it, not five steps from where we tussle.

If I had a hand available to slap against my forehead, I would do it now. Of course. We need to be in the convergence. That's how Xenia entered my body properly the first time. We need the connection of the earth cables to allow the shift.

I'm still halfway in the other body, and I have experience moving physical forms without being fully in them. I force my intent backward into the other body and forward into mine, and slowly, both clusters of human strands roll toward the convergence. Xenia's strands squirm as if in protest, but he clearly doesn't have full control of my body anymore. I've ripped enough of him out to loosen the hold.

We cross into the stream of glowing earth lauvan, and Xenia squirms even more. His presence pushes against mine with a force far greater than I've ever experienced in this plane. My hold on my body slips, and I scrabble for traction. He pushes again, harder, as if sensing my weakness.

I can't let him force me out. If he does, that's it. I don't know if I have the strength for another round, and he will run far away, where I can't find him. I need to end this now.

Light and sounds flicker in and out as Xenia and I wrestle for dominance of my body.

"Merry!"

"…do it…"

"Come on…"

My friends are cheering me on, and the sound of their voices spurs me to greater heights. This is my body I'm fighting for, and I'll be damned if I let this power-hungry elemental take it over. I push forward with all the will I can muster, bolstered by the increasingly loud voices of my friends as my ears become my own once more. Xenia holds on with the tenaciousness of a mountain.

The body I inhabit shudders, and it draws my attention. Its legs wobble. Have I pushed it too far? But I can't let it die—I need it for Xenia.

Xenia senses my momentary weakness and pushes with relentless force. I'm losing my grip, and I start to hear sounds from the ears of the other body. I dig deep, but the weakness of the body gives me nothing to draw on.

Someone slams into us, then a voice shouts in my ear.

"Damn it, Merry! Hang your misplaced compassion. I never wanted it. Put Xenia into my body now!"

I'm fully in the borrowed body now, and my eyes open to March's furious face in mine. I don't want to let her die, but should it be my choice? Perhaps it's finally time to give her the desire of her heart. I close my eyes briefly in acceptance.

"All right."

I dig into my pocket to extract the goddess then grab Xenia's arm as he attempts to rise in my body.

"Not so fast," I say. With a deep breath that rattles in the dying body's chest, I force my conscious back into the fray.

Xenia must have thought he'd won, for I'm able to push quickly into my body with the element of surprise. He fights back with a swift counterattack, but not before I gain control of an eye and arm.

It's now or never. The tomato red strands of the borrowed body are already fluttering away in the final throes of death. Xenia pushes against my strands, but he forgets that he's in a human body. I never forget.

With the arm that I control, I shove my fingers into the sword wound on my leg and twist. Excruciating pain lances through my thigh and Xenia and I scream as one through my throat. Xenia's strands spasm, but I don't hesitate. I've felt enough pain in my long life that I can push through it when needed.

I blast Xenia's lauvan with all the intent I can muster and

push into the wound again. Little by little, Xenia's strands crawl off my body and slither toward March. They're not moving fast enough, and my mind races over March's instructions. She isn't fully ready for Xenia, not until I can connect her to the earth in an essential way.

When I look at the goddess in the elemental plane, rainbow strands of the statue dazzle my senses. Clear among them are brown earth strands. I twist around them and coax them to the earth cable, a simple task since they yearn to join their fellow strands that loop and curl sinuously on the forest floor.

Bringing them toward March's body is a different matter, and it takes every fiber of intent I can muster to encourage the earth threads to join with her burgundy lauvan. I push and pull, twist myself around the coils and yank them upward.

Use it as a conduit, March whispers in my mind. Am I trying to force something that should come easily? In this form, I am earth. Between me and the tiny goddess, can we act as a bridge between earth and her body? I am of both worlds, after all.

I wrap my lauvan tightly around the strands of March's body and the threads of the statue. Visions of the physical world flicker in and out with my partial entry into my body. At the connection, power thrums through me—the power of thunderous landslides, of the crack of monstrous trees falling, of the shake of an earthquake. The shock nearly loosens my hold on March's strands, but I hang on. As best as I can, I filter the power through myself, only allowing a dribble of the force through me into her body. Pressure builds and I release a little more, then more. Her body, when my awareness fills it, jolts and seizes with the increase of power, although it feels stronger with every burst that I feed it.

More and more power runs through me, until the full force of the earth fills March's body. There. She's at full connection.

Xenia must sense the welcoming vessel, so different from my hostile presence, so he flows easily into her. The release of his strands from my body is blissful, and I enter my own body fully for the first time in too long.

Now that both eyes are mine to look through, I rake my glance over March. She sits up with a dazed look, then she stands above me with a wobble.

"March?" I whisper. "Is that you?"

"Yes," she breathes. "Yes, I have control." She laughs in disbelief. "This is amazing. The power is immense. I've never felt anything like this before. Oh, I'm going to enjoy this."

Her eyes roll back in her head and her limbs shake. I would jump to my feet, but my wounded legs scream at the movement and I desist.

"March," I shout. "What's going on?"

When her convulsions cease, she opens her eyes and looks at me with a calculating gaze.

"You and March are clever," Xenia says. "I'll give you that. But neither of you understand what it means to be the earth fundamental. That's all right. I will teach you both."

For a moment, I lie on the ground, stunned. The cable pulses beside me. Xenia starts to walk away in March's body.

"After her," I shout to whoever of my friends might be listening and haul myself to my feet despite the pain. Xenia looks back then touches the ground with firm hands.

The forest floor shakes, far stronger than anything else tonight. Alejandro shouts and falls to the ground, and I stumble, unable to keep my footing. The trembling lasts for minutes, and it's impossible to move while the ground is so unstable.

When the shaking finally stops, Xenia is gone. There isn't even a trace of excited strands hanging in the air to indicate in what direction she went. She must have covered her tracks to prevent me following her.

My heart squeezes with fear and regret. Xenia is now in a stable body, but at a cost that was too high. For all our differences, I never wanted to see March trapped in a body she can't control, forever at the whim of another. For March, and for Morgan, it sounds like the worst hell she could imagine. All I can hope for is that she might claw her way to the surface of her mind. If anyone is determined enough to do so, it's March.

No one runs to embrace me, and I wonder why until Wayne holds the sword to my throat.

"Who are you?" he says with a grim expression.

"Gawaine," I say in Brythonic. "You couldn't stick a sleeping pig with that sword. Don't pretend you're threatening me."

Wayne stares for a moment, then he lets out a surprised guffaw filled with relief.

"You were always jealous of my sword work," he says in English. "You've had more practice since, that's all."

A body thumps against my side, and my heart races until I realize that Minnie clutches my chest. I grip her tightly and lie back on the mud-streaked grass to look up at the clouds, tinted orange from the city lights. Everything aches, and with every passing moment, more parts of my body chime in with their ailments. I look at the others.

"What the hell did you do to my body? I hurt everywhere."

CHAPTER XXIX

We're all a little battered, although I have the worst of it. Minnie winces as she checks me over.

"It's even worse now that I can see the lauvan," she says. "Now there are bleeding wounds and snarled knots. You look terrible."

"Thank you very much," I say. "At least I look like me. That other body was too rough for my taste."

Minnie takes my head carefully in her hands and kisses me gently despite my split lip.

"I'm glad you're back."

I give her a half-smile—the best I can do with my beaten-up mouth—and turn to the other two.

"Anything major that needs healing? I'll fix you up better tomorrow, but basic triage can happen now."

"I might have a few broken ribs," Wayne wheezes. "Didn't notice until now. Funny what adrenaline can do."

"I'm fine," Alejandro says through gritted teeth. "Nothing that can't wait."

"Stop being a bloody hero," I say. "I can see the knots from here. Come on, I'll do enough for both of you to get some sleep tonight."

"Can we do it in the van?" Minnie says with a glance around. "I know it's the middle of the night, but I still think we've beaten the odds having nobody come across us during all this ruckus. I don't know how we'd explain any of it."

"I could talk us out of it," I say. "But I don't have the energy right now. Come on, lead the way. I can patch us up in the back of the van while you drive."

It's a quick ride to Wayne and Alejandro's neighborhood of Kitsilano with the three of them chattering like birds, filling me in on what happened during my abduction. When I didn't come home from work today, Minnie contacted the others. It was obvious to them that Xenia had nabbed me, and the only clue they had was Xenia's need for a connection to earth for the ritual. Minnie pulled out my old cable maps and they narrowed the location down to three likely spots. Jen, Cecil, and Liam had traveled to the next closest location. When I call Jen, her relieved voice assures me that they are safe and heading home now.

The others listen raptly to my tale of abduction and the clues that led me to understand how to finish stabilizing March's body for Xenia, and I fall into storytelling mode. The others glance at each other with amusement, but I don't stop. This is who I am. After filling someone else's shoes for a while, I'm happy to be me.

"We got you back," Alejandro says. "And Xenia doesn't need to kill anyone else because she has a stable body, thanks to March, but she's still out there."

I sigh and focus on working the knots out of my sliced leg. Minnie pulls onto the road that leads to Wayne's house.

"I can only hope that Xenia's bloodlust is sated," I say. "At least we know what she looks like, now. If you see March again, call me. We do need to stop her, but perhaps we've given ourselves some breathing room. We still don't truly know what she wants. Perhaps, now that she has a body to explore the world with, she's harmless."

I say the words, but I don't truly believe them. The others don't either, by the skeptical looks in their eyes, but no one refutes me.

"However," I say. "I don't like the thought of leaving March to her doom. Given how she prepared her body for possession, and the fact that she was still sentient for a moment after Xenia possessed her, there is a strong possibility that she can be recovered."

Alejandro sighs.

"On the hunt again for March. It's what we do, right?"

"We're here, Wayne," Minnie says from the front.

221

"Thanks, Minnie. Night, all. Just another day on the job, right?" Wayne grins at me. "It's never boring, being your friend, Merry."

"Happy to spice up your life," I say with a wave.

We drop Alejandro off at his home then speed through the empty streets to my apartment. Minnie helps me to the elevator—my wounds are better, but not fully healed—and lowers me onto the couch once we're in the apartment. I sigh with relief, and Minnie kneels on the floor next to me.

"It's as easy as untangling a knot?" she says in question, staring at a snarl above my sword slice. I nod.

"Just do it gently. If you yank too hard, you can cause more damage."

We set to work. Minnie's slender fingers are nimble, and before long she picks apart knots as quickly as I do. The intimate sensation of her hands on my lauvan goes a long way toward easing the pain. In half the time, the worst of my injuries are healed, and I draw her onto the couch and into my arms. She wraps herself around me.

"I was so worried," she murmurs into my chest. "I only just got you, and I thought I'd lost you for good. Just because I have multiple lives doesn't mean you necessarily do."

"I know," I say quietly into her hair.

"I guess I need to trust that you can take care of yourself." She readjusts so that her face looks up into mine. "You've lasted this long."

"You were right to be worried. It was a close one."

Minnie frowns in question, and I sigh.

"I almost let him take over, willingly," I say quickly, needing to get the words out there, needing Minnie to hear me and absolve me of my guilt for almost leaving her. I don't know if she'll be able to. "Ever since you and Arthur and Guinevere came back—after a fashion—I've been feeling lost." Minnie strokes my arm in recognition, but I plow ahead. "The only thing that has kept me going for so many years was waiting for Arthur to return. It was my life's purpose, as absurd as that might be. I needed a reason to keep going, so I latched onto that faint hope. Now that my dream has come true, and more," I squeeze Minnie's shoulders to indicate that she is the more I speak of. "I don't know what to do with myself. Isn't that ridiculous? Then Xenia came along and wanted my body for himself, and I thought, why not? I'm half-elemental. Perhaps I could join that world and learn that part of myself. I've wanted to know about my father's world for centuries, and this was a chance to do that."

"You've always been a wanderer," Minnie says quietly. I nod.

"I wouldn't have considered it for even a moment, if I hadn't known that you were half-elemental, too. I thought you could join me, when you were ready. I could stop the killings by giving Xenia my body, explore a new chapter in my life, and have you by my side. It made sense, at the time." I squeeze her tighter. "Now it seems like folly, and I hope you can forgive my momentary foolishness that almost cost us so much."

Minnie reaches up and touches my cheek with soft fingers. I gaze into her blue eyes, now wide and clear of strands.

"We're all searching for our purpose on Earth," she says. "Trust me, I see plenty of people at work with the same concerns as you." She laughs lightly and corrects herself. "Similar concerns. It's something we all have to work through. But I'm glad—so glad—that you decided against giving your body up. I'm not ready to lose you, and I still like being human. We've had such a short time together—truly together, in full knowledge—and I want more. I want to keep being like this with you. And we can figure out our lives' purposes together, here."

"I realized I'm more human than not," I say with a kiss on Minnie's forehead. "Being strictly elemental isn't for me. I got a panic attack just trying it out for a minute."

Minnie's eyes turn from thoughtful to coy.

"If we were both elementals," she says, her fingers running down my neck and unbuttoning my shirt. "Would I be able to do this?" She slides her delicate hand inside my shirt and lightly strokes my chest. A slow smile creeps across my face, and I reach for her.

"No. Nor this."

CHAPTER XXX
Dreaming

The winter rains have finally arrived in earnest. While I never enjoy the cold, dark, wet days, the change of season means that campaigning is over for another year. I revel in battle as much as the next man and more than some, but even I weary of endless riding and nights on the hard ground.

And, now that a beautiful woman waits for me, the time away is far less appealing. By the end of summer, I itch to ride home as fast as my horse will tolerate.

I don't know how Nimue knows, but a scant two days have passed after we arrive at Arthur's villa when she appears like a vision. I sweep her off her horse with a squeeze that takes her breath away.

We walk through the forest the next day, and it is as if the long summer of campaigning never happened. Nimue's fingers are entwined through my own, and our hands swing idly between us as we walk. During this small window of clear skies, leaves drift from the trees and crunch underfoot. The forest smells damp and earthy, and I draw in deep breaths with pleasure.

"I've missed you," Nimue murmurs to me. I squeeze her hand in reply.

"Summer was far too long this year."

"Will you leave for the winter, as you used to do?"

Nimue refers to my escape of the desperately dull confines of Gwentish winter to the warmer south. I used to travel extensively, once Arthur was settled in his role on the local war council.

"Why would I do that?" I say in genuine surprise. "The only reason I went was to relieve my boredom. Well, and for the warmth. But how could I ever be bored or cold with you in my life?"

"But Arthur's villa is so far from my lake, once the roads wash out." Nimue strokes my fingers. "How will we see each other?"

"I made it last year, didn't I?"

"But it was a mild winter."

"So much worry." I raise her hand to my lips and kiss it. "If the roads wash out, I will transform myself into a deer and bound my way to you. Nothing will keep me away. I would stay at your lake the whole winter, but I fear your regard for me would wane if you should see the petulant child I become when cooped up for too many days in a row."

Nimue giggles.

"Never. And there's too much to do at the lake, you would never get bored. Because we're up in the mountains, the lake freezes early. I always know when the ice is strong enough to walk on."

"Because of your abilities?" Nimue has a connection to the element of water. I don't understand it, and sometimes I wonder how real it is, but she believes it fully and I would never contradict her.

"Yes, exactly." Her eyes brighten. "We slide all over the ice and pull each other on sleds across the lake. Sometimes, we've even carved a hole in the ice and caught fish through it."

"That sounds like a job for a fishing line." I glance at the nearby stream and shudder at the thought of sticking my hands in icy water to tickle fish lauvan so that they swim into my waiting fingers. "I won't attempt my way of fishing."

Nimue's smile is so bright it rivals the sun. Without thinking, I gather her in my arms and press my lips to hers. Her mouth yields to me, then her body melds against mine, and we sink to the carpet of leaves under our feet.

My hands roam her perfect body, all over her waist, her breasts, her hips, and I marvel that I stayed away from her for so long. What was I thinking? Her eyelids flutter closed, and I pull up the hem of her dress. When my fingers brush the soft skin of her thighs, she moans and throws her arm out to the side. The edge of her hand splashes in the water at the stream's edge.

I need more of her, and my mouth covers hers with desperate hunger. When she stiffens, I draw her skirt up further. She puts a hand on my chest and pushes me away.

"Stop," she says in a commanding whisper. "For a moment."

My breath is short, and I watch her closed eyes with increasing frustration. What is she doing? Why is she denying this? It's with immense willpower that I follow her request, even as every part of me screams to kiss her again.

"Saxons," she whispers finally. With that one word, my drive to make Nimue mine dampens. I look at her with confusion.

"What do you mean?"

She sits up and pushes her skirt down.

"There is a group of Saxons upstream. A few hours' ride away, perhaps? They are crossing the river at a ford, I think. I can taste metal on them, and leather."

"Are you sure?" My conviction in her ability wavers, but I recall the tests we've performed in the past, when I whisper secrets to the river and Nimue can hear them from far away. What if she is right?

"If you're correct, then Arthur needs to know." I sigh out my frustrated desires and get to my feet. "They are far too close. How did they even find their way in so far? They must be scouting for next year's push."

"I can help," Nimue says from her seated position at the water's edge. Her eyes are frightened but determined. "I can ask the river to wash some of them away."

I stare at her. Do her powers extend that far? It seems far-fetched, but what harm will it do? If it fails, we are no further behind than we already were.

"Do what you can, then we must run back to the villa."

Nimue nods then kneels on the bank and thrusts her hands

into the water. She closes her eyes.

I wait with bated breath for a few moments. When Nimue doesn't move, I cross my arms and look around. By the time she pulls her hands out of the water, I'm nearly dancing with impatience.

"What happened?" I ask. "Never mind, tell me on the way. We need to let Arthur know."

"I think seven drowned," she says in a small voice. Her sky-blue lauvan droop and writhe with emotion. I set aside my exasperation and wrap my arm around her shoulder.

"You did well." I kiss her hair and lead her along the path homeward. "If they have crept in this far, they were up to no good. Any Saxon who wanted to legitimately settle would have approached Guinevere's father first. They were a raiding party, I'm sure of it."

Nimue nods, and her strands relax a little. I'm not sure of anything—if Nimue really did sense the Saxons, or if she had some part to play in the demise of seven of them—except that Nimue needs comfort. That, I can do. If she is proven wrong, then Arthur and I can have a pleasant ride through the woods. If she is right, then I will have to adjust my belief in her abilities.

CHAPTER XXXI

My close encounter with the death of my human life has made me appreciate it even more. The day after the Xenia debacle, I come home straight after my morning classes—marking can wait until the weekend—and start preparing for the impromptu party I've arranged for this evening. To my surprise, given the short notice, everyone I invited can come.

My mood is buoyed even further by news from the admin assistant when I stopped in at the departmental office. My missing student Carson has been found, after an unintended bender at Whistler that his friends hadn't known about. I have enough deaths on my conscience without Carson weighing it down.

I set myself to cooking. Only some will appreciate a few of these dishes, but I don't aim to please everyone. One last run to the grocery and liquor stores, and a last-minute pick-up of a specialty item that makes my pulse race, and I am ready for my guests' arrival. Candles and lamps light the living room without the aid of electricity, and the scent of beeswax and burning wicks fills the room. Minnie comes home first, sniffing appreciatively at the air.

"Just a taste?" she says when she enters the kitchen. "Please?"

I place a final spring of parsley on a plate and grab one of the crab cakes. "You know I can never say no to you." I place it on her waiting tongue and am rewarded by a groan of pleasure.

"That's so good. Just one more?"

"Get out of here."

Minnie turns and I lightly smack her bottom as she leaves to change out of her professional attire. When she returns, my face breaks open in a smile.

"You know that matches your lauvan perfectly," I say when

I grasp her by the hips and pull her close.

"Actually, I do know," she says with a kiss on my lips. "I chose this dress especially. It looks like it shimmers now. Only to you and me, though. I'm sure it looks like boring navy blue to anyone else."

"Never boring. Not when you're in it."

A loud hello announces Wayne's arrival, followed by Alejandro and Liam. Wayne offers a box of baked goods, and my eyes narrow at the insignia on the box from a particular coffeeshop on Broadway.

"Another visit with Anna?" I say. Wayne shrugs and doesn't meet my eye. I put the box on my kitchen table and stare at him. "Are you really going to make a move on her?"

"Maybe," he mutters. "I don't know. I like her. And she has a history, too. I like that."

"She's a handful," I say. My warning makes Wayne tighten his lips with unspoken remonstrations. I sigh. "But, hey, if you like her, go for it. New leaf and all that, right? Perhaps you can be her second chance."

"Yeah," he says, his voice heartened. "That's right. A new leaf. I really think she's a different person now."

"Go for it, then." I clap my hand on his shoulder. "But don't wait too long. Women like boldness."

Wayne rolls his eyes at me.

"I forgot who I was talking to. Forgive me if I take your female advice with a grain of salt."

"Merry," Alejandro interrupts. "Is that mead in your fridge?"

"It doesn't taste much like what I remember, but it's the best I could find," I say.

"It's great." He beams at me while Liam looks on with confusion at my words. Damn, I forgot he was here. So many people know, now, that it's hard to keep straight who is who. Perhaps I should run an advertisement in the local newspaper, declaring my past. It might be simplest.

Gary and his wife from next door arrive next, closely followed by a gaggle of Minnie's friends. Jen and Cecil enter a few minutes later. When Alejandro sees her, he whispers something to Liam, who then approaches the two and engages Cecil in conversation.

"What's that about?" I say to Alejandro.

"I want to help Jen with her past lives," he says quietly to me. "I know she doesn't want to be with me, and that's okay." He catches sight of my raised eyebrow. "No, really. It took a while for me to see that, I admit. But I want her to be happy, more than anything else. If being apart from me will do that, then I can accept that. Maybe next life, right?"

I chuckle.

"You're really that patient?"

"I'll be honest, I don't think all hope is lost. Maybe destiny will push Jen my way eventually. But I want her to reach that decision herself, not be forced into it."

"Very wise," I say. "But she might come to that decision more quickly if she is comfortable with her past lives."

Alejandro winks at me.

"Exactly."

Jen looks bored as Cecil and Liam speak animatedly beside her. Alejandro saunters away from me. When he reaches Jen's side, he sidles close to her and starts to speak.

"What is this dish, Merry?" Minnie's friend Inna distracts me from my preoccupation with Alejandro's plotting.

"Have you never had almond gingerbread made with gum-dragon? It's nothing like the gingerbread we get today, but it was very popular in Elizabethan England."

"Oh?" Inna looks dubious but picks one up gamely and takes a bite. Her face clears when the flavor hits her tongue. "Totally different, but really good."

"Merry has a fascination with historical food," Minnie says at my side. She glances at me sideways with a quirk in her smile. "It's his thing."

231

"A man who can cook? I don't care what it is," Inna says and takes another bite. "I have friends with stranger hobbies."

"Really?" I'm intrigued. Inna thinks for a moment.

"Okay, not really, but cooking as a hobby is easy to swallow." She smiles at her own pun. When Minnie pulls her away to speak about a common acquaintance, Gary comes up to me.

"Thanks for inviting us, Merry," he says. "Great idea, inviting the neighbors. Then we can't call you in for the noise!" He laughs heartily then coughs when his wife glances his way. "Don't tell the missus, but this is my third ale. It really hits the spot, doesn't it? And I don't have far to toddle home." He laughs again.

"Enjoy tonight," I tell him with a slap on the back. "Help yourself to as much ale as you want."

The party gets louder as my fridge is depleted of alcohol. With my eyes at half-mast, the candlelight flickering, and a hum of voices in the air, I am transported back to many past gatherings. They meld and fuse into one, just like Alejandro and Jen and Wayne and Minnie are each many memories and yet one person. I can live in the past and the present, and they are the same.

"Wake up, Merry." Jen's voice jolts me out of my reverie. "It's not that late, old man."

I glance sharply at her, but she merely smiles, her golden strands calmly swirling.

"I've chatted with both Minnie and Alejandro," she says. "They seem to think that this whole past-lives thing is not so bad. They've been trying to convince me, too."

"Were they successful?"

Jen sighs, but it's one of contemplation, not of defeat.

"I realized what my issue is," she says. "I am terrified of destiny. Am I doomed to repeat the past, over and over again, with no say in my future? I can't handle that. I need to know that I have control over my path in life. I make my own destiny, you know?"

She looks to me for confirmation, and I nod.

"Control is important. I understand."

"The others helped me to see that I can decide what I want, especially now that I know everything. Even if I do follow the same path with the same people." Jen's eyes flick toward Alejandro briefly. "It will be because I chose it. Does that make sense?"

"Absolutely," I say. "You'll have the same options as before, but you can charge forward with full knowledge that whatever you do will be your choice, not the blind following of a predetermined path."

"Exactly." Jen nods slowly. There is a pause, then she says, "I'm going to tell Cecil."

"About your past lives?"

"Yes. And I want to give him the option to touch the grail, if he wants."

I gaze at Jen in consideration. She looks back, determined and unfazed. Cecil, initiated, will make us six. I wonder, does he also have a past? Surely, not everyone I know was formerly connected to me, but with so many so-called coincidences already, can I discount the possibility?

"Why do you want to tell him?" I say. "Are you that close?"

"I don't know. Maybe." She dithers for a moment. "No, I'm being selfish. It's for me. I want to know if he is anyone from my past, make sure he's not—" Jen checks herself before saying the name we're both wondering. "I want all the facts before I charge forward. I want to know that I'm choosing Cecil for him, not just because I'm trying so hard not to be with Alejandro." She bites her lip and looks angry at herself then glances quickly at me. "Don't tell Alejandro I said that, okay?"

"My lips are sealed." I mime zippering my mouth shut. "But if you tell Cecil, make him sleep on the decision to touch the grail, all right? Bring him by on the weekend if he decides he wants to know."

Jen nods then folds her arms as she changes the topic.

"In other news, what's up with Xenia? Where is she now, and what do we do about her?" She looks inquisitively at me. I shrug.

"I'll try to find her through the lauvan. She has no need to go on a killing spree, now that she has a stable body, thanks to March. My guess is that she'll have a joyride, try out a few human things in the physical world, and realize that she prefers her existence as an earth fundamental. She'll be gone and out of our hair shortly, I don't doubt. If we catch wind of any trouble, we'll be ready. And if we find her before then, I'll consider ways to get her out of March. I'll keep tabs on my elemental contacts in the meantime."

Minnie's form in her shimmering blue dress catches my eye across the room. I wipe my suddenly sweaty palms on my trousers. Jen notices the motion and frowns in question.

"What's up?"

"There's something I need to do." I clear my throat in preparation. I would think, having done this so many times before—with the same person, no less—that nerves would not be an issue. And yet, here I am, hoping for a positive answer to my question.

"Have at it, then." Jen waves me forward. I step to the center of the room and clap my hands once. The room quiets and more than a dozen faces look my way, waiting.

"I have an announcement to make." I reach my hand out to invite Minnie to my side. She joins me with a quizzical look. "Firstly, thank you for joining us this evening. The older I get, the more I appreciate good friends around me."

I turn to Minnie.

"My next announcement is more of a question." I kneel before Minnie. A few of the women around us gasp and titter, but Minnie merely gazes at me steadily. "Minnie, my love, we've been together for such a short time in this life, but I feel that I have known you forever. I can't imagine my life without you, and I don't want to go anywhere without you by my side. The past is past, but the future holds so much promise. Minnie Dilleck, will you marry me?"

Minnie's eyes are bright with emotion.

"Always," she whispers, then her mouth quirks upward in mirth, and she pulls my arm for me to stand. "Get up, you foolish man. Of course, I'll marry you."

My grin is quickly hidden by her lips on mine. The room erupts with cheers and clapping. When we finally part, Minnie's cheeks are pink, and she squeezes my hand.

"Better put a ring on it," someone yells. Right. My special purchase this afternoon. I draw out a small box and open it to pull out a ring. Minnie holds out her hand and I slide it on her finger. She holds it up and peers at it.

"Sapphires?"

"A fitting blue for my lady of the lake," I whisper in her ear.

CHAPTER XXXII

We sleep late the next day, but modern Saturdays were made for late rising. When Minnie and I finally drift out of the mists of slumber, an autumn sun streams in through the half-closed blind. Minnie groans.

"I think I drank too much last night." She covers her eyes with one hand. "Be a darling and close the curtain, will you?"

"I can do better than that." I shuffle closer to her and pick at the knots that prevent the strands on her head from moving. Within a minute, Minnie's eyes open without discomfort and her strands swirl freely.

"So much better. I pity anyone who doesn't have you in their bed after a party." She smiles wickedly at me and I lean in to kiss her neck.

"As you should. They are all pitiable creatures. Be thankful that I grace you with my presence."

"How I put up with you is beyond me," she says with a laugh, then she coughs. "I need a drink."

"Here, let me." I reach over to pull the strands of water in her glass on the night table, but Minnie stops my hand. Her eyes are wide with excitement.

"No, I want to."

Between a gentle finger and thumb, she pinches a swaying water lauvan that extends past her glass. She pulls, and a stream of water flows along the strand. I hold my breath and watch as she brings it closer to her mouth. Her brow creases in concentration, and her other hand takes a different strand to end the stream and gather the water into an undulating ball. She pops it in her mouth, swallows, and grins from ear to ear.

"You are amazing." I gather her up in my arms and kiss her wet mouth. She laughs with delight.

"This is so much fun. Did you see me the other night? Spraying water at Xenia? My aim is improving. Shooting him with water was perfect, really, because I wanted to distract him without hurting your body. I'm rather fond of it, you know. Wayne insisted on bringing your sword, which I didn't approve of."

"I did notice your performance. Your control is exceptional, especially considering that you only discovered your abilities the other day."

"I guess years of watching you helped. I can't wait to try out other things. What can I do on the ocean? And if there are earth cables and air cables, what do water cables look like?"

"It's not easy searching underwater," I say. "I've never been interested enough to find out."

"You're such an earth snob," she says with a giggle. "Watch, I'll make a water cable map to rival your earth cable ones."

"I look forward to it."

"Teach me everything?" she says. "I want to move the wind, and shake the earth, and heal a body. I want to do it all."

"I will teach you everything I know," I promise. "And, who knows, you might have things to teach me too. Since I'm apparently very earth-centric, perhaps you'll have a water perspective to freshen up my view. Water cables, indeed."

"I'm glad you stuck around." Minnie admires the ring on her finger that gleams with blue jewels in the morning sun, then she tucks her head in the crook of my neck. I twist to kiss her hair.

"So am I."

Minnie wants me to take it easy today, but I've healed everything that needs healing, and I've never been one for lying around. Todd said he was available to meet after an extensive phone conversation explaining our encounter with Xenia the other night, so Minnie and I take our ridiculous van through the university and park at the top of a western cliff that drops steeply to the sea.

"Tell me again why we're meeting at Wreck Beach?" Minnie says as we unclip our seatbelts. "I know you're a hedonist at heart, but do we really need to practice our lauvan work at a nudist beach?"

"It'll be deserted this time of year. No one will be watching us wave our hands around. Trust me, there is rarely any 'scenery' to speak of when the weather turns frosty."

I zip my coat up tightly against the breeze. It turned chilly overnight, and autumn has become rather forthright. Minnie slips her hand into mine, her ring cool against my fingers, and we walk down an endless staircase to the beach.

The wind blows even more strongly down here, and Minnie tightens her hood around her face. A voice hails us from nearby, and Todd lopes toward us.

"No nudists today, hey?" He grins. "Freeze your balls off in this weather."

"Todd, meet Minnie, my fiancée." Minnie and I smile at each other at the word. "Minnie, meet Todd. I brought Minnie along because we just found out that Minnie also had an elemental for a parent."

"No, really?" Todd's eyes are wide in his lean face. He squints at Minnie and examines her strands. "Oh, yeah, I can see it now. Just water, hey? It's so hard to tell when you only have one element."

Minnie's eyes rake over Todd.

"Fascinating," she murmurs. "Three colors. This is all very new to me, Todd. I've been suppressing my abilities since I was a small child, so I couldn't even see lauvan until a few days ago."

"And you two just happened to find each other?" Todd looks skeptical. "How many of us are there?"

"I can't believe it was coincidence," I say. "But I don't have an explanation. And I've never, in all my long years,

238

encountered another like us. This is uncharted territory." I release myself from Minnie's grasp and clap my hands together in anticipation. "With that in mind, let's do some practicing. Between us, we cover all the elements. Let's see what we can do."

We start with earth, as earth strands are stable and slow-moving. They carpet the pebbly beach, and Minnie and Todd squat down and rake their fingers through the strands experimentally.

"Don't forget to touch them with intent," I say. "Otherwise, your hands will pass straight through."

"I got one." Todd holds up a silvery brown strand. Rocks tumble to the water's edge from the disturbance, and Todd drops the strand with a guilty expression. "Was that me?"

"Everything is connected," I say. "With enough practice, you'll figure out what goes where."

"I can do it," Minnie says. She gingerly pinches a strand between her fingers. "But it doesn't feel as natural as when I was pushing the water around the other night. That was easy. This is strange."

"Good to practice, then. But we can move onto water, if you like." I point at a runoff stream that cuts a path through the pebbles to the sea. "Let's make a splash."

As predicted, Minnie manipulates water with more ease. Where Todd struggles with his task, Minnie creates a tiny fountain on her third try. When we move to wind, though, Todd shows his affiliation strongly.

"Whoa," I shout as a powerful gale bears down on us. Air lauvan surround me like tiny shards of glass, and I hold my hood close to my head. "Tone it down, Todd!"

Todd brings his hands down, and the wind dies.

"Sorry," he says, but his eyes gleam. "That was amazing. So much power at my fingertips. Did you see that? And I didn't even try hard. Can you imagine what I could do if I really wanted to?"

Todd turns his gaze to the clouds roiling in the autumn sky. Minnie and I share a glance. There was never any question that I would contact Todd when I discovered what he was, and it was a natural decision to mentor him as he grows into his abilities. A faint twinge of unease ripples down my spine. I know very little about Todd. What sort of man is he? Will he treat his abilities with the respect they deserve? I know I haven't always done so. How can I expect Todd to be a better man?

ALSO BY EMMA SHELFORD

<u>Immortal Merlin</u>
Ignition
Winded
Floodgates
Buried
Possessed
Unleashed
Worshiped

<u>Nautilus Legends</u>
Free Dive
Caught
Surfacing

<u>Breenan Series</u>
Mark of the Breenan
Garden of Last Hope
Realm of the Forgotten

ACKNOWLEDGEMENTS

A hearty thank you to the usual suspects: Gillian Brownlee, Steven Shelford, and Wendy and Chris Callendar for editing, and Deranged Doctor Designs for the cover.

ABOUT THE AUTHOR

Emma Shelford feels that life is only complete with healthy doses of magic, history, and science. Since these aren't often found in the same place, she creates her own worlds where they happily coexist. If you catch her in person, she will eagerly discuss Lord of the Rings ad nauseam, why the ancient Sumerians are so cool, and the important role of phytoplankton in the ocean.

Emma is the author of the Nautilus Legends (a marine biologist discovers that mythical sea creatures are real), the Immortal Merlin Series (Merlin is immortal, forever young, and living in the modern day), and the Breenan Series (a young woman follows a mysterious stranger into an enchanting Otherworld).

Printed in Great Britain
by Amazon